UNSWERVING

UNSWERVING

BARBARA RIDLEY

THE UNIVERSITY OF WISCONSIN PRESS

Publication of this book has been made possible, in part,
through support from the Brittingham Trust.

The University of Wisconsin Press
728 State Street, Suite 443
Madison, Wisconsin 53706
uwpress.wisc.edu

Gray's Inn House, 127 Clerkenwell Road
London EC1R 5DB, United Kingdom
eurospanbookstore.com

Printed in the United States of America
This book may be available in a digital edition.

Library of Congress Cataloging-in-Publication Data

Names: Ridley, Barbara, 1950- author.
Title: Unswerving / Barbara Ridley.
Description: Madison, Wisconsin : The University of Wisconsin Press, 2024.
Identifiers: LCCN 2023041528 | ISBN 9780299348144 (paperback)
Subjects: LCSH: People with disabilities—Rehabilitation—Fiction. |
BISAC: FICTION / General | LCGFT: Fiction. | Novels.
Classification: LCC PS3618.I392253 U57 2024 | DDC 813/.6—dc23/eng/20231016
LC record available at https://lccn.loc.gov/2023041528

Dedicated to the staff and volunteers at
BORP (Bay Area Outreach and Recreational Program)
in recognition of their work for adaptive
sports and recreation.

UNSWERVING

I

Tave told him she couldn't remember a thing. One moment they were getting into the car at the restaurant, and the next thing she knew, she was staring at a grid of square ceiling panels. A swarm of strangers' faces hovered overhead, and then she was plunging, tumbling into a muffled gray fog.

"That's all I got," Tave said. "Until I woke up in this place."

"Very common," the new doctor said, pushing his spectacles up the bridge of his nose. There was a mole above his left nostril that looked big enough to hold the glasses in place but didn't. "Retrograde amnesia. Having no memory of events immediately prior to or after the accident. A protective mechanism."

He nodded in agreement with himself, as if to compensate for the fact she could not, with the hard collar around her neck. He inched his chair forward, bringing his face closer into her field of vision. "Don't force it. You may never recall the details."

Tave had stuck to this story for the past two weeks. But the truth was she remembered more than she let on. She remembered the dotted yellow line down the center of the road, the way it danced toward her with its hypnotic rhythm: line-space-line-space-line-space-line-space. She remembered the blackness of the road, the warm, dark night, the stickiness of the steering wheel, the heaviness of her eyes, the irresistible urge to close them, close them, to lower her eyelids just for a moment.

"You all right, hon?" Les had said, shifting sideways in the passenger seat.

"I'm fine."

"Maybe I'll snooze. You okay with that?"

"Sure, go ahead."

The greasy burger sat heavy as a softball in the pit of Tave's stomach. She adjusted the air vents for a full throttle effect on her face and turned the radio to the station they'd discovered right before crossing back into

California; the signal was still strong. She caught the end of a Red Hot Chili Peppers number, but then it was whiny Mariah Carey and endless commercials. The only alternative was a religious nut going on about bestiality and sin, so she switched off the radio and reached for another stick of gum. She remembered the blinding lights of the oncoming traffic. She remembered blinking hard and stretching her eyebrows, trying to visualize her eyes propped open with duct tape.

Tave didn't tell the doctor any of this.

She closed her eyes now, hoping he would leave her alone. She couldn't recall this doctor's name; he was from another unit, the nurse said. He told her he'd seen her before, but she didn't remember. She didn't give a damn. She closed her eyes but could sense him sitting there; his aftershave had a rich, oaky fragrance that was not unpleasant. She'd never had a keen sense of smell before the crash, but now she could distinguish dozens of different odors. Her nose was about the only part of her body that still worked.

"Hey, sleepyhead. Wake up." Gloria, the nurse, was back. "Excuse me, Dr. Kramer."

She fussed with the tubes and wires she always fussed with. She pushed the button that raised the head of the bed, sending a jarring vibration through Tave's skull, as if the bones were being stretched in opposite directions.

"Come on, wake up." Her voice had a lilting singsong quality to it. She took Tave's shoulders in her hands and somehow adjusted her position a notch, enough to ease the pressure from the plastic neck collar. Her smell was sweet, like honeysuckle.

"Don't be wasting Dr. Kramer's time now. He's come to talk to you about going to rehab."

Tave opened her eyes to a view of a golden cross dangling a few inches in front of her face, framed in the V-neck of a blue scrubs top. Maybe Gloria wouldn't start up again about the Lord, not with the doctor sitting there. That was one good reason for him to stay.

"Have another sip of juice."

She flexed the straw and presented it to Tave's lips. The juice was lukewarm and sickly sweet. Tave grimaced.

"You need to drink more if we're going to get rid of that tube."

Gloria wiggled the overbed table into place and positioned the cup and straw in front of Tave's face before leaving. *Getting rid of that tube* was a passion of Gloria's, right up there with Jesus and *American Idol*. She spoke of it with great zeal, as if she were coaching a team to the playoffs. The tube was disgusting, for sure: sticking out through the skin, directly from Tave's stomach. Once, she'd watched as Gloria hooked up a bag of beige liquid, but she preferred to look away.

"You've made incredible progress, you know," Dr. Kramer said. "Surprised a lot of people around here. You'll soon be ready for rehab." He seemed to expect her to respond, but she did not.

He tried again. "How does it feel to be eating real food now?"

Tave could have shrugged. He would know she could—because he'd just been doing a bunch of stuff with her arms, moving them around, asking her to push here or pull there. None of which she could do. She could move her shoulders a tiny bit, and this seemed a big deal to him. She didn't want to encourage him. She opted instead for screwing up her nose. Most of the food here hardly qualified as *real*: soggy sandwiches, watery scrambled eggs, overcooked broccoli. She couldn't move her arms, so had to be spoon-fed like a baby, and she lost interest after a few bites. But yesterday, she'd tasted chocolate; now that was good. The thought of it brought a smile to her face, in spite of her best efforts.

"Chocolate brownie with vanilla ice cream was good," she heard herself say.

They hadn't stayed for dessert that night. She'd wanted to, but Les said no, they should get going. She'd heard nothing from Les, and nothing about her since the accident. She must have been killed and no one wanted to tell her; that was the only explanation. Tave didn't ask and no one said. For weeks, she couldn't talk anyway. She'd had the tube down her throat and was on so many drugs, everything was a blur. She saw people through a haze, their voices muffled and drowned out by the alarms and the beeps and the constant whir of the breathing machine.

She thought of asking Dr. Kramer what had happened to Les. But she was scared to find out. She chose instead to clam up tight, sink her head into the pillow, hoping he would leave her in peace.

"You have some nice cards." His blue eyes watched her from beneath bushy eyebrows. "One of them is new, I think."

He pointed at the display the nurse's aide had created. It hung above the bed where Tave couldn't see it except when she was hauled into the recliner chair once a day. It was a small collection. First to arrive had been the one from Mervyn's, its inside pages speckled with signatures of people she didn't recognize and who surely didn't know her—she'd been working at the store only a month. Later, a card from her mother, one from her former college roommate whom she hadn't seen in two years, and a ridiculous offering from her father: full of smiley faces and emblazoned with *Get Well Soon!!!*

And now Dan's.

"May I read it?" Dr. Kramer asked.

Tave said nothing, which he took as agreement.

"*Won't be able to make it back down for a while,*" he read. "*The Chevy's blown a gasket and I can't afford to get it fixed right now. We're all thinking about you, babe. Love, Dan.*"

Someone had held the card six inches in front of her face when it arrived the previous day. She'd never seen Dan's handwriting before and was surprised by the neat script, very un-Dan-like. His texts were always full of chat slang and his own unique abbreviations. Tave had lost her phone since the accident—stolen no doubt—so she had none of her contacts. In her mind, she could feel her thumbs tap, tap, tapping the keys fast as a drummer's sticks. But if she had her phone now, she wouldn't even be able to hold it. Asking someone to text on your behalf would be totally weird.

"Is he your boyfriend?"

Dan? Tave curled her lip. These people were clueless. "No," was all she offered in reply.

"I heard he came to visit soon after you arrived," Dr. Kramer said. "But you must have been barely conscious."

Tave had no memory of his visit. She remembered her mother coming: the first time they'd seen each other in two years. Tave had changed her legal name, which her mother had refused to acknowledge and never forgave, so when someone showed up looking for Octavia Greenwich, no one knew whom she meant at first. She sat at the bedside crying, reeking of cigarettes, and dabbing at the corners of her eyes with a tissue in a determined effort to protect her mascara. For once in her life, she was speechless. Tave still had the tube in her mouth so couldn't pick up the slack. Just as well. The memory of their last fight remained vivid: a no-holds-barred screaming match the day after Thanksgiving, when her mother figured out Les was more than a roommate; Tave vowed to never return.

Her mother hadn't visited again. She telephoned once a week and one of the nurses would hold the phone to Tave's ear, while her mother rambled on about her new job in Riverside and how she wanted to get away but couldn't. As soon as Tave could get a word in, she said she was too tired to talk.

Tave's father had left when she was in eighth grade. He'd never been around much, but finally he was gone—gone, as in run off to Phoenix with some woman he'd met at a conference. She was half his age, and Tave hated her; she giggled in the background, squealing *Hi Octavia*, whenever her father called. That was in the early days. After their twins were born, he could hardly be bothered to keep in touch; an email on her birthday and a fifty-dollar bill at Christmas was about it. But he must have heard about the accident and, along with the smiley-face card, had sent a bunch of balloons. He'd evidently clicked the wrong button; they were pink and heart-shaped and said *It's a Girl!*

Something itched Tave's cheek, a stray eyelash maybe. She tried to shake it off by twitching her nostrils, but it wouldn't budge.

"You don't agree?" she heard Dr. Kramer say.

She had no idea what he'd said. She tried to will the eyelash to fall off, scrunching up her cheeks, but it was stuck. It wasn't an eyelash, could be a crumb or piece of dirt—or god forbid, a bedbug or something. She wanted that thing off her face. But she would never ask this doctor dude to help. She hated having to ask anyone for help. She wanted to run away. She wanted this all to end.

"Well, I'll be following you," he said. "And when you get cleared by the ICU docs we'll transfer you across the way." He twitched his head to his left, as if Tave could see anything except the machines and the pink plaid curtain around her bed.

"Okay," Tave said and shrugged, before she remembered not to. She didn't know if he noticed. He stood and left her bedside.

Why the fuck hadn't they stopped to take a break that night? They shouldn't have tried to make it all in one day, after such a late start. They could have pulled into a motel for the night. Okay, Les wouldn't have wanted to spend the money. But if they'd known this was going to be the deal, they could have found a way to pay.

Gloria returned carrying a bundle of white packages and rolls of tape. She scrutinized Tave's face and, without a word, picked up a tissue and wiped away the wretched speck.

"Can I do your heel now?" she said.

"Do I have a choice?"

"No, but I like to ask anyway." Gloria grinned. She had a wide smile and perfectly straight bright teeth.

Tave closed her eyes again. She heard the ripping of paper and smelled the astringent odor of the impregnated dressings as Gloria prepared to work on the object that occupied the lower part of the bed, which was apparently one of Tave's legs. She felt nothing as Gloria gripped her heel, but she caught the sour smell as the bandages were removed.

"This is looking so much better," Gloria said. "You were in that place for less than thirty-six hours before they airlifted you down here, but they still managed to give you pressure ulcers." She tut-tutted in disapproval.

"How long have I been here?" Tave asked. She knew she was in San Francisco but had lost track of time.

"Your accident was May 7. So, I guess it's over four weeks now."

"Shit." Four weeks and still she couldn't move.

Gloria was focused on Tave's foot. "The left heel wasn't so bad, but this one sure was a mess. I get they were busy saving your life, but they must have kept your feet in one position the entire time. Could have led to bone infection, blood poisoning. Pressure ulcers can kill, you know."

"Sounds like a good way out," Tave said.

"Now don't you be talking that way."

"Why not?"

"You're doing great. Off the vent during the day, eating and drinking some, blood pressure stabilized. This is healing beautifully. You'll be off to the rehab unit any day now."

"Yippee." Tave sneered. They acted like rehab was a trip to Disneyland.

She winced as she felt a stab of tingling around her temples, a signal she'd come to recognize, a small protest her lower body sometimes mustered when the nurses prodded and poked. She looked down to the foot of the bed and saw Gloria working at her heel with something that looked like tweezers. Once upon a time, Tave's legs were her greatest asset: long and slender, yet strong; always a golden tan by June. Now they looked hideous: scarred, ashen, unshaven.

"Almost done here," Gloria said.

"I want to be done," Tave said. "I want to go to sleep and not wake up."

"I said none of that talk. Only the Lord can decide when it's time for you to go."

The Lord is getting a helluva lot of help—or interference—around here, Tave thought. From the machines, the tubes, the lines, the wires. And from Gloria herself, for that matter.

"Besides, you can't only think about yourself. You have to consider what your dying would do to other people."

"No one would care. Not for more than five minutes. They'd soon get on with their lives and forget about me."

Gloria stood at her side and scooted the bed table aside to move in close. She ripped off her gloves and looked Tave square in the eye.

"I tell you one person who'd care."

"You'd get over it."

"Well, yes, I would care, and I would eventually get over it, but I'm not talking about me. I'm talking about the other driver."

"What?" *Other driver?*

"The driver of the other vehicle. Rumor has it he was drunk."

Other vehicle? Wait . . . she thought she'd fallen asleep at the wheel.

"He's gonna be in enough trouble as it is," Gloria continued. "You croak, sweetheart, and he's looking at manslaughter."

2

On Monday morning, Beth pedaled the last two blocks uphill to the hospital, her thighs strong, her skin tingling from a week backpacking in the Santa Lucia Mountains, the best possible vacation. The wildflowers were spectacular and the creeks full, and Katy perked up as she always did in the wilderness. After the first two miles on the trail, they saw no one else for days. They'd made love on a ledge overlooking a gorge, Beth's back soft against the mossy groundcover, a sliver of moon overhead. She'd said *hush*—out of habit—and Katy had made fun of her; *only the coyotes can hear us.*

She was still smiling as she reached the parking garage and maneuvered her bike into one of the lockers. The parking attendant waved. "Someone's in a good mood this morning," he said.

She removed her helmet and ran a hand through her hair, rearranging her pixie cut. In the lobby, she grabbed a cup of coffee from the cart and rode the elevator to the third floor. A new coat of paint spruced up the hallway on the rehab unit. Located in the older annex, it was buffered from the noise and bustle of the acute hospital. The artwork on the walls had been updated too; Beth recognized a watercolor one of her stroke patients had painted last month: an abstract splash of greens and purple.

"Hey! Welcome back."

"Look at your tan!"

Hugs all around as her colleagues greeted her in the crowded physical therapy office.

"Did you hear about the new patient? She's a mess: throwing up, grouchy as hell." This was from Stan, who was one year shy of retirement, as he liked to remind everyone at least once a week. "Linda's assigned her to you, babycakes. You're going to need that post-vacation glow to cope with her." He swaggered out the door with a campy wave of his wrist.

"Don't listen to him," Kristy said. "You'll like her."

Beth had seen the text from her department manager as she was eating breakfast at home. Linda must have sent it late last night.

Got a new spinal cord injury patient. Saving her for you.

Spinal cord injury was her specialty, and Linda had assigned the patient to her, in recognition of her expertise, which Beth appreciated. She'd even felt—she couldn't deny it—a twinge of excitement and an eagerness to return to work. Good thing Katy had slept in; she would have given her a hard time: *How can you be excited that someone just became paralyzed?*

Even her friends from physical therapy school didn't understand. They considered the plum jobs to be in sports medicine or orthopedics, but Beth found those uninspiring. Seven years ago, she'd been thrilled to land a position on the spinal cord unit at the Rehab Institute of Chicago, her first job out of school.

"What level is she?" she asked Kristy.

"They said C4–5 but I think she's getting return below that. See what you think." Kristy scrolled through the screens on the monitor at her desk. "She was transferred over from the ICU on Thursday, but we didn't get to complete the eval. She kept getting nauseated. But I see from the nurses' notes she was better over the weekend."

So, Beth would be starting from scratch. Yes, she *was* excited at the prospect. It would be a challenge, a welcome change from the routine broken hips and strokes. She missed that since moving to San Francisco. Katy had insisted they return to California; she could no longer endure the Chicago winters and wanted to be closer to her family.

People always asked: *Isn't spinal cord injury depressing?* Beth was accustomed to this but always surprised by its assumptions. No, it was amazingly rewarding—though always difficult to explain. Mostly, Beth enjoyed the teamwork. Everyone had to pull together: no retreating into your own little silo when working with these patients. Linda insisted they work as a team with all patients, and to a certain extent they did, but it was more focused somehow with spinal cord injury. Had to be. As a physical therapist, she couldn't do her work unless the physician had stabilized the patient's blood pressure, the nurse had managed the skin and bladder, the respiratory therapist had worked on breathing, and the occupational therapist had adjusted the wheelchair seating. And the payoff for all the hard work: watching your patient gradually recuperate and blossom and adapt to life after injury. It was thrilling.

Beth skimmed through her inbox and checked her schedule for the day. Tave Greenwich: that must be her. "This new patient—is she off the vent?"

"Yes. She's young. Healthy lungs. She was a softball player."

"Great." Beth smiled. She could hardly wait.

~

She had to wait until eleven o'clock. First, she was scheduled for family training with a stroke patient, showing his wife how to transfer him into the car, followed by a session with Billie, a woman with multiple sclerosis back for her third admission—Beth got her to take a few steps in the parallel bars, which was an achievement—followed by half an hour on balancing exercises for a man in his seventies who had Parkinson's.

Finally, she prepared to meet the new patient. Tave: *Rhymes with Save,* someone had written in the Comments field. Her legal name, not a nickname apparently, which was interesting, Beth thought. She sat at the nursing station and skimmed the history: unrestrained driver—*goddamn it,* another one not using a seat belt—airlifted down from Siskiyou County, a rough course in the ICU, eventually stabilizing enough to make it to the rehab unit.

Beth's phone buzzed in her pocket. She was not supposed to take calls at work, but she flipped open her phone, keeping it hidden on her lap. It was a text from Katy.

Guess what? Indigo Girls new album coming, tour in Sept. Wanna get tickets?

She couldn't believe Katy was doing this. Of course, she would love to hear the Indigo Girls, their favorite band. They'd seen them at the Chicago Auditorium on their first date. But Katy should be getting ready for her new job, as she promised she would, not surfing the web for ticket sales. And not pestering Beth at work. She'd better not screw up this opportunity, as she had so many others. When they first moved here, Katy had hoped to get into acupuncture school, but that hadn't worked out. Nor had her pottery studio idea or her plan to be a freelance wellness coach. She'd drifted between part-time gigs and hadn't contributed to the rent for months. Now finally, she was supposed to be starting at a gym in the Marina District. The vacation had been their last getaway before Katy began a steady job.

Beth tapped a quick *Sure*, switched off her phone, and walked to Room 3306.

The record showed Tave to be twenty-three, but she looked younger. Slim build, about a hundred and thirty pounds, Beth estimated. Her reddish-brown hair tumbled in chaotic waves down to her shoulders, framing a narrow face with prominent cheekbones. A healing scar at the base of her neck revealed the site of the tracheostomy tube. She sat in a highbacked manual wheelchair, her legs elevated on extended footrests, her hands supported in arm troughs on each side.

Beth sat on the bed and introduced herself, bringing her face level with Tave's. "I know you've met a couple of different physical therapists since you came over to rehab last week," she said. "They were filling in until I got back from vacation. I'm going to be your regular PT from now on."

"Whatever."

Her eyes were downcast. Not surprising: a typical reaction from the newly injured in Beth's experience.

"I'd like to take you down to the gym and get you onto the mat table."

"You asking me or telling me?"

Beth couldn't suppress a light laugh. She had some spunk, this one. "A bit of both, I guess."

"Whatever," Tave said again, but she looked up and made eye contact for the first time. For a fleeting moment, before her gaze returned to her lap.

In the gym, Beth and Duane, the PT assistant, secured a transfer belt around Tave's waist, placed her feet on the floor, and with Beth bracing Tave's knees between hers, safely tipped her forward and pivoted her onto the mat table. They carefully laid her flat, Duane supporting her neck and shoulders while Beth took her legs and positioned pillows under Tave's knees and elbows.

"Thanks," Beth said to Duane. "We're all set here."

"Sure." Duane gave Tave a thumbs-up sign and turned to leave. His broad shoulders and chiseled muscles made him intimidating at first glance, but he had a relaxed manner and soothing baritone voice, often able to cajole the most reluctant patients with his dry sense of humor.

Beth sensed he would work well with Tave, but for now she wanted time to establish her own rapport.

She asked Tave, "Have they explained to you what your injury is?"

Silence. Tave stared up at the ceiling.

"You broke your neck."

"Duh."

Beth took a deep breath. *Okay, so this is not going to be easy.* But it was not up to Tave to make it easy; that was Beth's job. And Beth preferred to work with someone who was appropriately depressed rather than blithely in denial about the extent of their injury. Or angrily lashing out at anyone within range. She recalled the South Side gang member who had intentionally tipped the full urinal from his bedside table, aiming for Beth's shoes— about the only time she'd lost her professional composure.

"Do you know the level of your injury?" she asked now.

"C-something. I don't give a shit." But Tave looked up at Beth. Her eyes were a striking green-hazel color. "What difference does it make?"

"It makes a lot of difference. The lower the level the more you'll be able to do with your arms. I'm going to do some testing to determine exactly what level you're at right now." Beth positioned herself on the mat, kneeling at Tave's right shoulder. "Did they tell you if you're complete or incomplete?"

"I'm completely fucked, I know that much."

"I'm sure that's how it feels right now." Beth placed her hand on Tave's shoulder and lowered her voice to a more soothing pitch. "Can you shrug your shoulder for me? Like this?" She demonstrated. "Good. Now let's try the other side. This isn't bothering your stomach, is it? I heard you've been feeling queasy."

"I'm okay." Tave continued to stare at the ceiling.

"Good. Your shoulders are strong. Now let's try your elbows. Try to pull against my hand here." There was a definite contraction in Tave's right biceps, even stronger on the left. "Good. Now try to lift up your wrist."

Beth wasn't sure if she'd imagined it. Maybe it was a spasm, an involuntary twitch.

"Do that again."

No, there it was again: a trace, barely a trace of wrist extension. On both sides. A great sign.

She completed the rest of the evaluation, testing for strength and range of motion in every muscle, and assessing sensation to light touch and pin-prick in Tave's arms and legs. She knew Dr. Kramer, the rehab doctor, would have completed his assessment but it would be good to compare notes. And at this stage of Tave's recovery, things could change from week to week.

"You're definitely incomplete," she told Tave. "That means you have some slight movement and a bit of feeling coming back below the level of your injury. That's good."

Now Tave looked at Beth and maintained eye contact. "So, am I going to get to walk out of here?"

Not likely, Beth thought to herself, but she wanted to be gentle. "I can't promise you that," she said. "Right now, I'm not seeing any movement in your legs. But it's early days yet. This is what I can promise you. I'm going to work like crazy to get whatever muscles you can control as strong as possible. And I'll ask the occupational therapist to set you up with some special devices so you can do more with your arms. Like feeding yourself, for a start."

"Whatever."

"I'm going to need you to work with me on this. Okay?"

"I guess."

Good, Beth thought. A small victory for the morning.

〜

By the end of the day, Tave felt wiped out. God knows why. All she'd done was sit in this goddamn wheelchair. Or get lugged onto the mat in the gym, back to the wheelchair, back to bed, and now up again in the chair for dinner. Sarah, her evening nurse, insisted she go to the dining room to eat with the other patients.

"I don't want to," Tave said. She wanted to zone out, watch some mind-less shit on TV.

"Sorry, hon, you got to. I can't spare anyone to feed you in your room." Her tone was not unkind, but firm. She was a redhead, with a long pony-tail and cheeks dotted with freckles, and super tall with a long, thin neck, which boosted her air of authority.

Sarah pushed Tave down the hall, past the nurses' station and the rows of open doors of other patients' rooms—all emptied out now for dinnertime—

down to the large dining room with its windows looking out to an expansive view of the city. Rows of tables, about a dozen in total, filled the room. It bustled with patients in wheelchairs and visitors and noise. As Sarah maneuvered Tave into position at the far end, carefully easing the bulky extended footrests under the table, Tave looked down at her useless legs. Encased in white support hose, they were like uninvited strangers, hollow objects, feeling nothing, yet somehow still attached to her body: if her feet were not propped up, she felt dizzy.

She found herself next to a middle-aged woman. All the other patients were old.

"This is Billie," Sarah said. "I'm going to have Rowena come set you up once she's finished over there." She pointed at the neighboring table, where three old guys sat stooped over their trays, bibs around their necks. An assistant was moving from one to the other, wiping chins, repositioning food items, steadying cups of juice.

"Welcome to the non-droolers' club," Billie said with a grin. "Glad to have the company." She raised a forkful of iceberg lettuce in salute. "What you in for?" She was also seated in a wheelchair, but Tave stole a glance at hers and noticed it had a low back and her knees were fully bent, her feet close to the floor.

"Car accident," Tave said. "Broke my neck."

"Bummer." Billie gently shook her head. She had a square jaw and thin lips, a face rough around the edges. Her black hair was short, unruly, tucked behind her ears, with hints of gray at the roots. She reminded Tave of someone, but she couldn't place who.

Billie said, "So, you just came over from the main house?"

"The main house?"

Billie's mouth twisted into a lopsided grin, the left side lower than the right. "The main hospital. Across the way." She pointed with her chin to the window, where a tall building reflected a stream of bright sunlight. "I know it all too well. What unit were you on?"

"I was in the ICU for weeks, I guess. Don't remember too much about it to tell the truth."

Billie nodded. "Best forgotten, I bet. You must have been beaten up pretty bad."

"Yeah. Guess I was in bad shape. They had to transfer me down here. From up north."

"You've been through a lot, then. Glad you made it over here, kid." She lifted her glass of juice like she was making a toast.

"Thanks." Tave paused, before adding, "It wasn't my fault." The words tumbled out, as though shot from a pitching machine.

"Okay."

"When I first woke up, I thought I must have fallen asleep at the wheel." Tave had never met this woman before but for some reason she couldn't stop blabbering. "I don't remember much about the crash. I just kind of figured I blew it. But my ICU nurse told me there was another driver. He was drunk and he hit me."

"That must make you mad," Billie said.

"I guess. Mostly I'm glad that for once it wasn't me who screwed up."

"Hmmm." Billie nodded.

Okay, she was going to shut up now. "What happened to you?" Tave asked.

"I have MS. Multiple sclerosis. Also a bummer. You never know when it's going to slam you next. I'm a regular in here. A repeat offender, you could say." She laughed, surprisingly loud. "Last month I was walking fine. Now my legs are useless again." Her accent was vaguely Southern. She stabbed at another piece of lettuce.

Tave realized she was hungry. "At least you can move your hands."

"For now. My mother had MS too. Couldn't move much of anything by the end. So, it's not like I don't know what's coming."

"Wow. Yeah, bummer." Tave didn't know what else to offer.

She thought of what that physical therapist had said earlier in the day. That Tave was getting some movement in her arms. And something about fitting her up with some special stuff so she could feed herself. And that Tave was in the early stages of recovery. Tave latched on to the possibility she might get to move her legs and walk out of here.

"Got family around here?" Billie was asking. She smiled and her face did that lopsided thing again. Miss Dee, that's who she looked like, Tave's high school softball coach. The first person who ever believed Tave might be good at something.

"No," Tave said. "I'm not exactly close to my folks. My mom's supposed to be coming up next weekend. She's in Riverside. My friends are all up in Humboldt."

"That's tough. A gal needs a lot of support to get through this stuff."

"Yeah, well. I'm kind of used to doing things on my own," Tave heard herself say.

She wasn't certain that was true. Sure, she'd cut herself off from her family when she got out of high school, went up north to Eureka and bummed around for two years before going to college, paid her own way through school. Until she dropped out. And had a huge fight with her mother, who disapproved of what she called Tave's *lifestyle*. They never got over that one.

"Be there in a sec," Rowena, the nursing assistant, called over to Tave, as she cleared away trays from the other patients. One was a woman, Tave saw now, with gray hair so thin she was practically bald; a bib smeared with food covered her large boobs.

Billie pushed herself away from the table. "I'm going to leave you to enjoy your dinner. I'm waiting for a call from my sister." With a nimble motion, she pirouetted her wheelchair 180 degrees. "Good talking to you. Hang in there, girl." She turned her chair back to face Tave. "Who's your PT, by the way?"

"Beth, I guess."

"She's the best," Billie said with a nod of approval.

Tave watched as she spun toward the hallway. Her upper body looked flabby and out-of-shape, but she picked up speed as pushed her wheelchair with sweeping movements of her arms. How could she remain so fucking cheerful? She said she'd been in this goddamn place several times, and still she could joke about it. And her disease was going to get worse. Tave didn't know how she could face that. It struck her that Billie was on track to get weaker, but she, Tave, was going to get stronger. She could work at it, get a bit stronger day by day, the physical therapist gal said. For the first time, she felt a tiny speck of hope. She conjured up an image of moving toward Billie and passing her, of them moving in opposite directions, like traffic on a country road—and shook herself to stave off another image, one she wanted to banish but couldn't: the dark night, the mesmerizing yellow line, the oncoming headlights.

"Sorry you had to wait so long." Rowena stood at her side, lifting the cover off Tave's meal tray. She gave Tave's shoulder a gentle squeeze and smiled. She was a petite woman, aged about forty, with light-brown skin and gold-rimmed glasses, her eyes encircled with black kohl, her hair pulled tight into a bun on the crown of her head. "Are you okay?"

Tave's shoulders twitched in an involuntary shiver. "Yes, I'm fine." She caught a whiff of the chicken potpie in its oblong plastic dish; it was pasty beige but smelled okay.

"You want to start with the salad?"

Tave chewed her way through three bites of lettuce and a cherry tomato. At the next table, one of the old geezers sat with his face dropped forward on his chest, snoozing after the effort of eating; the bald woman had chocolate pudding drooling down her chin and the other guy stared rheumy-eyed into nothingness. Tave looked away so as not to lose her appetite; she'd have to eat if she was going to build up her strength.

Billie said you needed support to deal with this shit. Someone else—a social worker lady or something—had said the same thing, when she went on about why Tave's mother hadn't visited. Like her mom was going to be of any use. But Tave did have a pretty tight-knit group of friends up north: well, mostly Dan, Sammy. And Les of course.

Oh my god: Les. She squeezed her eyes shut and then opened them wide. She felt she was emerging from a dense fog, and only now beginning to think straight. The rehab doc said he was cutting down on a lot of her meds, so maybe that was it. A whole bunch of stuff was slowly coming into focus. What had happened to Les? She sort of figured Les must be dead but couldn't understand why no one had told her. But—she hadn't asked. She was so used to being secretive—not holding hands in public, hiding all evidence from Les's parents, tiptoeing around pronouns once she realized the name Les could be interpreted either way. She'd never been with a woman before, was always afraid people would disapprove, remembered the slurs shouted by the bikers down by the riverfront. Everything was cool if they were hanging out with Les and her friends; Les had sauntered into the bar where Tave worked and swept her off her feet, pulling her into her small circle, a safe cocoon. But anywhere else, like when she started the new job at Mervyn's, she evaded all questions about whether she had a boyfriend. Her supervisor—big hair, purple eye shadow, shrill voice—reminded Tave of her mother, and was constantly on her case about how to fold the denim jeans or when to tidy the fitting rooms. Tave wasn't going to give the woman something else to rant about. Les teased her, threatened to come into the store at the end of Tave's shift and fling her arms around her. But Tave made her wait outside.

Tave had quit her job at the bar so she and Les would have evenings together. She could see Les now, picking her up after work, sitting in her truck, arm perched on the open window, hand beating time to the music playing on the radio, the wide leather bracelet around her wrist, her big brown eyes smiling. Big, strong, vibrant. "Hey, girl," she'd say when Tave emerged.

Then it hit her. "Shit," she said.

That ICU nurse, Gloria, had said something last week, right before she transferred over here, something hovering around the corners of her brain that had not sunk in until now. That must have been when she was waking up, when everything was pretty much a blur, when the doctors had first told her she was paralyzed from the neck down, when she had wanted to go to sleep and never wake up. But now Gloria's words came back to her.

Tave could hear that soft lilting voice in her head again. *You croak, sweetheart, and he's looking at manslaughter.*

"Fuck," Tave said.

Rowena sucked in her breath in disapproval. So much crap going on in this place and this stupid woman was worried about Tave using the f-word. She offered Tave another tomato.

If he was looking at manslaughter only if Tave died . . .

Wait a minute . . . The fog was lifting as if to reveal a whole new vista.

"Holy shit," Tave shouted, loud enough for the whole room to hear. And then silently to herself—because no one else gave a damn: *Les must be alive.*

3

"Do you have any clothes here?"

Tave blinked at the woman standing at her bedside, fighting off the urge to go back to sleep. She'd had a rough night, thinking about Les, trying to guess where she was, and what had happened to her. She didn't know how to find out, who to ask.

"You'll need something to wear for therapy. We don't want you in a hospital gown."

This woman was older than the other staff: plump, with mousy hair escaping from an untidy bun, broad cheeks splattered with age spots, and eyebrows plucked into a pencil-thin arch that gave her a permanently startled expression. When Tave didn't respond, she said, "Do you remember me? I'm Laurel from OT."

"*O tea?*" Tave croaked. Her throat was dry.

"Occupational therapy."

Tave didn't understand what occupation she could possibly do in her present state, but she said nothing. The woman jabbered on and on about a daily schedule and something she called activities of daily living. She opened the door to the closet next to Tave's bed and closed it again.

"Nothing here. You'll need to ask your family to bring in something loose and comfortable. Sweatpants and T-shirts are best."

"How the fuck can I do that?" Tave said. "I don't have anyone. I mean, no one close by."

"Oh, that's right." She scooped some stray hair behind her ear. "Okay, not to worry. I'll see what I can rustle up."

She disappeared and Tave's mind returned to Les, trying to piece together what had happened the night of the accident. She remembered leaving the restaurant and the dark, dark road, the long drive back from . . . where? *Wait* . . . Oregon. Yeah, that's it. They'd gone up to Bend for a long weekend, to hang out with Les's old buddies from way back: Meg and Raven, who were living off the land, in the mountains outside of town. They'd seemed scary to Tave at first. Les had been lovers with Raven years ago, and Tave thought it weird they were friends. Back in high school or college, two people who'd broken up would run into each other in class or whatever, but they wouldn't *speak*. And everyone else had to choose sides. Sure, if parents got divorced, like Tave's mom and dad, they had to kind of stay connected, although in Tave's family that had hardly been an amicable arrangement. But if two people didn't have kids, weren't married, she didn't see why they would stay friends. She'd never heard of such a thing.

And she worried Les would want to sleep with Raven again. Raven: what kind of name was that anyway? She feared she'd be expected to do a swapping thing, where she would be expected to sleep with Meg. A prospect that was even more terrifying once they arrived at the ranch, and Meg came striding out to greet them: huge and butch, with dark whiskers on her chin and snake tattoos on her arms, definitely not Tave's type. She fretted they would make fun of her for not knowing how to approach the goats or being unable to hide her fear around the beehives. She thought it would be weird to be hanging out with all girls, two couples. They usually hung out in bigger groups, and mostly with guys. Mostly Les's friends.

But Meg and Raven turned out to be super friendly. There was no mixing up of the couples. Les pulled Tave close, her arm resting across Tave's shoulders, as she chatted with her old friends. Tave found it comfortable to be with them. They cooked together, fixing a delicious vegetarian stew and roasting foil-wrapped potatoes on the bonfire, and they told stories. Well, Meg and Les told stories; Tave continued to feel shy, and mostly listened, hearing tales of Les's past. Some she'd heard before; some were new to her. She loved learning more about Les's time driving a truck for the landscaping company out of Fortuna, and her run-ins with aggressive pot farmers in the hills. Les had a hilarious account of the day she and her crew stumbled upon a huge spread of marijuana plants under glass, way up in a remote area. She had to bomb down a steep track while two guys in dungarees and straggly gray beards fired shotguns into the air. Sounded terrifying to Tave, not hilarious at all—but Les made a joke of it.

Les thrived at times like these, being the center of the group, cracking everyone up with her wicked sense of humor. Tave tried to tell one of her favorite jokes about three girls stranded on a desert island, but as she approached the punchline, she knew she was going to mess it up, and she sure did. She winced at the memory. She should have kept her mouth shut and sat quiet, and just laughed at Les's jokes. Les would have been fine with that.

They had a blast at the ranch. They'd smoked some weed and drunk some beer—not too much, enough for a nice buzz. Meg and Raven had a large collection of CDs, mostly blues singers and folk artists Tave didn't know, but she enjoyed listening to them. Les was in a good mood most of the time, and very affectionate. They made love under the rafters in the converted barn that served as the guest room. Tave peeked out through the small window above the bed and saw a mass of bright stars in the black, black sky.

"It's awesome," she said. "Thanks for bringing me here."

She lay in the crook of Les's arm, her head nestled on her breast. The memory was still vivid: the feel of Les holding her close, kissing the top of her head, Tave pulling the covers up over her shoulders and sliding her legs over Les's thighs. Simple movements, made without thought, taken for granted.

Now look at her. Lying in this damn hospital bed. Leticia, the day shift nursing aide, was waving something in front of Tave's face. "Take your pick," she said, holding up two T-shirts. One looked about Tave's size, faded maroon, with a Donald Duck logo, the other much bigger, bright green, with *Kelly-Moore Paints* in white lettering; both were hideous.

"Whatever," Tave said.

"Let's go with the green," Leticia said. She was a tall, lean, Black woman with smooth, youthful skin and beautiful hair, which she wore in an elaborate swirl of fine braids. She raised the head of the bed and removed Tave's gown. "I'll work on getting you something better." She squinted at Tave, like she was sizing her up. "I'd say you're more of a blue person. And maybe purple. My daughter's about your build, and she's got way too much stuff."

Tave was about to protest that she didn't want anyone's trash, but hell, she didn't care. She allowed herself to be turned and twisted, leaned forward and back, in a series of deft movements, as Laurel and Leticia dressed her in the T-shirt and pulled a pair of hospital pajama bottoms over her white support stockings. They also insisted on wrapping something they called a binder around her stomach; it looked like an ugly corset, but it would stop her blood pressure from plummeting, they said. They seemed determined to make her as dorky as possible.

Once they got Tave into the wheelchair, Laurel wheeled her down the hall to a small room off the main gym. She spent the rest of the morning working through what Laurel called her "bag of tricks," a box of weird-looking splints, straps, and curved silverware, experimenting with various options for Tave to feed herself. At first, Tave couldn't see how that was possible, but after much trial and error, Laurel set her up with a wrist splint with a slot that could hold either a fork or spoon, and a plate equipped with a semicircular plastic ring to prevent food slipping off. With one hand supporting Tave's elbow and the other at her shoulder, Laurel had Tave practice small swinging movements of her arm to scoop up bite-size pieces of banana.

Tave tensed her jaw in concentration, as she tried to bring her arm down and across multiple times, missing completely. Laurel bent the spoon to adjust the angle and had her try again. Eventually, Tave managed to snag a slice of banana.

"Good job!" Laurel said, clapping her hands. "Now lift up."

Tave jerked and the banana fell to the floor. On the next attempt, it stayed in place, but Laurel had to give Tave's elbow a boost for her to reach her mouth. By the time the banana reached her lips, Tave scrunched her nose and turned away. It was as appetizing as pummeled Play-Doh.

"We'll work on this every day." Laurel placed the splint, the utensils, and the plate guard in a tote bag attached to the back of Tave's wheelchair. "But what a great start!" she gushed. Tave felt like she was back at her third-grade end-of-season softball party, where everyone received a medal simply for participating.

～

And it seemed Tave had no choice but to participate. There were days when she wanted to draw the sheet over her head and retreat into the shell she'd hidden behind when she first woke up in the ICU. But that wasn't allowed. Every day, Leticia pulled back the covers to get Tave ready for a full schedule of therapy, like back-to-back classes in high school. And in spite of the goofy devices and the overbearing cheeriness that drove her nuts, she found herself playing along. And she noticed tiny improvements in her arm strength.

"Try that again," Beth said, placing her hand on Tave's biceps. It was the morning PT session, toward the end of Tave's first week on rehab. Beth was intensely focused on the muscle-testing routine again.

Beth had a square face with a strong jaw, bright-blue eyes, and brown hair cut short on the sides and layered on top, with bleached blonde highlights. Her left ear was decorated with a row of silver studs, and she wore a thin silver ring on her pinky finger. She was dressed in olive cargo pants and a short-sleeved black polo shirt revealing strong, bronzed forearms: a body tight and compact, like she worked out a lot.

She motioned for Tave to flex her left arm. Seated in the wheelchair, Tave raised her wrist toward her shoulder. She couldn't hold a dumbbell, as her hands were still useless, but Beth had secured a weighted strap around her forearms. It was a pathetic two pounds—Miss Dee from high school would have sneered—but yesterday she couldn't do it and now she could. The tingling tension in her biceps felt good, made her feel alive. It also triggered a weird burning sensation in her fingers and a spasm of pain in her neck, but she decided to ignore those.

"That's good," Beth said. "See how your biceps are coming in on that side?"

"I guess. So, the doctors were bullshitting when they said I was paralyzed from the neck down?"

Beth scooted in closer and placed her hand on Tave's shoulder. "You broke your neck. You have a cervical spinal cord injury, so you're considered a quadriplegic. But like most quadriplegics—or "quads"—you're getting some return of movement in your arms. It's limited movement right now. And we don't know how far it'll go. But we agreed to work together to get you as strong as possible, right?" When Tave said nothing, she added, "They say you were a softball player. Is that true?"

"Yeah." Tave curled her lip. "Can't see me doing that again anytime soon."

"But you understand applying yourself, working out, building strength. That's what we're doing here. We're on a team together, okay?"

"Whatever."

Beth looked at her notes on the computer screen. "Are you right- or left-handed?"

"Right," Tave said. "For most things. But I bat left. I mean, I used to," she added.

She closed her eyes and could feel the bat in her hand, planting her feet and driving a hit far into right field, the thwack of the ball settling into her glove, the power of her throw to get a runner out at second, the thrill of sliding into score at home plate. She'd been determined to make the team at Humboldt, working out every morning, lifting weights, running three miles on the treadmill, going to the batting cages every night for a week before the tryouts, swinging like crazy, turning up the speed on the pitching machine, self-correcting her stance, Miss Dee's voice in her head: *Wider, more weight on your back leg.*

How fucking ironic this accident happened right when she'd been try-ing to get back into playing again. She knew Les would disapprove, but she planned to stand up for herself for once. Les was always jealous of the time Tave spent with her teammates. Tave had never admitted this to any-one, or even to herself, but it was the pushback from Les that led her to drop out of school. She told her mom the classes were boring and so her grades fell, and therefore she was no longer allowed to play on the team. But in reality, it was the other way around. She stopped going to practice because Les made a fuss. *You have to go every fucking day?* So naturally, she was cut from the team. And if she wasn't playing softball, she had no inter-est in being in school.

But two years later, she missed it too much. She heard about a new coed rec team in town. They were recruiting players. They needed a catcher. She said she was interested. But she hadn't told Les. She was going to. She'd planned to tell her on the road trip. That goddamn road trip. But she still hadn't fessed up by the time they were driving home.

"Good," Beth was saying now. "Means you're pretty versatile. For sure, you have more return on the left."

"I'm using my left for eating," Tave said. At breakfast, she'd managed to get some scrambled eggs to her mouth with only a slight lift from Leticia at her elbow. Pathetic that this was where she was at now, but it was true her strength was improving day by day. She could almost do it unassisted—after someone cut the food, placed the cuff around her wrist, inserted the spoon or fork: a fork for foods that were easy to spike, a spoon for soft or slippery stuff like scrambled eggs.

"I think you're ready to drive," Beth smiled.

"Drive?"

"A power wheelchair," Beth said. "Let's talk to Laurel."

She pushed Tave down to the occupational therapy room, where they met up with Laurel, who led the way to a storeroom next door. After some rummaging, the two therapists emerged with an enormous-looking wheelchair. With a high back and a rear platform supporting a huge battery, it reminded Tave of a beat-up old pickup truck, ugly as shit. But she said nothing as they pushed her out into the clinic area again, positioned this new monster next to her current wheelchair, and gently transferred her from one to the other. Beth adjusted the footrests at an angle halfway between horizontal and vertical.

"This okay?" she asked. "Not dizzy?"

"I'm good." Tave was doing much better with the dizziness. Dr. Kramer had started her on a new medication for that. Tave couldn't remember the name, although she was supposed to. The nurse subjected her to a quiz each morning.

Beth was busy now with a screwdriver, moving the drive mechanism to the left side of the wheelchair and adjusting the armrest, while Laurel fussed with a white plastic splint secured on Tave's forearm with wide Velcro straps. Her hand lay immobile in this splint, fingers slightly curved, thumb outstretched in its own little trough, like a lonely soldier separated from his regiment.

"Try this," Beth said.

She guided Tave's wrist, encased in the splint, into a U-shaped handle mounted on the armrest. Tave couldn't move her hand but with a forward motion of her shoulder and elbow, she could push the lever. The wheelchair lurched forward as soon as she touched it.

"Oops." Beth fiddled with something below the handle. "That's better. Tortoise setting for now. Try again."

She once again placed Tave's hand over the controls and scooted out of the way on her rolling stool. Tave gently pushed forward on the lever and the wheelchair inched forward, creeping across the room.

"That's great!" Beth said. "Now turn around."

Slowly, carefully, Tave made a wide circle. Then she reversed and turned counterclockwise, pushing the lever more assertively—but she overdid it, jerking the handle too hard. The chair jolted to the side, banging the footrests into the wall, jarring her whole body. When she tried to reverse, she spun around and bumped into a trash can, tipping it sideways, spilling its contents onto the floor.

"Shit. I can't do this."

Laurel scooped up the trash while Beth adjusted the armrest again and did something to the handle. When she repositioned Tave's hand at the lever, her wrist felt better supported.

"Give it another go."

This time she was more in control. She guided the wheelchair out into the hall, smoothly navigating past another therapist accompanying an old man hunched over a walker, before circling back the way she'd come, continuing past the OT room, toward the main gym, gradually picking up speed. She had to admit this was kind of cool: moving herself, without someone pushing her, the first time she'd done anything on her own since the accident. Caught unawares, she felt a smile creep across her face.

A memory surfaced: running on the beach. She closed her eyes for a moment and could feel the sand between her toes, the pressure on her palms as she did cartwheels—though she was never any good. Les was the pro, showing off to impress the guys they hung out with, tumbling over again and again, in a dizzying whirl, her strong arms and legs in perfect alignment, running back to the group, covered in sand, and throwing herself down next to Tave, pulling her into a hug.

"Shit, how d'you do that?" Sammy said.

"Gymnastics. I started when I was four. I loved it. But I got too big. *Not ladylike enough*, my coach said."

"Too butch, you mean," Dan said.

"Damn right." Les tickled Tave's ribs, rolling over on top of her, acting like they were making out.

"You crazy lovebirds."

"Ee-ew," said Dan's new girlfriend. Tave couldn't remember her name. Patti or Polly . . . something like that.

"Shut up," Dan said. "You think it's contagious or something?"

Patti or Polly didn't last long. None of them did. Except for Sammy's girlfriend, Rosie. And of course, Tave herself. Les had been hanging out with those guys long before the two of them got together, and Tave got to join the gang. That's how they thought of themselves: a gang. Not like they were into heavy drugs or anything, but they formed a tight-knit group, like family.

Beth ran to catch up with her. "I think you've passed your test," she said. "You can keep this chair for everyday use in your room if you like."

Tave looked up at her and smiled. "Thanks."

But halfway back to her room, she couldn't hold her arm in position any longer. Her neck and shoulders ached. She let go of the control lever, and the chair jolted to a halt.

"That's okay," Beth said at her side. "You're doing well for the first day." She took over, propelling the chair forward with only her index finger.

Tave leaned back against the headrest and closed her eyes. When she opened them again, she said, "I want to ask you something."

Beth looked at her and took her hand off the controls. They had stopped by the door of the patient dining room, empty at this time of day. Tave took a deep breath. "How could I find out more about the accident?"

"You mean . . ." Beth frowned.

Tave nodded. Yes, the accident. All those weeks ago, miles up north.

"You don't remember much about it, huh?"

"No." Her voice came out in a whisper. It was a tiny first step, like opening a door a crack. She didn't know what was behind that door; she was frightened, afraid to mention Les, didn't know how bad the news might be. "I don't really know what happened."

"Let's see what we can find." Beth steered Tave over to the computer terminal in the dining room. "There's something in the admitting note from when you came to the ICU."

She pulled up a bunch of records on the computer, scrolled through screen after screen, white pages covered with dense text that Tave couldn't read. "Uh, ha," she muttered. "No, that's not it. Oh, here we go. *Twenty-three-year-old female admitted following an MVA in Siskiyou County . . .*"

"A what?"

"MVA. A motor vehicle accident. Let's see . . . what else? . . . *A two-vehicle collision; the other driver was believed to be alcohol-impaired . . .*" Beth scrolled some more and turned to Tave. "Doesn't give any more details about the accident itself. Maybe we can find something online, from news reports."

Tave couldn't control the mouse herself, so Beth googled it every which way they could think of. Nothing came up. Finally, right before she was going to say *forget it*, on the fourth page of the search results, they found a small item in the *Mount Shasta Herald: May 7, 2006, in the early hours of the morning, a two-vehicle accident on Highway 97, three victims transported to hospital, two listed in critical condition.* No further details.

Two in critical condition. Must be herself and Les. Or maybe the other driver?

She knew if Les had recovered, she'd have made contact. She would have visited or at least called or something.

"Doesn't say which hospital the others are at?"

"No," Beth said. "But it's six weeks ago now . . ." She placed her hand on Tave's shoulder. "You want to find out what happened to the other people in the accident?"

Tave nodded, mute now. She bobbled her head in a stupid repetitive motion.

"Maybe the social worker can check on that for you," Beth said with a gentle squeeze.

She didn't press her to talk more and Tave was grateful. She wasn't ready. Les always screamed at her when they got into fights, accusing her of being useless at saying what was going on with her. Yeah, okay she was. There was a lot she'd held inside, she realized now, a lot they never talked about. Like why Les, who was shameless around their friends, cared so much about what her parents thought, or why Tave was afraid of Les sometimes, afraid of her anger.

But now she wanted to talk to Les about anything, or nothing. She just wanted to see her big brown eyes and feel those strong arms tight around her.

4

At the end of the day, Tave was back in her room, with nothing scheduled until dinner. The sun streamed in, casting oblong patterns on the wall above the sink. All week, Tave had insisted on returning to bed immediately after her last therapy session. She liked to retreat into a silent shell, to space out watching the shadows inch toward the corner, refusing all offers of *Judge Judy* or the afternoon soaps from the TV mounted on the wall. But today she wanted to stay up and have another go with the wheelchair.

She steered toward the window. The main wing of the hospital dominated the view across the courtyard, its eight-story tower sleek and shiny, its tinted windows preventing nosy eyes from peeking in. Somewhere over there lay the ICU in which she'd apparently spent five haze-filled weeks. To the right, she caught a glimpse of a residential area in the distance, with streets climbing the hill in grid formation. Tave was unfamiliar with the city; she'd visited Fisherman's Wharf as a child, and somewhere downtown once, fake ID in hand, for a spring break trip during her senior year in high school. She wondered about the lives contained in the little houses ascending the hill and beyond. They were as mysterious to her as her own life moving forward.

The nurse stepped into the room, stood near the doorway. So many people in this place, Tave couldn't keep them all straight; this was the redhead with the ponytail, but she couldn't remember her name.

"You're staying up until dinner?" the nurse asked.

"Yeah."

"Great. Do you want to wear your collar?"

"Sure."

Tave hated the hard collar she'd worn for weeks, but this soft one was optional, and it did help when she was tired. The nurse—Sarah, her name badge said—applied the soft foam, securing the strap behind Tave's neck.

"I'll help you with a weight shift after Tracy has been in to talk to you," she said.

"Who?"

"Tracy. The social worker. She wants to talk with you. Ah, here she is."

A middle-aged woman entered the room, wearing loose-fitting black pants and some sort of weird smock-type thing that hung below her knees. She had salt-and-pepper hair styled in a bob cut, and bright-red lipstick; her perfume smelled like sage. Tave vaguely remembered meeting her a few days ago. The woman obviously didn't think she had to reintroduce herself. She pulled a chair opposite Tave and settled with some papers on her lap.

"I hear from the therapists that you are doing very well," she said. She smiled and Tave could see lipstick smeared on her front teeth. "Super, super," she said, sounding like she was about to break into song. "We need to start planning for your going home."

"I just got here," Tave said.

"Oh, it's never too early to start planning. You'll only be here a few weeks," she added breezily. "And then you'll go home."

Home? "I've no idea where I'll go."

"Where were you living at the time of the accident?"

"In Eureka. But I can't go back there. I don't suppose anyone's been paying the rent." She didn't add that it was a second-floor apartment. She hoped she'd be able to walk by the time she got out of here, but stairs: she recognized that might be difficult. And she suddenly wondered what had happened to all her stuff. She and Les didn't own much, mostly IKEA junk, but she had a good bike and her catcher's gear, and a great set of skis she'd found for nothing on Craig's List.

"Okay," Tracy was saying. "Can your mother take you?"

"No," Tave said without hesitation. "That would never work." The social worker scribbled on her yellow lined notepad.

Tave took a deep breath. She couldn't put this off any longer. "I need to find out what happened to my friend."

Tracy looked up. She lowered her reading glasses from the tip of her nose, allowing the green cord to dangle over her breasts. "Your friend?"

"My friend was in the car with me," she said. "In the crash. Leslie Saunders." She bit her lip to stop crying, but it was no use. Tears rolled down her cheeks, damn it. She lifted her arm and bent forward, wiping her face with the crook of her elbow. "No one has told me what happened to her."

The social worker put her glasses back on her nose and ruffled through a red folder on her lap. "I don't see anything here about . . ." she said.

"She was in the car. Beth helped me find it online. It said two seriously injured."

The woman closed her folder and reached for Tave's hand. Or rather, the white plastic splint in which her hand was encased. Tave felt only a vague sense of pressure there but looking down she saw the bright-red fingernails resting on the Velcro straps. When she looked up again, Tracy held her gaze. "I'll see what I can find out," she said.

~

Beth intended to skip the gym after work. She wanted to get home in time to eat dinner with Katy. They'd hardly seen each other all week. And Beth had her board meeting tonight. She ought to go, as she missed the last one while on vacation. The major fundraiser of the year was coming up in September, and there was a lot to do. They had to make up for the cuts in the city budget for the disabled sports program.

Her schedule was getting full, and she and Katy were slipping back into the same tension that had hovered over them before vacation. Beth wanted to make this relationship work. They'd been together four years now. No one had lasted long before Katy. Pam, her first lover, decided monogamy was an instrument of the patriarchy, so Beth should accept a threesome with Linde; Gjerta moved back to Denmark; Susan freaked out when Beth said she wanted more commitment. Yes, Beth wanted commitment. She'd now turned thirty-one: time to settle down. She thought she'd found that with Katy.

Their big fight in Chicago about moving to the West Coast had been hard, for sure. The second winter they were together was unusually cold, even by Midwest standards. Katy couldn't stand it; she hated the bitter wind blowing off the lake, the icy chill that filled your lungs with every breath, the frozen grayness that prevented her from running or biking for weeks on end. When the temperature didn't rise above freezing for the entire month of February, Katy rebelled.

"I've got to move back to California," she said.

But Beth was settled in her job and had planned to supervise a fresh batch of PT interns the following year. She'd grown up with the wind barreling across the Iowa plains and accused Katy of being a wuss, and Katy said Beth was being selfish and rigid and not valuing their relationship. Katy almost left one night—did leave for hours, didn't come back until midnight. But they agreed to take a trip out to California in the spring and check out the options. Beth promised to keep an open mind.

A gray chill hung over Chicago that April, but California was blooming. Beth marveled at the kaleidoscope of flowers in every front yard, the palm and eucalyptus trees swaying in the breeze in the park, the brilliant sunshine as they sat on the patio of the neighborhood café with lattes and buttery croissants that melted in her mouth. She checked out the rehab units at the local medical centers, and held an informational interview with Linda, who made it clear there would be a job for her anytime. Katy took her to meet her welcoming family, and they borrowed her father's new Prius to drive all around the Bay Area. They rode the ferry over to Sausalito. Beth hadn't realized how cold it would be on board, and was ill-prepared, her jacket much too thin. But she didn't want to stay inside where the stuffy heat made her nauseous. They braved the gusts blowing across the stern, Katy enveloping her, protecting her from the wind, adorning her with salty kisses. As the ferry sped past Alcatraz, Beth decided: yes, they should move out here. They would make it work.

They'd been here two years, and Beth was happy. She'd quickly fallen in love with the city, the coast, the mountains, the immense scale of everything in the West—and the climate, of course. But she wished Katy could find meaningful work. She seemed to be settling into this new job. The shifts were all over the place, but at least she was sticking to it.

Beth couldn't remember Katy's schedule this week, and if she'd said when she'd be home. Katy might have told her, but Beth knew she'd been distracted. All week, she'd found it hard to put work out of her mind when she got home. Now, at the last minute, she changed her mind about the gym, and veered right at the bottom of the hill. Thirty minutes on the treadmill, she thought. She needed to clear her head. She couldn't stop thinking about Tave. Beth didn't usually get so affected by her patients, but there was something haunting about this one. Tave was settling into the routine after her first week on rehab, getting more recovery in her arms every day, getting stronger, remaining medically stable. And gradually coming out of her shell. But she'd had no visitors. And no calls, as far as Beth could tell. The cards above her bed were from weeks ago. Tave had given Beth permission to look at them: one from each of her parents and one from a friend, but when Beth asked about this friend, she clammed up. She said only that her mother was coming up from Southern California sometime soon, scowling at the prospect.

Beth worried about her. She had a great team here on rehab, but she was going to need support once she left. The proverbial village, in fact. Tave seemed to have no one.

Beth found an open treadmill and selected her favorite workout playlist. She picked up her speed to seven miles an hour to the beat of "Heart of Glass." She was glad Tave had opened up in asking about the accident. Too bad they hadn't been able to find much. Maybe Beth should do more searching when she got home. There must be a police report. She could find out which hospital the others were taken to. *No*, she thought to herself. *Stop it, let it go.* Got to maintain some boundaries. Even if she were able to identify the hospital, she wouldn't be able to get any information. Privacy rules and all that. Tomorrow she would ask the social worker to look into it, go through the official channels. Tracy must be working on tracking down family and friends anyway. She would have to figure out a discharge plan.

When Beth got home, there was no sign of Katy. Only a note on the kitchen table.

Back by 11. Leftover pasta and salad from last night in fridge.

She couldn't remember Katy saying anything about going out. Had Katy gone out by herself? Unlikely. Beth tried to wrap her head around this as she stood at the kitchen counter, chomping on the salad. Then she froze, fork in midair, as she noticed the beer bottles. Four empties tossed in the sink.

"Goddamn it," she said, pushing the food aside.

5

According to the day's schedule taped to her armrest, Tave had *SW* at ten thirty.

"What the hell's that?" she asked Laurel after their occupational therapy session.

"The social worker. Tracy."

"Oh, right."

The social worker who said she was going to try to find out what had happened to Les. Tave's stomach churned. It was odd: if she placed her wrist over her belly, she couldn't feel its touch. Her whole body was dead below the chest, with only the occasional twinge of burning pain from her feet. When she prodded her legs, she might as well be poking a lump of wood. But her insides could still twist and gurgle, as though to remind her they could spring to life at any moment.

She tried to steady her breathing, fighting off the urge to fall asleep sitting in the wheelchair. Again, she'd not slept well the night before, haunted once more by images of the accident—or the moments leading up to the accident, because she still couldn't conjure up the impact itself, or the immediate aftermath. But she saw the dark night, the black road, felt the heaviness in her core, and Les sitting next to her, nodding off. Having finally plucked up the courage to ask about Les, she could think of nothing else. She had to find out what had happened to her, and where she was now.

A whiff of perfume and a rustle of material meant someone had entered her room. Tracy pulled up a chair to face Tave. She wore a shapeless knee-length tunic similar to yesterday's outfit, but this one was bright turquoise, with a matching turquoise cord around her spectacles.

"Good morning, sweetie," she said, peering at Tave over the top of the glasses. "How are we doing today?"

"Fine."

"Lovely, lovely." She smiled. "I hear you've been driving the wheelchair all over the place. Good for you!" she gushed.

Tave stared at her. Her earrings were also turquoise, for fuck's sake.

"I spoke to your mother this morning," she continued. "She confirmed she's coming up next week. So that's wonderful. Lovely, lovely." That was her chorus.

"Don't count on her showing up," Tave said.

"Oh, sweetie, don't say that. Of course, she's coming. She was so happy to hear how well you're doing. And I told her we'll talk more about your discharge plan." She patted the yellow writing pad on her lap. "Oh, and I have some news about your friend."

Tave's heart jumped in her throat. "What?"

"Leslie Saunders was injured in the crash and hospitalized in Redding. I haven't been able to verify the extent of her injuries. But she was released three weeks ago. Apparently, she's back at her parents' home in Chico."

"Oh," Tave said. "Wow . . ."

"Do you have her parents' phone number?"

Tave shook her head. She'd lost all her contacts. But she wouldn't have their number anyway.

"Maybe they're listed," Tracy said.

Tave grimaced at the thought of Les's mom. Darlene would descend upon them once a month, bustling into the apartment like a tornado, her mouth going nonstop. The shit they had to go through to prepare for her visit. The den, which normally was jammed full of Les's elliptical machine and all sorts of junk, had to be converted into a convincing bedroom for Tave. Les had her list. Move Tave's clothes from bedroom into den: check. Drag elliptical machine into living room: check. Make futon into bed: check. Stuff gear into closet: check. Hide the framed photograph of them embracing on the Santa Cruz boardwalk: check. Remove the *Hers and Hers* mugs from the kitchen cabinet: check. Hide the vibrators: check and double check. All this for a couple of hours, at most. Les's father stayed in the truck; he couldn't make it up the stairs, was the excuse, his breathing being bad. Darlene sat at the kitchen table, boasting about nieces and nephews who had gotten engaged, or were expecting twins, or who'd won a football scholarship to Cal State Long Beach, ignoring Tave most of the time.

"Would you like me to try to find their number for you?" Tracy was saying.

"No, they won't . . ." Tave began, but added, "Yes. I mean . . . could you call them and find out how Les is doing?" Tave was pretty sure they wouldn't want to hear from her, but maybe they'd talk to this social worker woman.

"Yes, of course, I can do that." She patted her notepad again. "Now, we'll need to identify a wheelchair-accessible place for you."

She droned on and on, but Tave tuned her out.

~

The floodgates were open now and the questions swirled around Tave's head. She couldn't understand why the fuck Les hadn't called if she'd been home almost a month. She needed to know how Les was doing, how she was coping with being home. Her mother must be driving her nuts. Maybe no one had told Les that Tave was down here. But surely she could have found out if she wanted to.

"You're very quiet," Billie said. It was lunchtime. They sat in what had become their usual spot by the window, their backs to the old geezers in their bibs. Tave had been self-conscious at first about her feeding getup, but Billie waved off her concerns and praised every tiny achievement.

"What's on your mind, kid?"

"I just found out about my friend. She was injured in the crash too, but she's back home with her folks now."

"That's good news, I guess."

"You don't know her folks," Tave said.

"Oh."

They sat in silence for a while as they ate. At least, Tave tried to. She could feed herself now with her special utensils. Leticia had cut up the fish and potatoes into small bites and left her to it. But Tave didn't have much of an appetite. She was supposed to be eating her main meal of the day at noon, to avoid the late-night nausea.

"What about your other buddies up there?" Billie said. "You talk to any of them?"

"No, not yet. I will . . . Fuck. I should have thought of that. I'm such an idiot."

"Relax, kid. Go easy on yourself." Billie bent forward and adjusted the position of one of her footrests. "You're dealing with a lot of shit, okay?"

"Yeah, I know."

"Your friend who was in the accident—what's her name?"

"Les."

"Could some of your other friends go visit Les at her parents' place, see how she's doing?"

"I don't know about that. Her parents are totally uptight. But I should talk to someone, see what they can find out."

Tave scooped up some potatoes with the curved spoon secured into her wrist cuff and swung her elbow up, bringing the food to her mouth. She was getting better at this. The peas might be a challenge, though. Hell, forget the peas. She was never much of a vegetable fan.

Dan, she suddenly remembered. "Dan sent me a card. I forgot about that. It came while I was over there." Tave looked at the gleaming windows of the main hospital building across the courtyard. "Shit, I don't even know how to reach him. I lost my phone."

"Ask the social worker to find him," Billie said.

"She drives me crazy," Tave said. "And those outfits of hers."

"I know." Billie grinned. "But she's okay. A bit ditzy, but she gets stuff done." She pushed back from the table. "I gotta go, girl. My sister's coming in. I've got *family training*"—she made air quotes—"this afternoon. Looks like I'm going to be stuck using this chair for a while, so they have to train my sister on how to help me into the car, and all that jazz." She swiveled her wheelchair to face the door, but turned back to Tave and said, "I get to blow this pop-stand the day after tomorrow. But I just might have to come back in here and check on you. So you let me know what you find out about your friend. Okay?"

"Sure. Okay."

Tave tried to scoop up some peas, but they cascaded onto her lap.

～

Beth had been stuck in the office all morning. Linda, the department manager, had grabbed her in a panic the moment she walked in the door. "The State" was in the main hospital. This meant the inspectors might come over to the rehab unit at any moment. HR was in a tizzy about the employee files for the new rehab aides hired earlier in the year, so Linda had to work on those. She asked Beth to fix the quarterly quality reports that had not been updated since December. "I need someone I can trust to get this done in a timely manner," she said.

Beth tried to focus on the data entry sheets, but her mind wandered. She caught herself chewing on her lip and digging her fingernails into the palm of her left hand. She couldn't understand what Katy was up to, sneaking around behind her back, staying out late. When Beth had returned from her meeting at ten thirty, there was no sign of Katy. She'd gone to bed, and tossed and turned, but when Katy tiptoed in at one o'clock, she'd pretended to be asleep. Even with her back turned, she could smell the alcohol on Katy's breath. Katy had slept in, as usual, and when Beth left for work, they'd not yet spoken.

She remembered the fight they'd had on vacation, about which route to take on the backcountry roads to the trailhead. They usually did well together on trips, but Katy, who was driving, had insisted on going left at the intersection, when Beth knew they should go right.

"You always think you know best," Katy had snapped.

"Well, in this instance I do," Beth said. "Look, this road is veering off far to the west. We need to turn around."

Katy wouldn't admit she was wrong until they'd gone miles out of their way. They had to backtrack, and therefore made a late start on the hike. Beth didn't like the way they'd gotten mean with each other. Something in the way Katy acted had reminded Beth of her father. Growing up, he never listened to her. He always sided with Mike or Jason, her older brothers, letting them choose which pizza to order or which video to rent, none of them believing her when she remembered the location of the best camping site or the rules to *Clue*. Bumping along that dusty dirt road hedged in by dense chaparral trees, she'd felt the same sense of anger and frustration with Katy. She wanted to talk, to figure out how to stop it happening again. But once they were hiking, and the breeze and sun and the smell of the ponderosa pine were so wonderful, she opted to forget it. It didn't seem important after all.

Linda popped in before lunch. "How's it going?"

"I'm almost done," Beth said. "I still have to finish the patient satisfaction surveys for May."

"I think we can get away with saying we're working on those," Linda said. "Thanks so much for your help. I know it's tedious. But I think we're ready for them. Phew." Her blonde hair was perfectly coiffed as always, cascading to her shoulders, but she had beads of sweat across her forehead, which she wiped now with the back of her hand. "If they even show. You know how it is. Might be a big fuss for nothing."

"So, I'm back on clinical this afternoon?"

"Yes, of course." Linda frowned. "Is everything okay? You seem down in the dumps. Is your spinal cord patient getting to you?"

"No. No, she's doing great." Beth shuffled the papers in front of her, avoiding eye contact. She hadn't realized her bad mood was on display. She looked up to see Linda's gaze fierce upon her. "Rehab-wise, she's doing great. She's had no visitors, though. She's estranged from her family, her friends far away." *I'm babbling,* she thought. *Keep it professional.* "I know Tracy is working on this, of course."

"Okay, sounds good. But let me know if you need a break from her."

"No, I love working with her." *Tave is not the one I need a break from,* she thought.

She returned to her own desk and reviewed her afternoon schedule: family training with Billie and her sister, followed by the new stroke patient who came in last week, and finally Tave for a joint session with OT. They were planning to work more on wheelchair mobility, maybe go outside. She looked up at the small window high above the bookshelf: the fog had burned off. It would be good to take Tave out into the sunshine. Maybe she would open up more, away from the hospital, talk about her friends, or anyone else she could look to for support.

~

Beth saw that Tave was exhausted. "Let me take it from here," she said. She moved Tave's wrist onto her lap and took control of the joystick to guide the wheelchair up the last block to the hospital courtyard.

"You've done very well."

"Thanks." The word seemed to stumble from Tave's lips on automatic pilot, hardly an enthusiastic endorsement. But there was a hint of a glow in her eyes, and she'd laughed at the antics of the kids shooting hoops in the park. Then she blurted out the news she'd received from Tracy: her friend had been discharged from hospital.

Laurel ran on ahead to get to her last patient of the day. But Beth had no one else on her schedule and could linger. Her charting wouldn't take long, as she'd been on office work all morning. And she was certainly in no hurry to get home.

"Would you like to sit in the sunshine for a bit?" she asked. They had reached the bench at the entrance to the rehab annex.

"Sure," Tave said. "Work on my suntan. Ha, ha." She looked down at her forearms crisscrossed with the splint straps. "These are going to leave a glamorous mark. Least of my worries, I guess."

"Yeah, I guess." Beth sat next to her. She turned her own face toward the warmth of the sun and stretched her legs. "What else did you find out about your friend? Is she okay? Have you spoken to her?"

"No . . . She's back at her parents' place. I don't have their number or anything. Tracy said she was going to try to get it. But . . ."

"But what?"

"Well, see . . . Her parents didn't exactly approve of me. Of us, I mean." Tave turned to her with a note of defiance Beth had not seen before.

"Wait . . . Les is your *girlfriend*?"

"Yeah."

"As in . . ."

"Yes. As in *girlfriend* girlfriend."

"Oh."

"What? Are you shocked, or something?"

"No, not at all." Beth grinned. It made sense. Perfect sense.

6

Beth cycled home that afternoon, her discussion with Tave buzzing around her head. So Tave was in a relationship with the other girl in the crash. And neither her family nor the other girl's approved of them being together. What a nightmare. The parents were probably awful Christian fundamentalists, insulated from everything Beth now took for granted here in the city. She'd seen those small towns, way up there in the boondocks: run down, nothing much left besides liquor stores and churches and Jesus billboards. She'd driven through them on the way back from Portland last year. They reminded her too much of Bramley, Iowa, and why she'd gotten out as fast as she could, more than ten years ago.

She stopped at the light at 18th and Market. The rainbow flags were up for Pride month. They flapped in the breeze gusting over the hill from the ocean. Beth loved this: the whole street decked out in celebration. The huge crowds on parade day. She always had the urge to pluck people from Bramley and plop them down here: Uncle Rick, for one, or Mrs. Rathbone, her high school counselor, who'd harangued her for lacking ladylike graces. *See: there are thousands of us.*

Her thoughts returned to Tave as the light changed to green. No wonder she was so reticent about her girlfriend; she was closeted. That explained a lot about why she was estranged from her family. But it made it even more imperative to sort out where she would go after rehab, and who would give her the help she needed. Beth—no, wait, the whole rehab team—would have to help her figure that out. Tave couldn't do it alone. The team would have to come together and step in. Beth would talk to Linda about Tave in the morning. And Tracy, of course. See what they could do. It might be above and beyond the usual call of duty. But this wasn't a typical situation. Beth couldn't recall a case quite like it.

She found Katy home, sitting on the couch, dressed in yoga pants and tank top, her face hidden behind the new issue of *Outside* magazine. Beth froze in the doorway.

"You didn't go to work?"

"I called in sick."

"Hangover, I suppose?"

"Yeah, I had a wicked headache."

"Surprise, surprise."

Oh my god, Beth thought: calling in sick the first week on the job. She threw her backpack onto the floor and went to the kitchen. She grabbed an iced tea from the fridge, and stood staring at the contents, not remembering what else she was looking for, not registering what she saw. The cold air sent a shiver through her. She slammed the fridge door shut and noticed the pot on the stove.

"You're cooking?" That was something, at least.

"I'm making chili," Katy called out from the living room.

Katy's specialty; always delicious. Beth lifted the lid. A huge stew of beans and vegetables bubbled at a rapid pace. It smelled good. She gave it a stir and lowered the flame. "This is enough to feed an army," she said.

"It'll freeze well."

Beth sat on the beanbag chair opposite Katy, who kept her focus on her magazine, her long legs sprawled in front of her. She was bigger and stronger than Beth, with a deceptively petite face and pert little nose that always seemed at odds with her solid frame, as if she were cobbled together from remnants at a thrift store. Her black hair was buzzed short around the ears, teased into spikes on top.

Beth took a swig of tea. "Where were you last night?"

"I told you. I went out with Angie and Jen."

"You never told me."

"I did. I told you on Monday. Angie wanted to check out that new place on the Embarcadero. They were having a two-for-one special." Katy flipped a page.

"Well, that's nice. Thanks for not including me."

"You had your meeting."

"And you couldn't wait until the weekend?"

"It was a one-night deal."

Katy looked up now and stared at her. Beth couldn't tell if Katy was bullshitting. She didn't know if she could trust her anymore. Katy had promised she would look for more stable work and pull more weight with the rent increase coming, but hadn't accepted anything offered her. None of it was good enough. Finally, she'd taken this new job—but now calling in sick already.

"You must have gone somewhere else after dinner," Beth said. "You got in way past midnight."

"Am I under curfew or something?"

"Why did you come home so late? You never called to tell me where you were." Maybe she was nagging, being unreasonable, but she couldn't stop.

"What is this? The Spanish Inquisition?"

Beth clenched her fists. "I want to know what the fuck is going on."

"Nothing's going on." Katy threw the magazine onto the floor. "Jeez." She went to the kitchen.

Beth followed. She leaned against the doorjamb, arms crossed, watching Katy as she stirred the chili. "And you were drinking beer here before you left," she said. "Four empties in the sink. You made quite a night of it."

Katy looked up, a spoonful of the stew poised in midair. "You're so full of shit. I told you we were going out. Angie and I had a couple of beers before we left. I didn't know I had to get permission from you. Jen was the designated driver, so she didn't drink. Hope that's okay with you, ma'am. We went to the tapas place, and then to a bar. I had a good time, okay? Someone's got to have fun around here."

"What's that supposed to mean?"

"What do you think? You're so fucking wrapped up in your work. It's all you think about. You come home and talk about that damned patient of yours, she's doing this and she's doing that, blah, blah, blah. You can't think about anything else."

"That's not true."

"It is."

Beth wanted to tell her: *Guess what? I've discovered Tave's a lesbian.* But now was obviously not the time.

"You don't pay any attention to what I'm saying," Katy continued. "That's why you had no idea I was going out last night. It's not like I didn't tell you. You didn't hear."

Beth stared at her in disbelief. This couldn't be true. She returned to the living room, slumped on the couch, and turned on the TV news. She stared at the images of more suicide bombings, the endless war in Iraq: a quagmire. Anyone with half a brain knew this would happen. It's what we were all saying three years ago, she thought, with those huge antiwar marches. Beth closed her eyes and groaned.

⌇

Saturday morning, Beth sat at the kitchen table, eating a bowl of granola, and scrolling through emails on her laptop. Kate shuffled in and poured herself coffee.

"Hey," Beth said. "Do you want to go to the farmers' market? The stone fruit will be in." She loved this time of year, with nectarines, apricots, peaches. And year-round farmers' markets: one of the many things she adored about California.

"Nah. You go ahead. I'm going to chill here for a bit." Katy's tone was flat. There was uneasiness between them since yesterday's argument. "I've got to go in for a half day, starting at noon."

"I didn't know you were working today. I'm so confused about your schedule. It would be great if you could put it on the calendar." Beth nodded at the Sierra Club calendar hanging next to the fridge.

"I don't always know in advance. This shift was added yesterday. The manager sent me a text."

"That sucks."

"I'm into it. I'm trying to get as many extra shifts as I can. And make up for my sick day. I thought you'd be glad. I'll be bringing in good money at last."

"Sure, that's great," Beth said. "I'm happy this job is working out for you." She put her arm around Katy and kissed her cheek. "I'm going to cycle over to the market. Any special requests?"

Katy shrugged. "Whatever looks good."

The market was bustling. Beth typically liked to browse all the stalls before buying anything, but halfway through the rows, she was seduced by the sweet smell of strawberries and juicy samples of nectarines waved in her face by one organic farmer. She loaded up on fruit, kale, and asparagus, and admired the gorgeous cage-free brown eggs on the neighboring stand—but decided they wouldn't survive the ride home. Satisfied with her purchases, she pushed through the crowd to her bike parked at the corner. As she squeezed her full bag into the pannier, she heard someone call, "Beth. Is that you?"

She turned to see Maddy, from the Disabled Sports and Recreation board, seated in her power wheelchair. She was a tiny woman, fair-skinned, with long, fine blonde hair down to her shoulders. Today, she wore a green baseball cap decorated with a yellow butterfly and *Life is Good* emblazoned across the front.

"Hi there," Beth said, happy to see her. "We missed you on Thursday. Is everything okay?" It was unusual for Maddy to miss a meeting. She and Beth were on the subcommittee organizing volunteers for the fundraiser in September.

"Yeah, I'm sorry I abandoned you. I couldn't make it. I'm okay now, but I had a big scare. Bad kidney infection." Maddy leaned forward and hooked her wrist around the long straw attached to the water bottle on her armrest. She took three long gulps. "I ended up in your hospital overnight."

"Oh, no. You should've let me know."

"I was in and out pretty quick. Just one night."

"How are you feeling now?" Beth realized she looked even paler than usual.

"I'm all right. A bit weak. But ho hum . . . I've been through this before."

"I hope they treated you right."

"For the most part." Maddy smiled. "You know there are always a few who don't get it. But I had a great ICU nurse. Gloria. Do you know her?"

"I don't think so."

"She was amazing. She got them to bend the rules all sorts of ways, helped me get out quickly, with home infusion set up. I'm still on antibiotics." She used her pinky finger to pull back her V-neck T-shirt, revealing a dressing over an IV port at her collarbone. Maddy's arms were very thin, with limited movement, and they were contracted into a bent shape at the elbow and wrists. Beth wasn't sure of her diagnosis. She had never said, and Beth would never ask. Not cerebral palsy, Beth thought, more like one of the muscular dystrophy conditions.

"I'm glad you're home," Beth said. "The best place to be."

47

"I was lucky I had Jess with me." She glanced up at a woman standing at her side. "I'm sorry, have you guys met?" she said. "Jess is with Independence Now. It's a great program, as I'm sure you know."

"Sure. That's cool," Beth said, introducing herself and extending a hand.

Jess towered above her, a big-boned woman over six feet tall, who appeared to be in her early forties, dressed in baggy teal pants and an oversize purple sweatshirt, with a teal-and-purple knitted scarf around her neck. She gave Beth a friendly nod.

"It couldn't have come at a worse time," Maddy said. "Getting sick, I mean. Ryan's out of town at a conference." Maddy's husband worked for a large educational nonprofit. He was suave and charming, and Beth was sure he would run for political office one day. Maddy wiped her forehead with the back of her hand and looked around. "Do you mind if we move into the shade?"

"We should be getting back," Jess said. "I promised Ryan you'd take it easy."

"See what I mean?" Maddy said to Beth with a light laugh. "Jess is looking out for me. In the hospital, she created a stink when they wouldn't let me use my own BiPAP. Their machine didn't feel right even when the settings were supposedly the same. And their masks are so uncomfortable."

"You were very capable of speaking up for yourself," Jess said. She turned to Beth with a smile and said, "Even with a temp of 102, she put up quite a fight."

"I'm sure you did," Beth said. Maddy's small stature belied her formidable presence on any committee, and she was passionate in her defense of programs she championed. "But I'm sorry you had to fight while you were sick."

"It comes with the territory." Maddy shrugged. "Listen, I wanted to ask you something. My ICU nurse told me about a patient with a new spinal cord injury, who's having a tough time. She's now on the rehab unit, I think."

"Yeah. Tave. She's my patient."

"I thought she might be. Gloria asked if I'd be willing to come in and speak with her." Maddy grimaced. "You know, I don't usually go for that kind of stuff—being held up as some sort of *super crip*. No thanks. But it seemed important to Gloria. I said I'd do anything for her."

Beth said, "That would be nice, if you're up for it."

"How's she doing?"

"Better. She's been on rehab for ten days now, and she's getting some movement in her arms. But she's isolated from her family, doesn't have any visitors."

"That's what Gloria said. So, you let me know when you think she's ready."

"I will. Thanks." Beth swung her right leg over her bike, preparing to mount.

"How's Katy?" Maddy asked. She and Ryan had shared a table with Beth and Katy at the Center for Independent Living awards dinner back in April.

"Good. She's started a new job. At the Fitness 21 gym on Chestnut."

"Cool. Tell her I said hi."

Cycling home, Beth considered Maddy's offer to meet Tave. This rehab unit was so different from the one in Chicago, a dedicated spinal cord injury unit with built-in peer support from the other patients. Here, Tave was by far the youngest patient, and no one else had a similar injury. She appeared to have hit it off with Billie, which was great, but Billie was twice her age, and was being discharged, and Billie didn't have a spinal cord injury. Nor did Maddy, of course. But Maddy was young, and active, and could introduce Tave to other people in the disability community.

But Beth wasn't sure Tave was ready to see herself as a long-term wheelchair user.

7

At first, Tave thought she was imagining it. But there again, during the night: her legs moved under the bedclothes, suddenly coming to life, jumping all over the place. Prayer sure wasn't her thing, but she couldn't deny she'd been secretly wishing for some sort of miracle, something to give her hope after all the gloom and doom talk about her never walking again. *This will show them*, she thought. The two weeks of hard work on rehab were paying off. She couldn't wait to tell Dr. Kramer. She imagined the look of surprise on his face. For once, she was excited for his routine morning show-and-tell.

Wanda, her morning nurse, had just gotten Tave dressed when he arrived, the usual entourage in tow.

"My legs moved," she announced.

"Good morning." He smiled. He was tall, with a crop of thick black hair, bushy eyebrows above blue eyes, and a square jaw, not bad-looking. He had new glasses, with thin wire frames; they made his face appear younger. He was old, but not real old. "Let's take a look."

Tave was ready for therapy in sweatpants and T-shirt, but in bed, on top of the covers. Dr. Kramer lifted her right leg, supporting her knee and calf. "Can you straighten your knee?"

She strained to push against his hand, her mind visualizing, willing, urging her leg to move. Nothing.

"Try to bend your knee."

Nothing.

"Bring your toes toward me."

No.

"Push your toes against my hand."

Nada. "I guess it was my other leg," she said.

But her left leg was equally oblivious. Like a spaceship that had lost contact with Ground Control.

"But I know . . ." She felt tears well up. She swallowed, forcing them back; she wasn't going to cry in front of them all: the doctor; his sidekick, whoever he was; the charge nurse; that stupid Tracy woman. "I saw my legs move last night. I saw the bedcovers move."

"Like this?" Dr. Kramer held her left leg and sharply bent the foot up at the ankle. It responded with a series of jerks, now suddenly awake with a mind of its own. He repeated this on the right: same deal.

"Was that what you saw?"

"I guess," she said, all her excitement dissipated.

"That's spasticity," he said. He moved her legs slowly now, bending, straightening, back and forth, out and in, like he did every day. He placed a hand on her shoulder, and held her gaze, his eyes gentle. "I'm sorry. Spasticity is very common, and it means your spinal shock is subsiding. But unfortunately, it doesn't mean you're regaining any voluntary movement. I wish it did." He gave her arm a squeeze. "It's less than two months since your accident. You're still what we consider newly injured. We may see more recovery over the next few weeks, but this here is reflex activity, I'm afraid. It's your nerves firing automatically. There's still no communication coming down your spinal cord."

He placed his stethoscope on her chest. "Deep breath . . . And again, breathe in . . . Perfect." He reached for his clipboard. "How's the blood pressure?" he asked Wanda.

"Good. She hasn't needed Midodrine for three days. I think we can stop it." Wanda was a new nurse. Not new; new to Tave. She seemed to know her shit. She was fair-skinned, in her thirties, Tave guessed, with shoulder-length dark-brown hair swept behind a headband, wide cheek bones, no makeup, and a solid, no-nonsense demeanor.

"Sounds good." Dr. Kramer nodded.

The telephone on the bedside table rang, loud and shrill. It startled Tave. She'd never heard it ring before.

Wanda picked it up. "Yeah, she's here. A moment please." She cupped the receiver. "You have a phone call."

"I do?"

Dr. Kramer said, "I think we're done here. I'll let you take your call. Keep up the good work. We'll see you tomorrow." He and his gang departed.

Wanda held the phone. "She'll be with you in a minute," she said, pushing the button to raise the head of the bed and move Tave into a seated position. She looked around the room. "This is ridiculous. How come they haven't set you up with a speakerphone?"

"I dunno. I guess I haven't gotten any phone calls. Who is it?"

"Who's calling? Dan? Okay, hold on a moment. How are we going make this work?" She grabbed an additional pillow and rolled it into a ball secured with surgical tape, placed the phone base on the bed, and propped the receiver against the pillow, wedged between Tave's shoulder and ear.

"Dan?" Tave said. "Oh my god."

"Hey there, girl."

Wanda adjusted the pillow again. "I think that will stay put." She placed the flat call light on Tave's chest. "Call me if you need help. I'm going to hunt down a speakerphone."

"Dan. I can't believe you called." A lump swelled in her throat. "Man, I've been dying to talk to someone."

"I came to see you when you were first down there. But you were, like, totally out of it. Guess you don't remember, huh?"

"No . . . but I got your card. Wow, it's good to hear your voice." Now the tears welled up with full force. She tried to hold her voice steady. "You know, I lost my phone, I don't have anyone's number." The receiver began to slip. She tilted her head and arched her shoulder more to hold it in place. "How are you?"

"I'm okay. You know, same old, same old. But how are you, girl? You sound a whole lot better. Are you, like, up out of bed and stuff?"

"Yeah, sort of. I mean . . . To tell you the truth, I'm pretty fucked up. I can't move my legs. I thought maybe I could but . . . Yeah, it's fucking bad, man. Anyway, like, they get me up in a wheelchair. And I have to get set up with all this special shit to do anything with my hands."

"Oh wow, babe. That sucks."

"Yeah." The tears streamed down her face. But she had to concentrate on preventing the phone from slipping.

"But, like, at least you can talk. Man—" He broke off.

"What?" Tave heard Dan take a sharp intake of breath. Then silence. Was he crying now? She'd never seen him cry. "Are you okay?"

"Yeah, I'm okay. Listen, I'm going to get back down there to see you real soon, okay? I got the truck fixed. Me and Sammy are talking about trying to make it next week."

"That would be good." She wanted to wipe her tears with her elbow but was afraid the phone would fall. The salty taste dripped onto her lips. "Listen, have you seen Les? I just found out about her. That she was injured, I mean, and that she's home with her folks now."

"Yeah, it's pretty fucked up, babe. She um . . . She's not doing so good."

"What do you mean?"

"Well, like, we went to see her when she was in hospital. Right before they let her home."

"And?"

"She was in a bad way, man."

"But if she was going home . . . ?"

"I know . . . But she was out of it. Seemed like she couldn't even sit up straight. She kept kind of falling to the side. And she never said a word. Seemed like she didn't even know who we were. And then her mom came in the room and ordered us out of there. It was fucking weird."

"Shit."

"Yeah. And, like, we haven't heard anything since."

"Oh my god."

Les. Now the tears streamed down, she could not make them stop. Her shoulders heaved, and the phone fell onto the bed. Tave sobbed in waves. She heard Dan on the other end of the line: "You okay, babe?" but she couldn't answer. She closed her eyes and tried to imagine what was going on with Les. She'd been sent home at least, but she must be in bad shape, if she hadn't called Tave or anyone else. She couldn't understand that scene in the hospital room Dan described, but it sure didn't sound good. Les not speaking? She must be totally fucked up. And her mom pushing Dan aside, taking control of everything: Les would hate that. She always wanted Tave to stick around when her mother visited, Tave pretending to be the little "roommate," but shielding Les from Darlene's overbearing chatter, changing the subject when needed, or coming up with some sort of joke.

Now Tave couldn't help her. She couldn't be of much use to anyone.

"Oh dear." Wanda returned and rescued the phone. "They're bringing up the speakerphone this afternoon. Yes, she's still here," she said to Dan, and then cupped the receiver. With her other hand, she wiped Tave's cheeks with a tissue. "Do you want to talk to him some more?"

Tave nodded. "Thanks." She managed to regain control of her voice. "Sorry," she sniffed.

"Hey," she said to Dan. "Sorry about that."

"No, I get it, babe. It's so fucked up."

"Yeah."

"But it's good to hear you, Tave. You . . . I mean, you sound like normal, do you know what I mean? That's such a relief."

Normal? This was normal? Fuck. But she had to pull herself together. Wanda was standing there, holding the phone. "So, when are you guys coming down?" she managed to say.

"We'll shoot for Friday. That's Sammy's day off. Will that work for you?"

"Any day will work for me."

8

Tave was so bored with these tests. Seemed like they went through this every other day.

"Look at that," Beth said. "You're getting some wrist extension."

"Say what?"

"Pull up here again." Beth had her hand on the back of Tave's. "Up, against my hand."

Tave hadn't been paying attention. Her mind kept returning to her conversation with Dan. She didn't understand what it meant that Les didn't speak when he saw her. Could be she was pissed off. But he'd said she was falling over. That didn't sound good. Tave thought about asking Beth what she thought was wrong with Les, but Beth was fixated on Tave's hand.

"This is great," Beth said. "Try the other side."

And indeed, Tave could bend her wrists back on both sides. Beth seemed jazzed; she scribbled some notes on her clipboard.

"So?" Tave couldn't see what the fuss was about.

"This is a big deal. It means your level is more like C6. Remember, we talked about this? How you might get more movement as the swelling in your spinal cord subsides."

"So, am I going to be able to walk?"

Beth placed her hand on Tave's elbow and shook her head. "I don't think so. We're talking about a tiny drop in the level of damage to your spinal cord." She held out her thumb and index finger, half an inch space between them. "There's no sign any signals are reaching your legs."

"My legs keep jumping at night." Dr. Kramer had said this meant nothing, but Tave could always hope for a different answer.

Beth did the same thing with Tave's ankles, and they did the same jerking.

"That's spasticity," Beth said. "Reflex activity. It's your legs responding on their own to touch or a change in position. It's like . . . you know how if you touch something hot, your hand pulls back automatically without you thinking about it? It's the same kind of thing: a reflex. It's like your legs are toddlers, running around a store wreaking havoc. Your brain can't be the parent bringing them under control because your spinal cord is damaged. The signals can't get through."

"So, I'm still fucked."

"I think you're still paralyzed. But we're working with what you do have, like we agreed, okay?"

"Sure. Whatever."

"And look at how much progress you've made. Remember when you arrived here you couldn't do much of anything. Now you're able to bend your elbows, lift your hands, feed yourself. You're working on combing your hair."

It was true. Tave could do those things now. Not like normal. She knew she looked goofy with all the weird shit they strapped on her hands for her to do stuff, but hey—it was better than nothing.

"And getting wrist extension is pretty exciting," Beth continued. "Opens up a realm of possibilities. We can get you working on finger grasp." She held up her own arm, the hand dangling down, and demonstrated how bending the wrist back had the effect of automatically bringing the thumb and first finger together. "Now, let's go over to the pulleys and have you work on your shoulder strength."

Tave could get into that. It was basically like working out at the gym. Well, not exactly. She couldn't get on the treadmill, of course. But the exercise got her blood pumping, her heart rate up. Beth secured her hands in the pulleys, and said, "I'm going to leave you to it. Duane can help you if you need anything."

Duane was working with another patient on the mat. He gave Tave a big grin and thumbs-up signal.

Beth said, "I'll see you this afternoon."

Tave pulled the weights, feeling her arm muscles tingle to life. Down and up, down and up. She could feel herself getting stronger, tougher. It was like the old days: Miss Dee from high school urging them on. She could hear her now: *Come on, girls, gotta build up that muscle if you're gonna hit. Come on. More, more, more.*

And Tave did. Became the star of the team. Batted .350 in her senior year. She knew how to push herself then and she could do it now. She was determined to get as strong as she could.

Duane came over. "You're doing great, girl. Look at you pumping iron," he said, flexing his own massive biceps. He looked like he could bench-press two hundred easy.

"Yeah, right," Tave said.

"Seriously, you're getting so much stronger. Wanna add two pounds?

"Sure."

He adjusted the weight and pulled over a stool next to her. His right forearm was covered with a tattoo of a bear, like on the California state flag. "You're acing this, girl. Think how excited Miss Laurel will be when you can brush your hair all by yourself. You'll make her day." He pumped his fist again and Tave laughed.

"Hey, sweetie! I've got a surprise for you."

Tave's back faced the door, but she knew that voice, that perfume, and the sickening singsong tone. *What now?* she thought.

"Look who's here," Tracy gushed, appearing at her side, an inane grin on her face.

Tave let the weight fall, but her arms were hooked into the pulleys, strung up like idiots in midair, partly blocking the sight before her: Tracy, in the most hideous outfit yet—a billowy, flowery, orange tunic thing—and standing next to her, Tave's mother.

"Oh," Tave said. "Hi."

Duane unstrapped her arms, giving Tave an excuse to focus on him settling her back into her wheelchair driving position. She fussed longer than necessary on the adjustments to her splints and the angle of her armrests.

"Octavia . . . Honey . . . Oh my god . . ." Her mother looked freaked out, her hand clasped to her mouth, eyes bulging.

Tave needed all her newfound strength to face her. Apart from the brief visit when Tave was in the ICU, which she barely remembered, she'd not seen her mother in two years. Tave accepted a kiss, an awkward peck on the cheek, her mother keeping her body at a safe distance. Even so, Tave got a strong whiff of her perfume, something cloying, too sweet, mingled with the tobacco on her breath.

"Oh, honey," she said again, pulling back. She looked as though she might burst into tears. She held a bunch of flowers—pink carnations—which she thrust at Tave's chest, but noticed her arms confined in their splints and withdrew. "Oh, sorry," she said, letting the flowers droop at her side.

Tave studied her mother. She had put on weight. She wore a tight-fitting, purple-patterned, V-neck shirt that revealed bulges of flesh around her midriff, and ample cleavage. The skin at her neckline was tanned and had that crinkled look from too much Southern California sun. As always, she wore a ton of makeup: purple eye shadow and false eyelashes and bright-red lipstick she'd managed to smear in spite of the years of practice. Her wrists jangled with a collection of gold bracelets adorned with charms.

"I was telling Mrs. Greenwich—er, Marjorie—how well you're doing now," Tracy said. She looked at Tave's schedule attached to the chair. "Looks like you're free for half an hour. Let's all go and sit in the dining room and have a little chat." She led Tave's mom out to the hallway.

Tave felt obliged to follow. She drove slowly behind them, watching her mother totter in high-heeled open-toed sandals and a tight black skirt. She recalled her last visit to Riverside, and the huge fights over the usual issues: Tave having dropped out of school; Tave wearing scuffed-up Converse high-tops and a baggy black hoodie, *ugly boy clothes* her mom called them; and always, inevitably, her *immoral lifestyle*. Things got worse and worse until her mom screamed at her to get out of the house. Tave did. And vowed to never return.

"Why don't you sit here, Marjorie?" Tracy arranged the chairs to allow space for Tave opposite her mother. But Tave kept her eyes on Tracy.

"Now, Tave," she said. "Your mother says she thinks she could make her house accessible for you. We have been talking about a ramp and widening the bathroom."

Tave shook her head vehemently. "No, no, no. I told you. That's not going to happen." She was not going to go back on the promise she had made to herself. No matter how much things may have changed. She looked across the table at her mother now. "You know as well as I do, that'll never work."

"Honey . . ."

"You have to be practical, dear," Tracy said. "You don't have many options."

"I'll figure something out. My friend Dan is coming down at the end of the week, and . . ."

"Octavia, stop being so stubborn." Marjorie turned to Tracy and gave a light laugh. "She's always been so headstrong, this one. But I'm sure she'll come to her senses. Maybe you could leave us alone for a while."

"Oh, yes. Of course." Tracy gathered her papers. "I'll check in with you later, dear."

Tave turned her wheelchair to face the window. The fog had burned off, leaving a few puffy clouds above the main hospital tower. She had an urge to swirl her chair around and escape, go out into the sunshine, get as far away as she could.

"Listen, honey," her mom said. "I know we haven't always seen eye to eye. But we'll get through this. We will, honey. I know we will. I'm praying for you. I pray for you every night. And Pastor Gregory—I've told you about him, right? He's amazing. He's been our pastor for going on three years now, such a wonderful man. He's been praying for you every night, too. He includes you in the blessing every Sunday. And you know what else? He knows someone up this way, in Danville, I think he said, a healer. A true man of God. No, don't make that face, honey. This man is a miracle worker. He does the laying-on of hands. He's healed people of cancer and all sorts. Pastor Gregory has spoken to him, and he's willing to come in and see you. He's a very busy man, so we were lucky to get him. But he'll come up here tomorrow and do a healing and a blessing, directly, right here. I couldn't believe Pastor Gregory was able to reach him. I'm so grateful. Like I say, he's a wonderful man. And this stuff works, believe me. Lillian Reaves—you remember, I told you about her, dear—she sprained both her ankles in a fall off the curb, and her knees being bad already, she could hardly walk, but Pastor Gregory had the whole congregation lay hands on her, and she was cured. It was a true miracle. Once we get you down to Riverside, Pastor Gregory said we'd do the same for you, but in the meantime, he has arranged for . . ." She finally paused for breath as she rummaged in her enormous purse and retrieved a card. "Here it is. *Darlington Abraham Chugwi-whatsit.* I don't know how you say it. Funny name, I know. Normally I wouldn't go for someone with a name like that, but if it's good enough for Pastor Gregory, it's good enough for me. Let's see now. Yes, it is Danville. *Believe in Miracles.* So, he's coming up tomorrow and . . ."

"Mom, stop. Stop, stop. I'm not doing any of that crap. It's not going to work. I'm paralyzed, okay? I'm trying to deal with it as best I can, and that bullshit doesn't help."

Tave turned and fled full speed ahead.

9

Three days later, in the late afternoon, Tave wheeled herself to the dining room. She was getting to be a pro at this. And her last therapy session of the day had been—well not fun, exactly, but pretty cool. Laurel had taken her outside, and Tave had navigated the sidewalks—cracks and all—down to the bottom of the hill and back. Now she rotated her shoulders forward and back and stretched her forearms. She had more movement in her wrists now, didn't have to wear those ugly white splints to control her chair. But her hands felt tight and tingled with pain. You'd think if she couldn't do a damn thing with her hands, and couldn't feel anything in the normal way, they wouldn't be painful. But that wasn't the deal, Tave was learning. Her hands hurt and her wrists were exhausted. It was crazy how sitting and driving a wheelchair could feel like hard work.

"Tell my nurse I'm going to hang out here," she told Feliz, the evening shift aide. "I'm expecting a visitor."

"Okay. Awesome," he said.

Yes, it was good to be able to say that—even if she knew nothing about this visitor. Beth had told her there was someone she wanted her to meet. She sounded kind of mysterious about it and said, "I think you'll like her," and that she would be coming at the end of Tave's day of therapy. Nothing more.

Everyone else had visitors, but Tave didn't—which made her feel even more like a freak. She didn't count her mother's visit. Tave wanted to blot out the memory of those dreadful two days: her mom going on and on about the faith healer and other delusional garbage. She'd shut up only for the fireworks: on the Fourth, the nurses had wheeled all the patients up to the rooftop garden for a great view of the show on the waterfront and across the Bay too. It was spectacular, and for half an hour they relaxed together in the *oohing* and *aahing*, mother and daughter, almost like they could be normal. Tave remembered one time they'd all gone as a family, she and her mom and dad, to see the parade and fireworks in Temecula. Tave was maybe ten years old. It was during one of the truce periods, a brief respite from the constant fighting. Her dad was in a buoyant mood, and everything was lovey-dovey, and Tave desperately hoped he would stay. But the arguments soon resumed, and by the end of the month he'd disappeared again.

As Tave and her mom had made their way back down to the rehab unit, her mom started up again about her minister's laying on of hands. Tave had to tell her to shut the fuck up. Her mom left in a huff, and the following morning flew back to Riverside, with no word about when she might return.

Tave positioned herself now in her favorite spot by the window and looked down on the courtyard below. A little kid was chasing the pigeons around the flowerpots while his mother tried to coax him back into his stroller. Billie would have made some joke, something about the kid not wanting to be in a "wheelchair" either. Didn't sound very funny when Tave tried saying it to herself, but Billie had a way with words, would have made it witty and cackled with that coarse laugh of hers. Billie had been gone over a week and Tave missed her. She was lonely in the evenings, nothing to do but watch *Jeopardy!* with Feliz, who was crazy smart and knew all the answers. He'd been a nurse back in his own country but there was some bullshit about him not being able to get a license here.

Dan was supposed to be coming down soon. *Never thought I'd miss that dude so much.* She hoped he would get it together, but you never knew with Dan. Maybe he'd run out of money. Or he might be freaked out at the thought of seeing Tave like this. Couldn't blame him. She kept thinking about the telephone conversation with him, the news about Les being so messed up. She was desperate to talk to him again, try to figure out what was going on.

Tave caught her reflection in the window. Her hair was getting long and straggly. Last week, the nurse had told her they have hairdressers who come in, but Tave said she wasn't interested. Maybe she should reconsider.

"Hey, there you are." Beth's voice came from the doorway.

Tave swirled around.

"Tave, this is Maddy," Beth said. "A friend of mine."

"Hi," Tave said. And clammed up. *Oh shit,* she thought.

She stared at the woman sitting in front of her. She looked weird, all shriveled and crooked, tiny, like no more than ninety pounds or something. But she wasn't old, not when you looked at her face. Her head was twisted to one side at an odd angle, like she was trying to wedge something between her shoulder and ear, and her arms were all skinny and bent funny, one of her wrists hanging down. She sat in a wheelchair much fancier than Tave's, with a bright-green frame and a full set of complicated control buttons on the armrest. She wore cropped pants and kid-size sandals with open toes. Across the top of one foot a tattoo read: *Out of*, and immediately next to it, on the other foot: *Order*. Ha! *Out of Order*. Funny. Billie would have loved that.

"Hi, Tave," Maddy said. "It's nice to meet you."

Tave looked up to see bright-blue eyes smiling under a baseball cap and wispy blonde hair falling in thin strands to Maddy's shoulders. Tave sort of expected her voice to sound weird, but it didn't. And she had a friendly smile.

"Hi," Tave said again. She was going to sound ridiculous if she couldn't come up with anything else to say.

"I heard about your accident," Maddy said. "I'm sorry."

"Yeah. Thanks."

"If it's okay with you, I'd like to hang out for a while."

"Listen," Beth said. "I'm going to leave you guys to it. I've got to finish my charting and get going."

"Sure," Maddy said. "Thanks, Beth."

Maddy had a long straw attached to a cup next to her armrest, and she hooked her wrist around it now and took a long drink. Tave realized she was staring—and looked away, out the window, checking the scene in the courtyard again. The kid was back in his stroller, his mother walking fast toward the bus stop at the corner.

"I know you're dealing with a lot of stuff," Maddy said. "Getting accustomed to using a wheelchair and all the other crap."

Tave turned to face her again. "Yeah."

"It's not a club anyone signs up for voluntarily. But there are a lot of good people in this club. And if you're willing to reach out, we're here to help."

"Okay. Thanks."

Maddy smiled at her but not in an overbearing, pushy way.

"What . . . er . . . what happened to you?" Tave asked.

"I have a rare genetic disease that makes my muscles very weak."

"Oh, wow. So, like, you were born like that?"

"Well, I was much smaller when I was born." Maddy laughed, tipping her head back, almost knocking her baseball cap off. Tave saw now it was decorated with the words *Life is Good* and she laughed too. "But, yes, I've used a wheelchair most of my life."

"Sorry. That's a bummer."

"I love my wheelchair. It allows me to get around and do the things I want to do."

Tave didn't know what to say to that.

Maddy patted her wheelchair armrest. "Yeah, this is my girl. I call her Thelma."

That is really weird, Tave thought.

"Beth tells me you're into sports," Maddy said.

Tave snorted. "I used to be. Can't see me doing any of that again."

"Not in the same way, for sure. But if you're interested, I could tell you about our organization: Disabled Sports and Recreation. DSR, we call it. I sit on the board. I used to play soccer."

"Soccer?"

"Power soccer. It's for people in power wheelchairs."

"Oh." *Weirder and weirder*, Tave thought.

"It's fun. We had a pretty good team. Went to the national championships in Indiana twice. But I took a couple of bad tumbles. Luckily, I didn't break anything, but my bones are soft. Mushy, my doctor says. So, I'm taking her advice and laying off that now. I'm doing cycling, kayaking. We have a bunch of trips and outings, that sort of thing."

Outings. Tave grimaced. She recalled the group that had come through the first week she'd worked at Wendy's, back in her senior year of high school. "It's the outing from Lakewood Manor," Mr. Stanton had said. "Be nice to them, now." And Tave tried to be nice, she did. But one of the guys screamed his head off, freaking her out, and another threw up outside the bathroom door, and Tave had to clean it up and it was totally gross.

"We could arrange for you to come out on a Sunday," Maddy was saying. "You could watch the cycling team practice. And meet some of the guys. And girls, I mean, too."

"How would I do that? I'm stuck in this place."

"Let's talk to Beth. I'm sure she could make it happen. She could say it's a therapeutic outing or something."

That *outing* word again. But Tave couldn't help being intrigued.

"Maybe," she said.

"I'll ask Beth to set it up."

10

Tave was rolling to the gym for her first physical therapy session of the day when she saw a sign she'd not noticed before: Social Work Dept., with an arrow pointing down a hallway to the right. The clock on the wall showed nine twenty-three. She had time.

She swirled and almost collided with Leticia propelling an old lady in a manual wheelchair with one hand, the other holding a breakfast tray high above her head, balancing it on her palm like a waitress.

"Whoa," Leticia said with a laugh, sidestepping out of the way. "Watch your driving, girlfriend!" The tray wobbled, but she managed to steady it with her other hand.

"Sorry."

"Where are you going in such a hurry? Don't you have PT?"

"Yeah, but . . ." Tave looked at the sign again. "Is this where Tracy's office is at?"

"Second door on the right, hon."

The door was open, and Tracy sat at her desk, in one of her crazy-shit outfits, this one bright green. She was on the phone. She held up one hand and covered the mouthpiece with the other. "Just a minute, sweetie," she whispered, and pointed at the phone like Tave was too dumb to get she was talking to someone.

"Uh-huh, uh-huh," Tracy murmured into the phone, beckoning for Tave to enter. Tave hesitated. She had only a few minutes.

"I'm going to have to get back to you on that," Tracy was saying. "I have someone in my office."

"Sorry . . ."

"No, come in, sweetie." Tracy had hung up. "What's up?"

"My friend, Les . . ." Tave said, continuing in a stronger voice: "You said you were going to call her parents, see if you can find out what, you know, what happened to her. And how she's doing and stuff."

Tracy patted a yellow notepad on top of an untidy stack of papers on her desk. "Right here, on my to-do list this morning," she said. "I've tracked down their number." She lifted her glasses onto her nose. "Lifton Avenue, Chico, does that sound right?"

Tave shrugged. "Guess so."

She'd never been to Les's parents' place. Never been invited. She'd heard Les describe it often enough: the ranch-style home where she'd grown up, the large oak in the backyard where her father had built a classic tree house, the creek two blocks away. Sounded idyllic to Tave, who had lived in a series of crummy apartments. But whenever Les went home, there was always some reason why it wasn't the right time for Tave to come along.

"I know they won't want to talk to me," Tave said. "But can you please call them and find out what's going on with Les?"

"Of course, sweetie." Tracy smiled. "Now, I did talk to your mom again. She feels bad about how things didn't go so well when she came to visit. But she loves you, dear, and she's trying. She talked to her landlord about building a ramp."

"I told you, I'm not going there."

"But you'll have to go somewhere, dear."

"No, no. Anywhere but there." Tave reversed, slamming her chair into a bookcase as she made her escape.

～

Tave was working in PT on the pulleys; Beth said she had to catch up on paperwork, so after a quick testing of Tave's arm strength, she left Duane to finish the remainder of the session. Tave wasn't in much of a mood to chat, and only smiled weakly when Duane made jokes about the Giants game the night before. She tried to get into the zone doing her exercises: up and down, in and out, same old, same old—but she couldn't stop worrying about Les, and what was going on with her. She'd have to keep bugging Tracy to get on it. All that idiot wanted to talk about was Tave going to her mom's place. Fuck that. She wasn't going there, no matter what anyone said.

After PT, she swung by Tracy's office again, but the door was closed, with no response when Tave knocked with her footplates. On her way back to her room, she ran into Wanda.

"Hey, Tave," she said. "You've got a visitor. I had him wait for you in the dining room. It should be quiet in there until lunch."

Him? Tave felt a surge of excitement. "Is it . . . ?"

"It's your buddy Dan."

"No way!"

Wanda smiled at her. "I know you've been waiting for him to come down." She examined Tave's schedule on her armrest. "I'm going to see if we can switch your OT session until after lunch. Give you more time with him. Go on, I'll take care of it."

Tave spun around and tore down to the dining room. She saw Dan from the doorway, standing in what she'd come to think of as her spot, his back to her, gazing out the window. Tall and skinny, with his long ponytail straggling down his back, the usual scruffy jeans. She was never so glad to see someone.

"Hey, dude," she said.

He turned and bounded toward her, all arms and legs. He came to a stop in front of Tave, looking unsure what to do next. "Hi, babe," he said.

Tave widened her arms. "Come give me a fucking hug," she said.

Dan leaned forward and nestled his head on her shoulder, his stubble scratchy against her neck. He smelled musty and sweet, with a hint of weed. *I could sure use some of that*, Tave thought.

"Man, it's good to see you," she said. "How you doing?"

"I'm okay," he said, pulling away and taking two steps back. "But shit, what about you? Oh god . . ." He gestured at Tave's wheelchair.

He looked like he was about to cry. Tave felt tears well up too, but she swallowed and pushed them back down.

"I'm okay. I'm getting better, stronger. That's what they keep telling me."

"But . . ." He pointed again at her chair.

"I know, it sucks, but hey . . ." She shrugged. "When I first woke up in this place, I couldn't do nothing. Now I can do this." She spun around fast, doing a 360 one way and the other, and laughed. "Come sit with me by the window. I'm free until after lunch. There's so much I gotta ask you." Tave looked around the room. "Did you come by yourself?"

"Sammy drove with me. But he's, like, kind of freaked out about hospitals. Since his mom died and all."

"Oh wow, sure." Tave remembered now that Sammy's mom had been sick with cancer for months last year.

"So, he's waiting in the truck. Good thing, because the parking's fucked around here, man."

"I guess so." Tave had no idea about the parking. But she was glad to have Dan to herself. "So, tell me what the fuck is happening with Les."

"I don't know." Dan drew up a chair next to Tave. "All I know is she got beat up pretty bad too. And when we went to see her in the hospital in Redding, like I told you, seemed like she didn't know who we were. She kind of stared at the wall or something and—well, she don't look good. I guess she got hit on the head and she's kind of messed up because of that."

"Shit."

"Her folks took her back home. That was like a while ago, so I don't know how she's doing now."

"Shit. Her mom . . ."

"I know. It sucks." Dan sniffed and wiped his nose with the back of his hand. Tave noticed soft wrinkles around his eyes she'd never seen before. She knew he was older than her—in his midthirties, she'd always thought, but maybe older than that.

"There's a dimwit social worker here who's supposed to be finding out how Les is doing back home," she said.

"That's good."

Dan crossed his legs and jiggled his ankle. He wore his usual beat-up, tan work boots, with the same splotches of paint across the top. It was comforting to see something unchanged.

"There's something else I gotta tell you," he said.

"What?" A knot of dread tightened in Tave's stomach.

"They cleared out your apartment."

"They?"

"Les's parents. I guess no one was paying the rent, and the landlord wanted everything out. So, they came and packed up all of Les's stuff and left your shit on the sidewalk."

"What the fuck . . . ?"

"I know, right? It would have been hauled off with the garbage, but Becky downstairs from you, she called and gave me the heads-up. So, me and Sammy picked it up. It's at Sammy's place in his garage. I don't know if we got everything. The apartment was all locked up by the time we got there, and we couldn't get in. It was mainly a bunch of clothes and stuff. And er . . ." Dan hesitated. "And, like, your catcher's gear."

"Right." Tave puckered her lips. "Don't suppose I'll be needing that." Tears were threatening again. "Fuck." She pressed her wrist to her mouth.

"I hope that was okay. To take the stuff to Sammy's."

"Sure. Thanks." Tave closed her eyes and nodded softly. Tears streamed down her cheeks; she couldn't stop them.

"I'm sorry." She could feel Dan's hand patting her wrist awkwardly. "I guess I shouldn't have said anything. Didn't mean to upset you."

Tave shook her head, unable to find words. She was mad and upset about everything: Les, and Les's parents, and the goddamn accident, and being in this fucking wheelchair. But she appreciated what Dan and Sammy had done. It felt like the first time she had someone on the outside rooting for her. Someone from her old life who might be able to help. Do whatever the fuck was needed for her to move on from here.

She opened her eyes and saw Dan had found a tissue from somewhere and was offering it to her. She grabbed it between her two fists and wiped her face.

"I'm gonna have to find a place to stay," she said. Her lower lip quivered. "When I get out of here. Where, you know, where I can get in with this thing." She pointed at her chair. "I'm gonna need your help."

"Got it." Dan nodded. "We'll figure something out."

They talked for what felt like hours. The guy came in with the lunch cart and they were still getting caught up: how Dan's work at the construction company was going, his latest fight with his ex about when he could see his son, Sammy and Rosie moving in together, Mitch's new job at the Botanical Garden that he was totally into, the bar on Third Street that had recently closed, the way the cops were harassing the guys who hang out at the waterfront, and the weird scene the previous night when they'd stayed at Sammy's cousin's place in Willits. Tave hadn't even thought about that, but of course they wouldn't have made it down from Eureka by midmorning unless they stopped somewhere. Sammy's cousin had a six-month-old baby and was very uptight, freaked out big-time when they smoked some weed.

"You got any with you now?" Tave whispered.

"Nah, sorry babe," Dan said. "We only brought a small stash. Sammy was paranoid about getting stopped in the city."

"Next time, okay? There's a park down the street from here. We could sneak out. I'd tell them I was practicing my *community mobility*," Tave said, trying to make air quotes with her fists.

Wanda came up behind her and placed a hand on Tave's shoulder. Tave wasn't sure if she'd heard them talking about the dope. But she acted cool, and said, "Great to see you guys hanging out. I hate to break up the party, but we've got to go back to your room before lunch, Tave. Do your cath and weight shift."

"Your what?" said Dan.

"Trust me, you don't want to know," Tave said. "This wheelchair ain't even the half of it. You wouldn't believe the other crap I have to go through."

"Tave will be back for lunch soon, Dan," Wanda said. "Do you want me to order up a sandwich for you?"

"Nah, I'm good. I'm going to check on my buddy. He's waiting in the truck." He turned to Tave. "We should hit the road, anyway. Gotta get back, you know . . ."

He shuffled and shrugged his shoulders, like he was kind of embarrassed to be taking off so easily.

"Sure, no problem," Tave said. "It was so good to see you. Thanks. Really."

Dan gave her a hug, less awkward this time—and he was gone.

Back in her room, Tave told Wanda, "Dan said he'd help me figure out some place to stay. I told Tracy there's no way I'm going to my mom's."

"That's good," Wanda said. "I get it. But don't forget, you'll also have to find attendant care for all your bowel and bladder and skin care needs. I'm not saying it can't be done. But it's tough."

Tave spaced out while Wanda did her thing. She knew Wanda was right. It wasn't only that she couldn't walk. She couldn't pee or poop like normal. Every six hours someone had to insert a catheter to empty her bladder, for fuck's sake. She didn't see how she would ever be able to do that herself. She knew she was supposed to pay attention and learn everything so she could tell others how to help her, but sometimes she wanted to tune out. She'd put on a brave face when talking with Dan, but now she felt empty, like a deflated balloon.

She was alone again, facing all the same old crap, staring at a giant mountain with no idea how to find her way up. And she couldn't talk to Les, wasn't going to be able to, by the sounds of it, couldn't look to her for help. For days or weeks—whatever it was—when she was first in the hospital, Tave had believed Les must have been killed in the crash. When she found out Les had survived, she imagined Les coming to rescue her and figuring out what to do next. Les always knew what to do. Sure, sometimes Tave hated the way Les would throw her weight around, act like she knew it all. But now, she'd give anything to have Les walk in the room and yell at everyone and help her get the fuck out of here.

But it didn't sound like that was going to happen anytime soon.

～

Tave was in her room at the end of the day after therapy, watching *Judge Judy*. There was some stupid girl whose boyfriend had broken her arm in a fight, and she was going on about how now she needed help to do stuff. *You have no fucking idea*, Tave thought.

"Hello, sweetie." Tracy came in and sat in the armchair next to Tave's bed.

"Did you get them?"

"Yes. Can I mute this?" Tracy reached for the remote and switched off the TV.

"What did they say?"

"I spoke to Leslie's mother. She's quite the talker, isn't she? She was reluctant to open up at first, but then wouldn't stop. It's not good news, I'm afraid. About your friend. It seems she sustained a traumatic brain injury in the accident."

"Oh my god." Tave clasped her wrist to her mouth. "That sounds bad."

"Yes. Brain injury can vary greatly in its severity, but I'm sorry to say that in Leslie's case, there appears to be major damage. She's unable to speak or eat food by mouth. She has a tube in her stomach."

"Oh no." With a surge of nausea, Tave recalled the gross tube poking out from her own stomach when she was in the ICU.

"I'm so sorry. I couldn't tell from what her mom said how much Leslie understands what's going on around her."

"Shit." Tave's eyes filled with tears. She bit her lower lip to stop it trembling.

"I'm sorry, honey," Tracy said again, squeezing Tave's hand. "They have home therapy coming out, and all-day attendant care. And it's still early. She could improve. Like you are," she added.

Tave shook her head. "Damn. This whole thing is so fucked."

"I know. It's tough." She sat in silence for a moment, before adding, "There's something else she said I think you should know."

"What?"

71

"She said they had gotten a lawyer."

Tave stared at her, bewildered. "A lawyer . . . So?"

Tracy shrugged. "Just saying. I thought you should know. It sounds as though they're looking at the other driver, seeing if they can sue. You might want to get yourself a lawyer too."

"How the hell would I do that?"

11

One afternoon the following week, Beth was maneuvering her bike out of the locker in the hospital garage when she felt long, cool fingers covering her eyes.

"Surprise!"

She spun around to see Katy grinning, radiant, clearly pleased with herself for pulling off this stunt. She was dressed in leggings, a loose sweatshirt, and her bike helmet. She came toward Beth to embrace her and kiss her on the lips.

"Hi!" Beth said, turning her head to receive the kiss on the cheek instead. She looked over to the garage entrance, where a steady stream of people walked by. "Careful," she said.

"What?"

"I can't . . ." She was out to most of her colleagues; that wasn't the issue. But there was Mrs. Maxwell, the wife of the stroke patient she'd been working with an hour earlier. Beth dodged all questions from her patients about whether she was married, or if she had a boyfriend. Katy liked to remind her she wasn't in Iowa anymore, but Beth believed in being discreet and maintaining the highest professional standards. She avoided any potential confrontations with patients.

"What are you doing here?" she asked Katy.

"It's such a gorgeous afternoon. I thought we could go for a ride together. Over to the park or something. And maybe get a beer at that place on 46th."

"You got out of work early?"

"I finish at four on Tuesdays."

"Oh. Okay." Beth couldn't keep up with Katy's new schedule. "Sure. Sounds fun." She looked up at the hill behind the hospital. No sign of any fog. It would be a nice day for a ride. "What's the occasion?" She couldn't squash a suspicion: there must be some ulterior motive.

"Nothing! It's a nice day, is all. Jeez. If you don't want to . . ."

"No, it's a great idea." Beth mounted her bike. "Let's go."

She led the way up the first block, but right before the stop sign, Katy overtook her, laughing, speeding through without slowing. Beth watched her pump her legs from a standing position, her hips swaying from side to side. By the time they reached the park, Beth was panting from the effort of keeping pace, her heart racing. She relaxed into the gentle glide down the bike path, meandering through the meadows and the eucalyptus trees. She turned her face into the sun. This *was* a wonderful way to decompress after work.

They stopped at the light at 19th Avenue. Beth eyed Katy's ass astride the saddle. She looked so damn cute. She indulged in a brief fantasy of swerving off into the bushes and making love right there. It had been a while, what with their different work schedules, the fight last week when Katy had stayed out late.

The light changed. "Race you to the windmill," Katy said, her cheeks flushing with the wind and sun. She took off.

Beth pedaled hard, keeping almost abreast with her. Katy seemed in a bubbly mood. She was holding on to the job at the gym, finally bringing in a regular paycheck. Maybe things would return to some sort of balance between them.

They got trapped behind two giant jogging strollers taking up the whole path. Katy swung out onto the grass to the right, Beth tried to do the same on the left, but her front wheel got caught in a patch of mud and she almost wobbled out of control. By the time she got back on track, Katy was way ahead of her. She saw her stop in front of the windmill and collapse on the grass. Katy was still panting when Beth reached her.

"That was fun!" Katy glowed.

Beth lay beside her. They were surrounded by tourists, so it was hardly the secluded setting she'd been fantasizing about. But she squeezed Katy's hand in hers.

"Yes. Thanks for this." She smiled at Katy and closed her eyes, feeling the warm sun on her face. She could hear the ocean roar a block away. Such a soothing sound; she imagined it coursing through her as she took long, deep breaths.

"I talked to my mom this morning," Katy said. "She said to say hi. She misses us."

Katy's family lived in the East Bay, at the end of the BART line, an hour away. They'd become a surrogate family for Beth, welcoming her into the fold. They were energetic and fun—so different from Beth's. Beth's mother was weak and timid, cowering in the shadow of Beth's father. He worked long hours throughout her childhood, and when he was home would slump in front of the TV, beer bottle in hand, watching his wrestling or football, engaging in conversation only when he felt the need to criticize what Beth was wearing or bad-mouth her friends. In contrast, Katy's father, Jim, had wrapped Beth in a hug the first day they met, and always wanted to hear her news. It had taken Beth aback at first, but she had come to love him and Alice, Katy's mom. She admired their patience with Katy's sister, Jenny, who was in her early twenties but had Down syndrome, with a mental age closer to eight. The last time Beth was at their house, Jim emerged from under the dining room table having constructed a "fort" where Jenny and Timber, the family dog, were hidden beneath a blanket.

"How are things?" Beth asked. She and Katy hadn't visited since before their vacation.

"Good. Jenny's all jazzed about her birthday. They're planning a barbecue for her. I promised we'd help." Jenny had formed a special attachment to Beth.

"Sounds good. Her birthday's next month, right?"

"The eighteenth. Five weeks away, but you know Jenny, she's getting excited already."

They laughed together. "We'll have to decide on a present," Beth said.

"As long as it's pretty and pink she'll love it."

"Let's try something different. Take her out to a movie. A date night with us. I hear the new Pixar movie is fun."

"She'd love that. Even if it doesn't have any princesses in it." Katy smiled and turned to face Beth, propping herself up on one elbow. "And let's plan a date for the two of us. I was thinking we could do a longer bike ride. Go over to Marin, snag some lunch at a place on the water in Sausalito."

"Yes!" Beth said. "And take the ferry back. Like we did on our first weekend here. That was so much fun." She had fond memories of that trip; she thought she'd landed in paradise.

"How about Sunday? I agreed to do a double shift on Saturday, in exchange for Sunday off."

"I can't do Sunday," Beth said.

"Why not?"

"I'm going to take my patient—Tave—out to the DSR cycling place on Sunday."

"What?" Katy sat up.

"It's a great opportunity for her to see the options out there. I want to hook her up with Maddy and Brent and all those guys."

"You've got to be kidding me."

"What?"

"It's fucking unbelievable. You work your ass off all week in that place and now on the weekends too?"

Beth wished Katy wasn't so quick to react. "Not all weekend. Just Sunday. Just this once."

"Why do you have to be the one to do it? Can't someone else go?"

"No, it's . . . It's not exactly an official thing. I mean, it's all aboveboard, but it was my idea, after I talked to Maddy, and—" Beth knew she wasn't explaining it well. "I think it's important for Tave to get some exposure to adaptive sports and the disability community."

"So that's what happened," Katy said, as if she'd stumbled onto a clue in a crime scene. "I thought you went to the farmers' market and ran into Maddy by chance."

"I did. For heaven's sake . . ." Beth had told Katy she'd seen Maddy at the market. But she hadn't told her they'd discussed Maddy meeting Tave. She wasn't sure why not. She must have feared Katy would accuse her of being too fixated on work.

"Why can't you do this trip to the rec center during the week, for fuck's sake?"

Beth sat up to face her. She tried to keep her voice calm. "Sunday's the only day they're all there."

"I went to all the trouble to get Sunday off so we could spend it together."

"Well, I'm sorry. I didn't know you were going to do that. You never said."

"I'm telling you now."

"I didn't . . ." Beth said.

"Can't you get out of it?"

"No. I promised her. I don't want to let her down."

"I want us to have some time together. Our schedules are so crazy these days. I miss spending time with you."

"I know. I do too."

"Seems like this patient is more important to you than I am."

"Of course not. It's . . ."

"I don't get why you're so obsessed with her. Isn't there supposed to be a whole team working together on rehab? That's what you always say. Why's it all down to you?"

"It's not. It's . . ." She wanted to tell Katy she felt a special connection to Tave, partly because Tave was a lesbian with no family support, but she sensed it wasn't a good idea to mention that now. "It's . . . she needs help, and this is a great chance for her to see what's out there and—"

"I'm very upset about this," Katy said. "I want you to change your plans so we can be together on Sunday."

"I can't. I've made a commitment."

Katy stood up and straddled her bike. "You've made a commitment, all right, and it's not to me." She took off in the direction of the beach.

Beth was stunned. She buried her head in her hands. She could still hear the ocean, but now it sounded like a roar of anger.

12

Beth sat at the terminal in the PT gym completing her charting when Linda walked by.

"How's it going?" she said.

"Good."

"I was looking through your notes on Tave Greenwich. Nice work. But I talked to Dr. Kramer this morning. It looks like she's reached a plateau. We'll have to start thinking about discharge."

"But she doesn't have a place to go."

"Tracy is working on that. She'll figure something out. You know we can't keep her here simply because we like her or feel sorry for her. She has to be making functional progress. Her FIM scores are flat."

"Of course they are." Beth tried to maintain a calm tone. Everything was focused on the FIM scores, the eighteen-item Functional Improvement Measure. Each therapist had to complete their section for each patient weekly. "The FIM is fine for measuring progress in patients with strokes or joint replacement surgery, but it's useless in spinal cord injury," she said. "You can't measure functional improvement in the same way. You know that. It's well established in the literature."

"You'll have to come up with concrete, achievable goals if you want to advocate for her stay to be extended. You know that." Linda repeated Beth's words with emphasis, mocking her.

Beth was ready with a comeback. "She's beginning to get C7 function on the right. I'm documenting that now." Beth nodded at her screen. "I want to work with her on sliding board transfers. With moderate assist, of course. But that would make a huge difference in her level of care wherever she goes. She would still need a lot of help but being able to transfer from bed to chair without a full lift would be huge. And I think we can work more with her in the manual wheelchair. Some limited household use is feasible."

"All right. Talk to Dr. Kramer and see if he agrees. It might buy us more time if you can document that. But I'm concerned about her length of stay."

"It's only been four weeks." Beth's stomach twisted in anger. She knew it was pointless to argue about "the old days" when spinal cord patients could stay on rehab for months. She would sound like a middle-aged grouch: *Everything was better in my day.*

Linda held up a bunch of papers in her hand. "Our stats for the quarter don't look good. I have to prepare my report for the senior management meeting next week. Even if I pull out Tave and that patient who got that bad infection in her hip—what was her name? Even if I treat them as outliers, our length of stay looks terrible. And our functional change ratio even worse."

Beth shrugged. What did she care about the stats?

"You may think you don't have to worry about that," Linda said, reading her mind. "But I have to. It affects our Medicare reimbursement rates, our capital budget, everything. It keeps the lights on. And pays our salaries—yours and mine." She turned away. "Now, please finish up soon. I can't have you run up more overtime."

Beth watched her walk across the gym, parroting her words with silent, mocking movements of her lips. *I can't have you run up more overtime.* If you left me in peace, she thought, I could get my work done in time.

At the end of the day, Beth was back in the PT office. She had to deal with the usual wrap-up stuff: a voicemail from Billie complaining she'd received the wrong shower chair, and an email about the authorization for the power-assist wheels for a paraplegic who'd been discharged months ago; *goddamn it*—it had been denied again, dismissed on a technicality. Beth groaned; all the paperwork would have to be resubmitted.

She hunted through her files for the original submission. She prided herself on impeccable organizational skills, all paperwork arranged alphabetically and by year of admission.

"Got plans for the weekend?" Kristy asked from the desk next to Beth's. Her desk was a mess, stacks of papers in chaotic piles.

"Not sure yet."

"Looks like the weather's going to be great."

"Yeah." Then she heard herself add, "On Sunday, I'm taking Tave to the DSR Rec Center. To get her introduced to the cycling guys, and the other activities."

"On Sunday?" Kristy said. "How did you get Linda to authorize that? She's been crazy about cracking down on overtime."

"Well, er . . ." *Shit*, Beth thought, *I should have kept my mouth shut.* "I'm doing it on my own time."

Kristy raised her eyebrows. "Are you sure that's wise?"

"It's a great opportunity. Tave seemed to connect with Maddy and—"

"I'm sure she did. But be careful, girl. Don't get overinvolved."

The *setting boundaries* lecture again. Hardly the first time Beth had been warned. Or worried about that herself. She remembered Curt, the ex-Marine who'd broken his neck in a motorcycle accident, her first quadriplegic patient, back when she'd just started in Chicago. He'd cursed and spat at everyone in his anger and frustration. Beth had been the only one to win his trust. She'd advocated on his behalf, convinced the neurosurgeon to repeat the x-ray of his neck earlier than planned, so his mobility restrictions could be relaxed. She worked with him day in and day out—for months. The spinal cord patients stayed much longer back then, back there, in Chicago. She could distinguish the particular sound of his power wheelchair coming down the hall and would jump up to greet him like a cheerleader. She was always coming up with new ways to engage him; she worried about him constantly, dreamed about him even—sometimes in very intimate ways, with fantasies she had trouble acknowledging. She'd been in the process of coming out, getting involved with Pam, who would have been insanely jealous if she'd had an inkling about the uninvited intruder swirling around Beth's brain.

"It's a lot to take on," Kristy was saying. "How are you transporting Tave?"

It was in fact more complicated than Beth had imagined. That morning, she'd searched for Dr. Kramer. She needed him to write an order for a therapeutic pass, and had hoped to snag him alone, before rounds. But Tracy was already at his side. Beth briefly outlined her plan.

"Sounds great," he said, readily agreeing, as Beth knew he would.

"But how will you get her there?" Tracy asked.

"Maddy Lohman, who's on the DSR board with me—she has a van. I thought we could get a ride with her."

"I'm not sure about that," Tracy said. "I'd have to check with Risk. I think there are liability issues to consider."

"You may be right," Dr. Kramer said. He turned to Beth. "It's fine with me as long as you get their blessing."

But Beth realized with a sinking feeling that she would not. "Maybe Paratransit then," she said.

"They have limited availability on Sundays," Tracy said. "But I can put in a call."

"Thanks."

At midday Beth learned Tracy had managed to book a ride. But this meant the whole outing would last much longer. At least an hour there and back, plus you always had to factor in delays when dealing with Paratransit. It was going to take up pretty much the whole day. Beth had been hoping to appease Katy by taking her out for brunch before she left. Now she wouldn't have time.

13

All of a sudden, Billie showed up. She zipped into the dining room as Tave was finishing dinner: lasagna, it being Thursday, a bit better than last week's effort. Billie greeted the staff like a rock star, high-fiving the nurses and the janitor guy, spinning 180s.

"How y'all doing?" she boomed.

"What are you doing back here, girl?" asked one of the aides.

"Here to check on my buddy, Tave."

Billie looked spiffed up in a white cotton V-neck sweater and black leggings, not the baggy sweatpants she'd worn for therapy. And she'd done something with her hair; it was shorter, with a purple streak on the side. Tave flipped her own hair away from her face. She'd finally relented and allowed for her bangs to be trimmed by the hairdresser ladies. They'd been bugging her for weeks, coming around every Tuesday night with their over-the-top cheerfulness and stupid pink-and-white striped tunics. Tave had always told them she didn't give a fuck. But the past few days, when OT was working with her at the sink on what they called grooming, using a hairbrush wedged into the cuff strapped around her wrist, she'd studied her reflection, and her hair sure was a mess: her curls drooping into her eyes, split ends all over. So, she'd agreed to a trim. But maybe she should get it cut shorter. Do something drastic, even. Like a buzz cut, ha, ha.

Billie parallel-parked next to Tave and leaned over to give her a hug. "How's it going?" she said. "You're looking good."

"You, too." Tave smiled. She felt her cheeks strain into a broad smile, like they were out of practice. "Those are cute," she said, pointing at Billie's gloves. They were purple, work-type gloves, but thin and with the fingertips cut out.

"My driving gloves," Billie said with a coarse chuckle. She raised her hands to reveal serrated ridges across the palms. "They grip real good. I see you're driving with a proper joystick now, no hand splints. Way to go, girl."

"Yeah. Thanks. My arms are getting stronger." She stretched her hands out in front of her and flexed and tightened her biceps.

"Look at you, muscle girl. What a champ," Billie said.

"Ha, ha," Tave said. "How are things going for you at home?"

Billie shrugged. "It's a challenge, to be honest. They sent me the wrong kind of shower bench, which is a hassle to sort out. And I can't walk much at all anymore, so I'm looking at having to make my place more accessible—or move. My sister and brother-in-law are offering to help me find a better place, do it up and all that."

She paused to wave to Rowena, who had entered the room. "Hey, how you doing?"

Rowena came over and gave Billie a big hug and admired her hairdo. They chatted about hairdressers before Rowena had to rush over to one of the old ladies wobbling back to her room.

Billie turned back to Tave. "What was I saying?"

"Something about doing your place up."

"Right. I'm not sure if I told you about my sister. My baby sister, Sandy, twelve years younger than me. By the time Sandy was in first grade, our mom was completely disabled with her MS. I told you my mom had MS, right? Sandy is okay, thank goodness. No sign of her getting it." Billie tapped her knuckles against the tabletop. "Anyways, I more or less raised Sandy, became like a mom to her. I guess Sandy feels like now she needs to help me out. They can easily afford it—her husband's loaded. But I don't like being a charity case, know what I mean?"

Tave nodded. "Sure do. But if the money's there, you might as well use it. What good would it do to say no?"

"That's exactly what Beth said. I'm thinking on it." Billie placed a hand on each wheel and pushed up to relieve the pressure on her butt. "Anyways, I want to know about you. Did you get to talk to your friend Dan? And what about your friend who was in the accident with you? Liz, is that her name?"

"Les."

"Any news of her?"

"It's not good. Tracy called her parents. I guess she got a head injury or something. She can't talk and she has a feeding tube in her stomach."

"I'm sorry, kid. That's tough." Billie shook her head.

"Sounds bad, huh?"

"Well, I can't say how things will turn out with Les, of course. But a cousin of mine got a bad head injury in a motorcycle crash many years ago. Never been the same since. I mean, he's there but not there, know what I mean? He don't remember a thing, doesn't have a clue what's going on. It's bad." She shook her head again. "Tell you one thing though, thinking about him made me grateful I got my noodle intact. More or less." She laughed. "I mean, I may not be able to walk, but I'm still me in here." She pointed at her forehead. "With him, it's like he's gone."

Tave nodded. Yeah—that's what she imagined about Les: that she was gone. And Tave hadn't even seen her yet.

"It's a real shame, for sure," Billie said.

"Tracy also said some shit about Les's parents getting a lawyer. To sue someone, I guess. I dunno. Do you think I can get a lawyer and get a ton of money, like you hear about on TV? Like, get rich? I saw something about this guy, he was injured by some piece of equipment, and he got fifteen million dollars. I sure could use that."

"I wouldn't count on it, hon. There has to be a deep pocket for that kind of settlement. Like a company or someone super rich who's liable. Whose car were you in?"

"Mine," Tave said. "Beat-up old thing."

"Right. Well, that's not going to help. What about the other driver? You know much about him?"

"I don't know. Tracy said something about Les's parents going after him. My ICU nurse told me he was drunk, but I don't know if that's true. No one's told me anything," Tave said. "Anyway, what the heck? It's not like money is going to get me walking again."

"No, but money could buy you state-of-the-art equipment, all the best help. But, like I say, most people get nothing. What does the police report say about the accident?"

"I don't know. Shit. No one's told me anything about that either."

Billie pointed to the computer terminal in the corner. "I guess we could try to find it. Hey, Rowena, can you log us on?"

She wheeled over and pecked at the keys while Tave watched. Billie peered at the screen and used only the pointy finger on each hand, like the little old ladies Tave remembered seeing at the library when she and Jimmy Spenger hung out after school on rainy days, pretending to do homework. They laughed back then, Jimmy copying their movements with exaggerated squinting and poking, but now it was way more than Tave could do, her hands being so useless. And truly, Tave had no idea how to get started with searching for a police report. But Billie navigated her way to the California Highway Patrol website and reached a page where you were supposed to enter the case report or VIN number. Tave had no clue about either.

"Okay," Billie said. "Looks like you can also search by vehicle type and location. Where exactly was your accident?"

"We were coming back from Oregon. On Highway 97, I guess. That's what Beth found in a news report."

Tave closed her eyes, squeezed them tight, trying to remember that fateful journey. Les was mad because they left so late. They didn't hit the road until four o'clock. She had to be at work early in the morning, Tave not until noon.

"I'll drive," Tave had said. "You can sleep."

But Les refused. "I can never sleep in the car. Gives me a cramp in the neck." And she always preferred to be in the driver's seat.

"You could climb into the back."

"With all that junk on the seat? I don't think so."

They were in Tave's car, because Les's truck needed new tires, but Les had driven most of the way up, and had insisted on driving most of the way back too. Until they stopped for a late dinner, right before crossing back into California, when she reluctantly handed over the keys.

Tave quivered. She still couldn't remember what happened next. It was late and very dark. But she shouldn't have been tired; she wasn't the one who'd been driving for hours. She remembered Les complaining it was getting late. Earlier, before Tave took over driving, there'd been delays on 97. One lane was closed over the pass, which made Les mad. They got stuck behind a huge RV.

"Why keep the lane closed on a Sunday night? They're not doing any work on the road now, for fuck's sake." Les banged the steering wheel in frustration. She honked at the driver of the RV. But there was no way for him to pull over.

Les always got mad when things were out of her control.

New images flashed in front of her—not images exactly, more a feeling: a scrunching, a roaring, screaming.

"Maybe we can get it this way," Billie was saying, still hunched over the computer.

"Stop," Tave said, shaking her head. "No. I don't want to see it." It was too much. She couldn't face it.

"All right," Billie said. "I get it. You don't have to do this right now."

～

On Friday morning, Tave was on her way to therapy when she was accosted by Tracy as she passed the nurses' station.

"Tave," she said. "We need to talk. Do you want to come to my office or go back to your room?"

Tave was heading off to the gym, in the opposite direction. No, she didn't want to go back. "I'm supposed to be in OT in five minutes."

Tracy looked at her watch. "It's ten minutes until the top of the hour. We've got time." She looked around her. "Let's go in here." She led the way to a room past the nurses' station, beyond the bank of computers. Tracy's outfit today was a bit more subdued: black pants with a green sweater. As she unlocked the door, Tave noticed she was, however, wearing humongous, dangling green earrings.

The room was small, packed with chairs around a table. Tracy rearranged the furniture to make room for Tave's wheelchair, dragging one of the chairs out into the hallway. "Come in, come in." The earrings bounced back and forth with the exertion.

Tave maneuvered her way into position at the end of the table.

"So, did Beth tell you?" Tracy said. "I've arranged transportation for you to go on this outing on Sunday."

"Yeah. It's like a bus or something?"

"Paratransit. It'll be good for you to try it. It's an extremely valuable service for people with disabilities."

"Okay. Whatever."

"You don't sound very enthusiastic. Are you sure you want to go? I know it's mostly Beth's idea. And I'm sure it's a good thing. But it's a bit unusual. You're going out for such a long time, and to a place not officially associated with the medical center. And not with a family member. I want to make sure you're not being forced into it against your will." She peered at Tave over the top of her glasses. Bright green, of course, with a green cord today. Tave was amused at the thought of the time and effort Tracy must put into these coordinated outfits every morning. "I know Beth can be strong-willed," she continued. "Are you feeling comfortable with the plan?"

"I guess. It sounds kinda cool. I mean, Beth will be with me the whole time, right?"

"Yes, of course, dear, of course, of course," Tracy said. It seemed like she was waiting for Tave to say more, but when she didn't, she pulled her yellow notepad out of her briefcase and said, "Right. We need to settle on your discharge plan. We need to know where you'll be living after you leave here, so we can plan for any modifications, and finalize your equipment list. It takes time to get those things lined up, so we have to begin in earnest."

She looked to Tave for a response, but again getting nothing, she plowed on. "Did you hear back from your friend in Eureka?"

"Dan?"

"Yes, dear. Didn't you tell me he might find you a place to live?"

"Yeah. He said something like that."

"Has he contacted you again?"

"No."

"Do you have his number?" Tracy reached for the phone on a low corner table behind her.

"I dunno. I guess. I mean, no."

Tracy returned the phone cradle to its base with a thud and fixed Tave with a hard glare. "Now listen here, young lady. We all understand your injury has been a great shock, and that you have a flimsy support system, but we have to move on. You've been on rehab for four weeks, and we must come up with a plan. You're an adult, and you need to start acting like one." Gone was her sickly sweet singsong voice. She wagged her finger in front of Tave's face. "We need to contact Dan today and determine if he has any realistic prospects for a living situation for you. Frankly, I think it unlikely. But if he can come up with something substantial today—or let's say by Monday at the latest—fine, we can explore that option. Otherwise, we need to look at alternatives."

Tave couldn't stand Tracy's beady eyes staring at her behind those ridiculous glasses. She looked around the room. There was a large poster on one wall, a print of a painting, a wooded scene with silver birch trees and golden leaves. On the opposite wall was a bulletin board covered with papers and notices, some tattered around the edges; one, covered in a plastic protective sheet, warned in large, printed block letters: DO NOT LEAVE CONFIDENTIAL PATIENT INFORMATION IN THIS ROOM; another, handwritten in red magic marker, said: Complete Your FIM'S!! with a yellow smiley face sticker attached. Next to that was a whiteboard, written on too many times, with layers of residual blue and red ink smeared into motley streaks, almost like an abstract painting. Tave squinted, trying to decipher remnants of something that might have been a list of names and dates. She searched for any trace of her name but couldn't see it.

"Are you listening to me?"

Tave had no choice but to look back at her. "Yeah. I'm listening."

"We need to discuss alternatives to Dan's plan, if that doesn't materialize. As I've said before, I've talked to your mother—"

"No."

"I know you don't like the idea. But it could be a temporary arrangement. Buy you some time to look into other options. Her landlord has agreed to construct a ramp leading to the back door, and your mom's been checking out resources. I'm talking about outpatient physical therapy and home care down in Riverside—all the things you're going to need. I'm impressed with all she's done. She wants to make this work, Tave."

"I told you, there's no way I can live with her. You don't understand. She . . . we don't see eye to eye on anything."

"I understand, I do." She turned on her sweet voice again. "But sometimes an event such as your accident can change the dynamic within a family. Bring out the best in people."

"That's assuming there's anything good there to begin with," Tave said.

Tracy shook her head. "You're very harsh on her, dear." She paused. "What about your father? We haven't talked about him. Could you go live with him? Again, maybe on a temporary basis."

"You've got to be joking." Tave felt the blood pumping at her temples; her jaw tensed. She raised her voice. She damn well wasn't going to play nice either. "Number one," she spat out, "I haven't seen my dad in, like, four years. Number two: he lives in some hellhole of a place in the middle of the desert. Number three: he has an idiot of a wife who hates my guts. *He* hates my guts, too, now that you mention it."

Tave was never good enough in her father's eyes. She always messed up. He never took much interest in her—even before he took to running off with women half his age. Once he started with that nonsense, her feelings for him turned to anger, rather than disappointment. Maybe it was different when she was tiny. Tave had vague recollections of playing T-ball with him, or tossing a football in the backyard in Fresno, but those memories were hazy, and sometimes she wondered if she'd imagined them. By the time they moved to Riverside, when Tave entered first grade, he was already pulling away. He made it clear he wished he had a son, someone he could roughhouse with, a boy to tag along when he went fishing with his buddies. He never took Tave fishing.

And he never took any interest in her softball. "You should come to the game, Ron," her mom said one time. This would have been the summer Tave played on the rec team that went all the way to the state championships. 14 Under. The Sharks. Her mom went to some of the games that year.

"Octavia is doing good, Ron," her mom said. "She can whack that ball."

"Oh yeah?" Dad looked surprised. "What position you play, Tot?" Tot had always been his nickname for her. *Tot.* So ridiculous.

He didn't even know she was the catcher. Mostly it was Megan's dad who took her to the practices and games. Tave's mom came occasionally, but she had weird hours at her job at the nail salon. She never came when they traveled. Megan's dad was the assistant coach, and he drove them all over, to hot, dry, dusty ballfields in sprawling suburbs. Her dad came to one home game, she recalled. Arrived late, in the sixth inning. Too late to see her RBI double in the third, too late to cheer her incredible throw to snag their lead runner stealing second base in the fourth. No, he missed all that. But there he was in the last two innings, shouting from the bleachers, too loud, taunting the other team's pitcher, insulting her for being fat. Tave was mortified. She wished he hadn't come. Megan's dad had to tell him to tone it down.

And at the bottom of the final inning, Tave came up to bat, bases loaded, two out, the final inning, and they were trailing by one run.

"You can do it, OG," her teammates shouted. She went by OG, her initials, on her softball team. This was before she had settled on Tave.

"You're a hitter, OG," the coach yelled.

And she was a hitter, she knew that. But this pitcher was huge and fast, brought in for the last two innings, and Tave hadn't faced her before. Her pitches came out of nowhere, curve balls dropping, fast balls spinning over the plate like lightning. She swung frantically and missed by a mile. Struck out.

She could hear her father cursing behind her. By the time she returned to the dugout and looked up at the bleachers, he was gone. By Christmas that year, he'd moved out and was gone for good.

"All right, all right, so not your father," Tracy was saying now, holding up her hand, calling a truce. "Sorry. It was just an idea. I'm really sorry, Tave." She was back in her good-cop routine. "I know this is hard. But we have to come up with something. The rehab unit is only short-term. Your insurance won't cover you to stay here much longer."

"Are you going to kick me out on the street?" Tave threw it out as a challenge. Surely, they couldn't do that. Or could they? What if they could? She would die, literally. She was suddenly very afraid, in a way she hadn't been since the accident. It had been terrifying, all of it, but there'd always been people, tons of people around her, fussing over her, taking care of her, taking care of everything. Without that . . . how could she possibly survive alone?

"No, we wouldn't kick you out in the street," Tracy said. "We can't do that. But if you don't want to consider going to your mother's, and your friend Dan doesn't come through, I'll have to start looking for a nursing home placement."

"A nursing home? What, like for old people?"

"Typically, a nursing home will have a lot of old people, yes. I can try to find one with a few younger residents, but we usually can't be too picky. We have to see what we can get."

"Shit."

"You should think about whether you'd prefer a placement down here, or up in Eureka, closer to your friends. I have less familiarity with the institutions up there, of course, but I can look and see what's available."

Tave couldn't believe she was going to end up in an *institution*.

~

Later in the afternoon, Linda stopped Beth in the hallway. "What's this I hear about you taking Tave Greenwich out on pass this weekend?" She was all dolled up in a suit and heels. *She must be on her way to a meeting with the big schmucks.*

Beth took a deep breath. "Yeah." She tried to smile, although she felt like gritting her teeth. *Was she going to get on her case about that too?* "I think it will be a great opportunity for her. To see what adaptive sports options are out there."

"You didn't think this was something you should run by me first?"

Er . . . no. "Dr. Kramer thinks it's a great idea."

"Maybe he does. But I think you're overstepping here. It's not your place to take her out on a pass. You're not family. And this is not an official medical-center outing. I'm concerned about liability issues."

"I'm doing this as a friend, on my own time. And Tracy has arranged Paratransit. It's no different than if it was a family member taking her out in a personal vehicle. Which happens all the time with other patients. But Tave doesn't have family."

"You've got to be careful, Beth." Linda placed her hand on Beth's arm and fixed her with a firm stare. "It's not your job to be her friend. You can't rescue her. Your job is to give her the best rehabilitation possible. And you're excelling in that. But you must maintain your boundaries. You can't save every patient who has poor family support or not enough resources. That's a recipe for burnout. I've seen it happen too many times."

"It's fine. I'm okay. I appreciate your concern." Beth smiled, hoping to end this conversation. *Thank you, ma'am.*

"I'm serious, Beth. This must stop. I'm not going to interfere with this outing, as the arrangements have already been made, and I don't want to see Tave disappointed. But I'm warning you, don't do it again."

Beth stifled a sarcastic reply as Linda turned and clattered down the hallway in her heels.

14

Tave sat while the van driver used the lift to hoist her into the vehicle. He took forever to secure her wheelchair into position.

"I got the power off," Tave said. "This thing ain't going nowhere."

"I know, hon. But regulations—got to strap you in." The driver crouched behind her chair. He was a burly Black guy with a wide smile that lit up his whole face. He rose and wiped beads of sweat off his forehead with the back of his hand. "All right. That's good and tight. Ready to roll."

"Let's get this show on the road," Beth said from across the aisle. There was an edge to her voice, Tave thought. She looked kind of wasted, like she'd been up all night drinking. Which didn't seem like her thing. Maybe she was tired, working her day off and all. Tave reminded herself to thank Beth later.

She thought they would drive directly to the rec center. But no. Turned out they had to pick up some other folks first. Tave had no idea where they were going, but she was thrilled at the change of scenery after all the weeks stuck behind hospital walls. Beth cursed softly and said they were going way out into the boonies, as she called it, although it hardly looked that way to Tave, just rows and rows of houses stuck close together like they were scared of standing on their own. They stopped at one of these houses, painted bright pink, maybe to stand out in the dense fog.

The driver jumped from his seat. A tiny old lady approached the curb, bent over like she was looking for something she'd lost on the ground, hobbling with a walker. A tall young man, her son, or could be her grandson, stood at her side. He said something to the driver as they waited for her to slowly make her way to the van. Tave couldn't see her face, but she wore a wide-brimmed blue hat, matching coat, and white gloves: her Sunday best. Her legs were swollen, her ankles bulging above tight white dress shoes. When she reached the door, she handed the walker to the driver and hauled herself up the steps.

"I got this," she said with a surprisingly loud laugh, making her way with the walker again, heading for the seat behind Tave. Her face was covered in wrinkles and her eyelids drooped, but her eyes shone bright, a vivid blue. Tave looked again at the young man waving from the curb: he looked Asian or something, while the lady was White. Must be a caretaker, Tave realized. Or not. Maybe families were mixed up any which way here in the city, as she'd seen in the hospital. Tave kind of liked that.

She thought briefly about her conversation with Tracy, about where she was going to live, who would give her the help she needed. And eventually she would have to face the police report of her accident and figure out what she was supposed to do about getting a lawyer. But it was all too much. She couldn't deal with any of it right now. She wanted to push it out of her mind and have fun for once.

The lady stopped when she got level with Tave, wheezing with the effort. Even though she'd appeared tiny on the sidewalk, she towered over Tave now. "Oh, honey," she said. "What happened to you?"

What happened? For a second, Tave didn't understand. She looked down at her sweatshirt. She'd had a minor mishap at breakfast; scrambled eggs were still a challenge to handle with the cuff and curved spoon. But she thought the nurse had cleared away the evidence: yes, all good. The old lady was still staring at her. Then it dawned on her. *Oh, that.* "Broke my neck in a car crash," she said.

"Oh, sweetie. I'm so sorry." She placed her gloved hand on Tave's shoulder, giving it a gentle squeeze. "I'm going to pray for you, dear."

Tave smiled faintly, not wanting to be rude. But that praying stuff was too much like her mother's talk. Once the lady was seated behind her, Tave caught Beth watching her. She straightened her shoulders, held her head up high. Goddamn it. She didn't want to be an object of pity, and sure as hell not from a shriveled old lady.

"Thanks," she said, likely not loud enough for the lady to hear, so she raised her voice and added: "I'm doing okay, thanks for asking."

~

They made three more stops, including dropping the old lady off at a church on top of a steep hill, and down to Grocery Outlet to pick up a woman laden with overstuffed shopping bags and an oxygen tank on wheels. Seemed like it was taking forever, but Tave kind of enjoyed the ride, watching the city slowly come to life, people of all colors and shapes emerging at a slow Sunday pace. As they crested a hill, she caught a glimpse of one of the bridges, she wasn't sure which; she was about to ask Beth, but her head was turned away, resting on the window, either dozing or spacing out, Tave couldn't tell.

Finally, they arrived. The rec center stood in a large park, surrounded by lush, green trees. Here, in this part of the city, the sun was beginning to burn through the fog, and as Tave was lowered to the sidewalk, she caught the scent of freshly mowed grass. She closed her eyes and inhaled the sweetness of it. *Damn*, she missed being outdoors. She wasn't sure what to expect from the day, but if nothing else, this smell made it worthwhile. She turned her head toward the sun, her eyes still closed, drinking it in, remembering long summer days by the lake, lying in the sun, or hiking behind Les, watching her calves, bronzed and strong above her boots, her purple fanny pack with twin water bottles around her waist, her damp shirt hugging her shoulders. Tave shook herself back to reality. *Fuck.* She was sitting here in this damn wheelchair, Les was in some sort of semi-coma, and Beth was fussing with Tave's foot straps, saying something about needing to move forward so the van guy could raise his platform.

"Come on. Let's go. Round this way." Beth seemed back to her cheerful self, leading the way to the side of the building. A large workshop opened out onto a courtyard spilling over with the oddest collection of bicycles Tave had ever seen. The bikes, if you could even call them that, came in all sorts of shapes and sizes: some low to the ground with reclining seats, one with two seats side by side almost like a golf cart, and several others with more of a tandem setup, two seats, one behind the other. Extra wheels and seats lay strewn all over the place. A guy in a manual wheelchair was bent double next to one of the tandems, wrench in hand, adjusting the gear shifter. He didn't look up as Tave and Beth approached, but a tall guy emerged from inside the workshop.

"Hey, you made it." He beamed. "Hi, Beth. And you must be Tave. It's so great to meet you. I'm Brent." He extended two hands and took hold of Tave's fist like it was no big deal she couldn't shake hands in the regular way. Tave squinted at him, and he moved so his shadow shielded her eyes. He looked to be about thirty-five, with dark hair and a closely cropped beard, thick eyebrows, and a friendly smile. He wore khaki shorts and a T-shirt, although the air felt chilly to Tave; she guessed this was his usual outfit as his arms and legs were deeply tanned, muscular, and covered with dark hair. No denying he was cute—if you were into that sort of thing. But Tave wasn't—never had been. In high school she and Jimmy Spenger had hung out and faked being an item to keep everyone off their backs, both knowing it was a charade. He moved away the end of junior year. She'd missed him like hell. They never did keep in touch. She suddenly wondered where he'd ended up and had the crazy notion she might run into him here in the city.

Brent was saying something about one of the bikes. "You could give this one a try. Or we could set you up with Beth on a tandem. It's up to you."

Tave looked at Beth, confused.

"This is a great handcycle for your first time," Beth said, pointing to the one Brent had selected.

Tave looked at the hand controls. "But how would I . . . ?" She raised her arms with their useless, curled wrists.

"You'll use quad grips. We'll strap them to your wrists, and they slot into the handlebars. You'll use the strength you have in your triceps and biceps, all that good stuff we've been working on, push and pull, push and pull." She made alternating motions with her own arms, circling in the air in front of her. "I'm sure you can do it. I think you should go it alone to get the feel of it. I'll walk beside you. Or run, if you get your speed up. We can ride tandem another time."

"You up for it?" Brent asked.

Tave looked again at the bike. It was low to the ground with a bright-red curved frame, a padded black seat reclined at an angle, and large wheels, one in front, two behind. The footrests lay either side of the front wheel. She wasn't sure how she would get into it, but she figured Beth must have a plan. *I've come this far,* she thought, *why not?* "Sure," she said.

"Great." Brent stepped to Tave's side, sizing her up. "Jorge," he called to the guy working on the other bike. "I think we should adjust this seat, more upright. Just a bit," he added. Turning back to Tave, he said, "You'll feel more comfortable sitting upright at first, but as you get into it, you'll find reclining will give you more strength and stability."

Jorge wheeled over and swiveled into position beside the bike. He smiled at Tave. "Hey," he said. "How's it going?"

"Good."

"This is a great machine." He adjusted the seat with an Allen wrench, tugged on it to check it was secure, and bent forward from his wheelchair to fiddle with something else low, near the gear shifter. "All set," he said, waving for Brent to come back over. He adjusted his position in his seat, pushing himself up off the cushion with both arms fully extended, in the way Tave had seen Billie do many times.

"Okay, Tave," Brent said. "Let's get you in."

He and Beth placed the bike next to Tave's chair and with a quick nod to each other—Brent at her shoulders, Beth with her legs—they deposited her into the seat in one smooth motion. As soon as she was seated, Tave's legs started their jumping thing again, twitching like crazy, triggering the weird pain in her feet, but mostly looking so damn stupid.

"I guess my legs are pretty excited about this," she said.

Beth pressed gently on Tave's thighs, putting a stop to the spasms and the pain. She smoothed Tave's sweatshirt behind her back while Brent adjusted the length of the leg supports and strapped in her feet.

"Looking good," Beth said. "Now these."

She applied rigid black braces to Tave's hands, which looked ugly as shit, with a three-inch rod sticking out from her palms. But when Beth showed her how to hook them into the cranks on the handlebars, she realized it was pretty cool. Brent adjusted the tension on the crank and cleared the way for her to take practice circles around the courtyard.

Damn. This could be fun.

"I've got to work on a new Quad Elite that's just arrived," Brent said, pointing his thumb toward the workshop. "Jorge here will show you the ropes. I'll see you later."

Jorge leaned across Tave from his wheelchair to show her how to use the gear shifter—disconnecting from the hand crank and pushing her wrist against a knob protruding at her right hip—and demonstrated how to brake by moving the hand controls backward.

"It's pretty flat around this section of the park, so it's a good place to start," he said. "Later, you can think about going up over the bridge. That's a real workout. But it's cool; you get to go around the other side of the lake. Maybe you can convince Beth to give you a push." He looked up at Beth with a grin.

"Let's see how it goes," Beth said.

Tave propelled toward the exit, slowly turning the crank. Down with her right, then the left; her right arm was still weaker, but she found she could compensate by pulling up more with the left on the upswing. Round and round. *Okay*, she thought, *I got this.*

"Wait," Beth called after her, running to catch up. "Helmet."

Tave pulled back on the handles to come to a stop. She scrunched her nose at the ugly black helmet in Beth's hands. "Do I have to?"

"Yes. Every time." Beth attached the strap under Tave's chin. "And this." She slotted a red flag on a long stick someplace behind Tave's seat.

"You think I'm going out on the freeway or something?"

"Come on, let's go," Beth said.

Tave wondered how she would make it out through the gate and onto the path—it looked kind of tight for the long, cumbersome contraption she was driving—but she turned the handlebar to the left, circling around with her arms, feeling the handcycle respond to her movements, and she made the turn just fine. She slowed to give way to a woman with a jogging stroller, and then went for it, full speed ahead. The path was smooth and wide, shaded by trees on one side, with a grass lawn coming up on the left, and beyond, a kids' playground. She got into the rhythm of her arm strides, exhilarated to be moving under her own steam, feeling the power of her muscles and the wind on her face. Sure, she would have liked to be moving her legs too and would have preferred to feel the wind in her hair instead of wearing a damn helmet—but hell, this felt good, the most fun she'd had in a long while.

She glided along, passing the playground, with more trees on both sides of the trail now. She saw the lake up ahead, and that must be the bridge the dude was talking about, with the path climbing up and over it. Disconnecting one hand from the crank, she waved at a little kid who had stopped to stare, wide-eyed; her fist in its clawlike brace probably weirded him out even more. Now she had to focus on getting her hand back into the crank, which was harder than she'd imagined, and she came to a standstill. Beth caught up with her.

"Wow, girl," she said, panting slightly. "You're a natural at this."

"It's cool." Tave grinned. "Thanks. On your day off and everything. I mean, I get it, you didn't have to do this."

Beth nodded. "It's great to see you enjoying yourself."

Tave managed to hook her wrist back into the crank, but she'd lost her momentum; it was much harder to get going again. It didn't seem like she'd gone far, but her arm muscles ached already, her left biceps twitched, and the tingling pain in her feet had started up again. "This is a workout," she said. She felt drained of energy.

"It is. You've done great for your first time. Do you want to turn back?"

"I guess." She was disappointed not to have made it to the bridge. And she needed Beth's help to turn around, to maneuver the bike back and forth a few times, blocking the trail, making people wait, having everyone stare. Going back was harder; it must have been slightly downhill on the way out, the kind of hill you only notice when you're going up. It took all her strength to keep pushing forward, turning the crank round and round. By the time they reached the rec center, Tave was spent.

She sat, catching her breath, waiting to be transferred back to her wheelchair. The place was buzzing now; more people had arrived, and Brent and some other guy were busy attending to them. Beth disappeared inside. Tave closed her eyes, tilting her face up to the sun again.

"Hey, is that you, Tave?"

Across the yard she saw one of the side-by-side bikes with a tiny woman, all twisted and scrawny, seated next to a buff-looking dude. The woman was waving at Tave, her arm making wild twitchy movements, but most of her face was hidden behind crazy, huge sunglasses, and Tave didn't recognize her.

"I'm Maddy," the woman said. "I came to see you in the hospital."

Oh, right. As she approached, Tave saw the same *Life is Good* baseball hat. And her face, which was so much younger than it looked from a distance. She was smiling.

"Hi," Tave said.

"Good to see you here. Have you been out already?" She jerked her head toward the path.

"Yeah, it was fun."

"Great. We're starting out."

Tave examined her setup. One of her hands appeared to be strapped onto the hand crank, but she surely couldn't do much with those arms; the guy had his feet on regular-looking pedals. He removed Maddy's cap and placed a helmet on her head, snapping the strap under her chin. He was in shorts and T-shirt, tanned like Brent, but a bit older, Tave guessed. He must be from the rec center, there to do most of the work for Maddy. Tave felt good she'd been able to propel herself, not just go along for the ride, even though her arms were trembling with fatigue.

"See you later," Maddy said with another weird arm wave, as the guy began to pedal. "Oh, and Tave: this is my husband, Ryan."

"Nice to meet you," Tave managed to mumble. Her mouth hung open as she watched them speed toward the lake.

～

They had to wait over thirty minutes for the Paratransit ride back to the hospital. Beth seemed grumpy again, but Tave was happy to chill, watching more people come and go. She'd had three glorious hours out in the real world and was in no hurry to get back to the pink-and-white-stripe ladies and their afternoon sing-along, followed by meatloaf for dinner— the same thing every goddamn Sunday. The thought of returning to the rehab unit filled her with dread. She didn't know how much longer she was going to have to stay in that dumb place. But it was much scarier to think about where she would go next.

She hooked her left elbow around the armrest and tilted her body to the side, doing her weight shift—*like a good girl*, she would tell nurse Wanda— relieving the pressure on her tush. But then she felt it, or rather, no, she didn't feel it; she felt nothing down there, only a vague tugging sensation, sort of a cramping pain in her gut, and a tingling at her temples. But she smelled it.

"Shit," she said. "Fucking shit."

"Now what?" Beth said.

"I've had a fucking accident, is what."

15

Beth delivered Tave back to the unit, and helped Leticia, the nursing aide, transfer her to bed. Beth felt obliged to help with the cleanup, although it definitely fell in the *not my job* category. If a patient had an accident in the gym, she would summon the nursing staff to handle it. But now, it seemed wrong to cut and run, like it would make Tave feel even worse. She was bummed the outing had ended that way. Tave had been mortified, of course, convinced she was stinking up the van and that the driver and other passengers would know what had happened. There'd been no way to take care of the situation at the rec center, even if Beth had thought to bring a change of clothes for Tave. Which she had not. Luckily, the Paratransit ride back had been much faster, with only one other stop.

Leticia was her usual calm, efficient self, and didn't truly need Beth's help. It was good to see how she put Tave at ease, asking her questions about the handcycling.

"Yeah, it was cool," Tave told her. "I had fun. Until this . . ." She stuck out her tongue in disgust.

"Hey," Leticia said. "You know what they say: Shit happens."

They all laughed. "Sure does," Tave said.

Leticia continued, more serious, "You be sure to let Wanda know about this. She'll figure out a way to get your bowel program back on track."

It was after three o'clock by the time they were done. Beth rode the elevator down to the parking garage to retrieve her bike, worried now about the shitstorm awaiting her at home. The night before, she'd proposed going out for breakfast at Olivia's, for Katy's favorite blueberry pancakes, but when Katy heard they'd have to be there by nine thirty, she'd gone all crazy, saying she sure as fuck wasn't going to get up that early on a Sunday morning. Which was nuts. She was always up by nine. And it wasn't like Katy had to get up at the crack of dawn during the week; her shifts were all over the place, but she never began before ten. So they'd had a huge fight, and when Beth left the house in the morning, Katy was sulking and had refused to say goodbye.

Beth stood at their apartment door now, bracing herself, before turning the key. "Hello," she called out.

Silence. Only the hum of the refrigerator. A few dirty dishes in the sink, Katy's pj's and a sweatshirt on the floor in the bedroom. Beth's stomach twisted. This was ridiculous, feeling like she'd done something wrong. She'd been gone only a few hours. Katy worked weekends sometimes. Three weeks ago, she freelanced all day Saturday as an assistant at a yoga retreat. And now, in her new job, she often had weekend shifts. Beth didn't see how today was so different.

Beth helped herself to an iced tea and sank into the beanbag chair. Relationships were so damn hard. With patients, it was easy, straightforward. You threw yourself into doing everything you could—and the rewards were instantaneous, and huge. They all adored you. But with girlfriends: different story. Recently, it seemed like everything Beth did was wrong. Last week, when she'd suggested meeting Katy after work, Katy accused Beth of not giving her any space. Now Beth had gone off doing her own thing and Katy was pissed. Beth felt she was stumbling around in a maze, making turns she hoped would work, only to bump into another dead end. She didn't know how to make it right.

The *Outside* magazine was on the coffee table; its cover photo featured a glorious lake littered with rock islands and surrounded by a high mountain cirque. Beth wanted to be there right now. They should plan another trip. It was Katy who first introduced her to the wilderness. Beth had been active in sports throughout her childhood, and her family had taken annual camping trips to Lake Macbride State Park, or Pikes Peak on the Mississippi. But on those vacations, Beth and her brothers had stayed close to camp, climbing trees, collecting bugs, swimming in the river, or paddling the old canoe through the weeds at the edge of the pond. They'd never done much hiking, and certainly never experienced being out in wild nature. When she first met Katy, she was enthralled with her descriptions of hikes in the Sierras or white water rafting on the Yuba River. It was a big part of the attraction of moving out to California. Katy would take her to all the amazing places she knew.

Beth immediately fell in love with the Western landscape and fell more in love with Katy in the process. The far corners of Yosemite became their playground, miles from the crowds in the Valley. Together, they became more adventurous, going deeper into the wilderness, embarking on longer backpacking trips. They hiked most of the John Muir Trail, nearly two hundred miles, taking it in sections, over two summers. Beth was the one who organized the logistics of the food and the resupply points—because she was good at that. She researched the best routes and read up on bear cans and proper food storage and the best equipment.

She smiled now remembering one close encounter with a black bear near Palisade Creek, more than twenty miles in, no one else around. They'd hiked ten miles the day before, with a steep climb up to Muir Pass, arriving at their destination late and exhausted, putting up the tent and fixing their freeze-dried chicken and rice right before dark. They'd collapsed into their sleeping bags, forgetting to put all the food and trash in the bear can. They awoke three hours later to the sound of huge paws rummaging through their makeshift kitchen wedged against the rocks ten feet away. They clung to each other in terror. Katy's teeth clattered and her whole body shook; Beth could feel her own heart thumping at a faster rate than she ever thought possible. She did a quick mental inventory, trying to remember if they had any food or scented items in the tent. She didn't think so; they should be safe. But for several horrifying moments, she couldn't be sure.

By the morning, they could laugh about it. They salvaged two granola bars and a package of freeze-dried apples the bears had somehow missed, and would have to survive on those for the hike out. The next day, they reached Le Conte Canyon, and met three guys, who gave them Ritz crackers and a tube of bologna, which normally Beth would have disparaged, but which she devoured with glee in her famished state. They told that story many times. It became famous among their friends.

They hadn't argued at all on that trip. The experience drew them closer. And made them paranoid about bear precautions on all future trips. They always carried two bear cans now, in spite of the extra weight, to make sure every single item, down to the lip gloss and tiny tubes of toothpaste, anything that might appeal to a hungry bear, was safely stashed away at night.

Beth realized she was hungry now. She returned to the kitchen in search of something to eat, dug out a protein bar, and considered the options from the fruit bowl on the counter: two overripe bananas and an apple.

She selected the apple, a crisp Fuji, perfect. She had an inspiration: she would make banana bread, a nice surprise for Katy, who was always impressed with her ability to make it from scratch. She didn't need a recipe; Beth would tap her temple and say it was imbedded in her brain, from the years in her grandmother's kitchen, where Beth and her brothers spent their after-school hours.

A quick survey of the cabinets confirmed she had the ingredients. No walnuts, which was a shame, but it would be good enough. Soon she was mashing bananas and beating eggs, immersed in the simple joy of baking the old-fashioned way, by hand, just like Grammy. She whisked hard with a wooden spoon, relishing the ache in her forearms, as if the effort would improve the flavor. A labor of love, she thought. Maybe she was being harsh on Katy. It must be difficult for her, having found no real career of her own, to see Beth engrossed in her work. She should be more sympathetic. Stop being so critical. Offer to make it up to her and plan a day trip somewhere fun for next weekend.

When the bread was in the oven, Beth sat with the latest issue of *Physical Therapy*. She was halfway through a complicated review article on the latest in neuroimaging techniques when she heard the building front door slam below. She flinched a little, an involuntary tightening of her neck and shoulders, but tossing her journal aside, she rose to meet Katy at the door to the apartment.

"Hi, honey," she said, moving toward her, opening her arms for a hug.

"You're back." Katy stepped into the hug for a fleeting moment before turning away. "I thought you were going to be there all day."

"No. I told you . . . it was only for a few hours." Beth followed Katy into the kitchen. "I'm making banana bread." The warm smell of baking filled the room. "Should be done soon."

"Is it gluten-free?"

"What? No, of course it isn't."

"I'm starting a cleansing diet. No gluten." She lifted a tote bag onto the counter and extracted three bottles of green liquid.

"What the . . . ?" Beth's jaw dropped. She was about to launch a tirade of protest. *Gluten-free isn't cleansing, for god's sake. It's for people with a genuine gluten allergy like Crohn's disease.* But she stopped herself. She remembered her vow to make peace. She took a deep breath. "When did you decide that?" she ventured, hoping her tone sounded light.

"This morning. I need to do something to turn things around." She rearranged the stuff on the top shelf of the fridge to make room for her green bottles. She rubbed her stomach. "I feel so bloated."

"Okay. I hope it helps," Beth said. *Let it go*, she thought. *It won't last long.* She checked the banana bread with a toothpick: it was ready, the top beautifully risen. "I guess I'll take this into work tomorrow if you don't want any. It'll be gone in a flash."

Katy leaned over to smell the steaming bread on the stove top. "It does smell good," she said. "Another masterpiece."

She looked up and made eye contact for the first time, with a faint smile. Beth moved toward her and pulled her into a hug. She felt Katy resist for a moment but then yield, as she held her tighter, kissed her neck, and licked her earlobe, biting it gently. Katy moaned softly. Their mouths connected, soft and moist, and their bodies rubbed together, rocking side to side. She felt Katy grab her butt in both hands, in the way that always turned her on, lifting her feet off the ground, thrusting her thigh into Beth's crotch, pushing hard against her. She loved that Katy was taller than her, more solid—unlike her previous lovers. Desire flooded through her; Beth was wet and throbbing as they fumbled their way into the living room, onto the floor, ripping off each other's clothes.

Makeup sex: always the best. She came quickly and rolled onto Katy to trade positions. But Katy murmured, "Oh, you're not done yet," flipping Beth back, caressing Beth's belly with strong strokes of her tongue, all the way down. Beth arched her hips to meet her, and came again and again, the orgasms rippling one after the other.

Later, as they lay spent on the rug, Beth watched the sun streaming across the wall above the sofa, casting rainbow patterns through the glass prism hanging in the window. Her head rested on Katy's chest, and she ran the tips of her fingers across the concave slope of her stomach, and down the strong muscles of her thighs. "I'm sorry I've been so wrapped up in work," she said. "I know you must feel neglected. We need to spend more time together. We talked about doing something special, like a day trip to Marin. But I was thinking . . . we could plan a whole weekend together. Maybe go up to the Russian River. Stan at work knows a cheap place to stay."

"Sure. It would be good to get away."

"Next weekend?"

"Yes, that would work."

"Great. I'll check with Stan." Beth smiled. "And we should go see your folks soon. We have to plan Jenny's birthday event, don't forget."

Katy kissed the top of Beth's head. "Yes, thanks for the reminder. I'll call my mom tonight." She turned on her side, propping herself up on her elbow. "How did it go today? Did your patient have a good time at the rec center?"

"Yeah." Beth smiled. She loved it when Katy took an interest in her work. "It was great. She totally got into it. She's a natural. I reckon she could be really good at handcycling. Or other adaptive sports." Beth swung herself up into a seated position, legs crossed. "She was a jock. Played softball in college."

"Wow. How sad."

"Sad?"

"Well, she's not going to be playing softball again, is she?"

"No. But that experience, being on a team, knowing how to push yourself—all that's a huge asset. Makes such a difference. She's able to draw on that in her rehabilitation."

"Well, I think it's tragic." Katy got up and pulled on her pants.

A distance opened up between them. It happened so often when Beth talked to people about her work. It always took her aback. Spinal cord injury had become normalized for her. She first met her patients when they were at their lowest point after their injury, and she moved onward with them, accepting them as they were—injured, yes, but urging them to look forward, not back, celebrating each gain, no matter how tiny. She was always surprised when those who didn't understand, who had no experience in rehab, focused immediately on what had been lost. She was used to that from strangers, from someone she might bump into at a party. But she thought Katy was different.

"Well, I'm glad it went well," Katy said.

"Yeah, she kind of blossomed in a way I haven't seen before."

"Was Brent there?" Katy had met him at fundraising events, and they had hit it off. It turned out they'd attended the same high school, though Brent was several years older.

"Sure. He was great with Tave."

"I bet she has a crush on him already."

"Maybe. But she marches to a different drummer." Beth grinned at Katy.

"What?"

"She's not into guys."

"Wait . . . What?" Katy glared at Beth. "Are you telling me this patient of yours that you spend all day, every day thinking about and talking about, that this chick is a dyke?"

"Yeah, she's a dyke. Totally closeted, living up north in some god-awful small town, but she was living with a girlfriend. Her girlfriend was in the car with her and—"

"No wonder you're obsessed with her." She stood, placing her hands on her hips. "It all makes sense now. Jeez. You have a crush on her."

Beth jumped up to face Katy. "Of course not. It's not like that at all. I just . . ."

"And you've been so sneaky about it. How come you didn't tell me she's a dyke?"

"I don't know. I wasn't trying to hide it from you." At least, not consciously. But she knew she hadn't told Katy.

"You have a fucking crush on her," Katy repeated. "No wonder you've been so wrapped up in *Tave this* and *Tave that*," she sneered. Her face twisted around the words. "Staying late, spending Sunday with her. I should have realized something was going on."

"Stop it. That's ridiculous." Beth gathered her own clothes, pulled her T-shirt down to cover her torso.

Katy, fully dressed now, swung her bag over her shoulder and headed for the door. "I'm going out. You can go back to the hospital and hang out with your girlfriend for all I care."

"Wait!" Beth shouted, running after her. She couldn't believe things had turned around so quickly. A minute ago, they had been making love on the floor. She felt the afterglow coursing through her.

Beth caught up to Katy on the landing, grabbed her elbow, and, still in her underwear, pivoted herself in front of Katy to block her escape down the stairs.

"Katy," she pleaded. But Katy stared back at her, eyes cold. "Get out of my way," she said, shoving Beth in the chest.

Beth felt the blow in her solar plexus and gasped. She grabbed for the handrail but missed and twisted somehow, and she was down, her hip brushing against the rough, industrial-strength carpet the landlord had installed last month. She caught a glimpse of the Picasso print at the bottom of the steps spinning in front of her eyes, her arms flailed, and there was a thump and a scream from somewhere and the most searing pain she had ever felt in her life.

"Beth! Oh my god, Beth, are you all right? Oh shit." Katy bounded down the steps to join her.

Beth tried to straighten herself out, but the pain bolted through her. She looked at her right ankle and knew immediately. It was contorted into a *c* shape. She could feel it throbbing like hell. There was no way she could bear weight on it.

"Shit. Ouch. Fuck!"

"Oh my god," Katy whimpered, her hand over her mouth.

Beth grunted and eased herself into a seated position on the bottom step. "You're going to have to take me to the hospital," she said. "I need to get this ankle x-rayed."

16

Of course the ER was packed, this being a Sunday afternoon. If Beth was hoping for some sort of VIP treatment as a member of staff, it wasn't happening today. There were two Code Threes that sent all the staff scrambling—all while Beth was in the waiting room. She sat squeezed in with a homeless guy wrapped up in a filthy blanket, rocking back and forth on his bare, blackened feet; a six-year-old with a bloody gash on his forearm, trying to be brave in his father's arms; an old lady bent over double, moaning softly while her husband tapped her on the back, looking embarrassed; and a young woman coughing and sneezing all over the place—why the hell hadn't the triage nurse put a mask on her?

Beth closed her eyes and focused on her breathing, trying to get a handle on the pain. She had Katy grab an extra chair so she could keep her foot elevated, but it was red and inflamed, and swelling up like crazy. She was dressed in an old skirt she hadn't worn in years; loose, with an elastic waistband, it was hardly flattering but seemed the easiest thing to pull on over her underwear as she crouched on the bottom step at home. Katy had managed to find it at the back of the closet.

The moment of her fall kept running through her mind, the moment when she could have stopped herself, made a better grab for the banister, caught her balance somehow, creating an alternative narrative: *It was scary, I almost fell down the stairs, but luckily Katy caught me. Not like it's a full flight of stairs, only seven steps down to the landing, and carpeted, thank goodness, but still, would have been awful.* For some reason, the image of the abstract Picasso print kept flashing before her, with more red in the picture than she'd noticed before. Had she fallen, a simple accident—or had Katy shoved her? She wasn't sure. Katy sat beside her, contrite, muttering apologies over and over until Beth had to tell her to quit. Hell, it didn't matter now, anyway.

"Beth Farringdon." A nurse appeared and called her forward.

Beth waved her arm in the air. "I'm going to need a wheelchair," she said. She'd told Katy to get her one when they arrived, but everything was pandemonium, and Katy was intimidated and didn't know how to be assertive enough, so Beth had hobbled in leaning on Katy's shoulders. But she sure as hell wasn't going any farther without one. She pointed to her disfigured leg. "I'm pretty sure I've broken my ankle."

"Oh dear." The nurse nodded. "Okay, hold on."

An aide appeared a few minutes later, pushing a wheelchair. Bless him; it even had elevating leg rests. He was a tall, Black, older guy, looked vaguely familiar. He helped her into the chair and gently raised her right leg.

"Wait—you work here, don't you?" he said, as he pushed her into the treatment area.

"Yeah." Beth managed a faint smile. "On the rehab unit."

"I thought so. Wow. That foot sure looks nasty. How'd that happen?"

"Tripped down the stairs." Beth avoided eye contact with Katy, who was trotting along beside her.

His name tag read Alvin. He deftly helped her up onto a gurney. "I'm gonna get the nurse in here right away. It's been crazy busy, as you can tell. But we need to get you something for that pain."

"Thanks."

She lay back and now felt woozy. It was bizarre being a patient, on the other side of the equation. Beth had never been in hospital, never been to the emergency room. She'd never broken any bones as a child. Her brothers had been the accident-prone ones. She'd been as active as them, played soccer, basketball, but she'd been careful. Or lucky. She had to live up to her mother's expectations. Beth's role in the family was to be the perfect one. "Why can't you boys be more like Beth?" was her mother's refrain. Jason had a bad fall from his bike when he was twelve, breaking his leg. He had it in a long leg cast for weeks. Mike was always getting into fights and scrapes, and once he got into high school, suffered at least two concussions playing football. Beth was convinced he'd never completely recovered. In her opinion, it explained his abusive outbursts over anything from someone bringing the wrong kind of beer to political disagreements, of which there were plenty. He was a strong supporter of the invasion of Iraq, which made Thanksgiving fraught with tension.

The nurse entered the cubicle. "Hi, I'm Carole. I understand you work here." She completed a quick assessment and started an IV. "Thanks for having such great veins!" she said. "What's your pain level?"

The zero-to-ten pain scale. Beth asked patients that same question. She thought for a moment. The pain was intense, but she didn't want to sound overdramatic. "Eight," she said. "Maybe nine."

"I'll get you an order right away. Are you okay with Dilaudid?"

"I guess." Beth had never taken anything stronger than Motrin.

"Good. And I'm going to see if Alvin can shoot you down to x-ray as soon as possible."

They were all very kind, but Beth squirmed in discomfort. She considered herself extremely sympathetic in her patient care, determined to treat each person as an individual. She hated it when she heard other staff members say, "Fifteen Door needs to go back to bed." *Fifteen Door? Are you talking about Mrs. Smith?* But it was inevitable there was always something *other* about the patient, the objectification: *The fifty-seven-year-old male in Bed 12W.* There was a divide as unassailable as the blood-brain barrier.

Now here she was on the other side of that divide: the thirty-one-year-old Caucasian female in Cubicle Seven.

With a fucking broken ankle after a stupid fall after a senseless argument. God, if her mother ever got to hear of this . . . Beth flinched at the thought. If she ever did something wrong, or wasn't as successful as she should have been, she felt obliged to hide it from her mother, so as not to disappoint. Like the time she tried out for track in sixth grade. She was already playing soccer in a rec league, and her mother thought track too much with the huge homework load in middle school, but Beth wanted to try out. Tanya, a cool new girl in her class, was trying out and Beth desperately wanted to become her best friend. She didn't tell her mother that part, of course. Nor did she tell her mother that when she ran the 100-yard dash, which surely she would be good at—she'd always been a sprinter—somehow the top part of her body got ahead of her feet and she stumbled forward, onto her face, looking up in time to see Tanya's long, ebony legs streak across the finish line way before anyone else.

She told her mother the scrape on her chin was from stumbling into an open locker door after second period. "That's so unlike you, sweetheart," Mom said. Tanya became best friends with Rachael Thompson, but she didn't stay long at Lakeside Middle School anyway; by seventh grade she'd moved to a private school in Cedar Rapids.

The nurse was back. "I have Dilaudid. The miracle drug," she said with a smile, holding a syringe in front of her like a trophy. "This should make you feel way more comfortable."

Beth felt a brief flush of coolness as the medicine entered her vein. Before she could tell if it was having any effect, Alvin appeared to wheel her to x-ray. He joked about the Giants and Barry Bonds's home run count, keeping up a constant banter Beth might have found irritating, but in fact enjoyed. Or maybe it was the high from the Dilaudid kicking in. The throbbing was easing. She felt she was floating, watching herself from above, relaxing as her ankle felt lighter, softer. It was almost fun.

But then she caught a glimpse of Dr. Michaels, the radiologist, as she was wheeled past the file room, and was overcome with embarrassment. She'd often discussed patients' images with him over the phone and had even sat in that same file room on occasion, peering at the screen, as he pointed out a suspicious shadow or she asked his opinion on a hairline fracture. *Damn.* Maybe she should have gone across town to St. Rose, to a hospital where she knew no one, and no one knew her. Last year, Laurel from OT had made that choice when she'd required abdominal surgery, and Beth understood. It was strictly forbidden for staff to access the computerized medical records for a patient not on their clinical caseload—but it was an irresistible temptation for some people. To this day, the precise nature of Laurel's surgery was a mystery she chose to keep to herself. Beth guessed hysterectomy, but recognized it was none of her business.

Beth looked around for Katy, then remembered she had stayed behind in the emergency room, with the nurse suggesting she go get coffee. They had to get their story straight. She had tripped on the stairs. That's what she'd told the intake nurse. They surely wouldn't be interviewing Katy separately, Beth hoped. This was hardly a grand jury case.

The x-ray tech was not someone Beth recognized, which was a relief. No chitchat from her, for which Beth was also grateful. She took one look at Beth's foot and made no attempt to get her to sit or stand for the x-ray but took care of it with her lying on the gurney. Beth could tell it would be pointless to ask what the x-ray showed; she would have to wait for the verdict from the ER doc. But she already knew the news would not be good.

~

Tave was surprised how exhausted she felt after her return from the rec center. She'd been working out in physical therapy every damn day for weeks, and it didn't seem like she was on that hand bike contraption for long—but now she was spent, and asked to be transferred back to bed right after dinner. She tried watching TV, but Rowena had left it on Channel 5, which was now playing 60 *Minutes*; she couldn't change the channel herself, and didn't feel like calling for help.

Tave tuned out the dude going on about North Korean nuclear missiles. She preferred to lie with her thoughts. Going to the rec center had left her with a jumble of emotions that bounced inside her like those brightly colored balls at the giant ball pit she used to play in at the shopping mall. Her mother would leave her there with Megan, the girl next door, while she got her hair or nails done. Tave marveled now that her mother had left them, knowing they wouldn't wander off, or get abducted by some weirdo. They stayed put, playing for hours, trying to separate the balls into colors: the yellows in one pile, the reds here, the blues there. They would never stay apart; one slight movement, or another kid jumping into the fray, and they tumbled into a random mix.

Being out in the fresh air had opened up a light inside her. She had forgotten how much it was part of who she was. The sun, the trees, the feel of the wind on her face. Made her think of the ocean. *Damn, she missed the ocean.* Those days—and nights—when they all drove out to Samoa Dunes, built a fire on the beach, smoked pot, roasted hot dogs, and played music, Dan on his guitar, Sammy with his harmonica. Or the winter nights they drove to the redwoods, found shelter from the rain under the huge, majestic trees. Those were good times. Last year, they did family-style Thanksgiving, Mitch doing the turkey, Les just about everything else. Tave tried her hand at pumpkin pie, but of course it was a disaster: the filling was burnt at the edges and undercooked in the center. She always messed things up. But with those guys, it didn't matter. They laughed it off and picked at the crust—which was store-bought, so hard to ruin—and ate it with pumpkin ice cream Dan found in the freezer.

And now that was all gone. Tave wasn't sure she could go back; it would never be the same. Les was staying with her parents, and god knows if she would ever return to Eureka. Without Les, Tave didn't know if she would have a place in the group. Even if they let her tag along, she'd feel out of it, an object of pity, needing help with everything, slowing them down.

Sure, it would be great to see them all again. But she'd heard nothing from Dan since he visited. He'd promised to figure out where she might live, but truthfully, Tave couldn't see him getting anything together. He meant well, for sure, but he was spaced out a lot of the time, and she couldn't see herself living with him; his apartment had steps like every other place she could think of. And she cringed at the thought of Dan doing her attendant care. She could see him transferring her in and out of bed; he was strong as an ox. But having him doing her bladder and bowel care: no, yuck, that would be too weird. So, realistically, she couldn't see how she would manage.

She had to stop living in a fantasyland. That Tracy woman would be on her case again tomorrow morning about where she was going to live, and she knew she had to come up with a plan. All she knew was that she was *not* going to live with her mom. She literally would kill herself rather than do that. She let out a bitter laugh, and then started crying. She wiped her face with the back of her hand, but some tears had escaped down the back of her neck, onto the pillow.

Rowena came in to help Tave get settled for the night. Perfect timing.

"How are you doing?" she said with a smile that quickly dissolved. "Oh, hon. What's up?"

"Oh, nothing much. Nothing new. Me just lying here paralyzed and not knowing where I'm going to live. No big deal, ha, ha."

Rowena took a tissue and wiped Tave's cheeks. "It's tough," she said.

Tave was grateful she didn't come out with some bullshit about everything going to work out okay. "Thanks. It's damp on my neck too."

"Time to turn you. Which way do you want to face?"

She positioned Tave on her left side. She always knew exactly how to make Tave comfortable, pillows between her legs, her top arm supported, nurse call light secured in reach. Tave now lay facing the window. The sun was setting, and she could see a sliver of crimson clouds between the buildings. A beautiful sunset. She could see shadows, reflections of the branches of the tree in the courtyard below, fluttering on the opposite wall. She thought again about the trees in the park, the path she had taken toward the lake, the green calm of it. She wanted to go back and get on that weird bike again, cross the bridge, explore more.

She loved that sense of moving freely, pumping her arms, feeling the strength in her body. Like her best times on the softball field. She remembered how she'd been trying to return to playing right before the accident, how excited she'd been to find a new team, pulling her gear out of the closet. And the glove. *Oh my god.* Tave had forgotten about the glove. She needed a new catcher's mitt. Her old one was in shreds, the same one she'd had since high school. She searched online and found a good one, a Rawlings Liberty, for only ninety-nine dollars. Tave didn't have the money. She'd just started the job at Mervyn's and had received only one paycheck. But she would soon be able to repay Les. Tave squirmed now at the memory: she'd sneaked behind Les's back and used her credit card, the one Les kept in the desk drawer and used for her online purchases. Tave had hoped she could find a way to hide the glove when it was delivered, and—well, she didn't have a clear plan for what to do when the credit card bill arrived.

She didn't know whatever happened to the mitt. Maybe the car crash was punishment for sneaking behind Les's back. No, that was ridiculous. But she felt guilty—and how convenient that now she'd never have to answer for the ninety-nine-dollar charge. Les's parents must have paid off her bills. They would never know to question that item.

Rowena finished tidying up Tave's bedside area. "You have everything you need before I leave?" she said, placing a soft hand on Tave's shoulder.

"Thanks. I'm good."

"Okay, hon. You rest now. I bet you're tired. But sounds like you had a good time on your pass this afternoon."

"I did." Tave smiled. Yes, she liked the vibe at the rec center. Everyone seemed relaxed and friendly. Being in a wheelchair was no big deal there. That guy who was working on the bikes from his wheelchair, he seemed cool. And that Maddy woman. She looked weird but she was cool, too. And married to such a hip-looking dude! Tave didn't know how that was possible. She would never have imagined such a thing. *Did they have sex?* She couldn't help wondering about that. She hadn't thought to ask anyone, but she kind of assumed that her days of hanky-panky were over. She had no feeling *down there*, as her mother used to say. Well, not exactly no feeling at all; she did sometimes have a burning sensation or a sense of pressure when the nurses touched her, but it sure wasn't normal. And she would never be able to return any favors. So surely no one would want to do it with her. She would be sort of useless. But she would have thought the same was true of Maddy.

And where did Maddy live? And that other guy, what was his name? Jorge, that was it. He seemed real nice, super knowledgeable about the bikes and how to fix them. She wondered where he lived and how he got the help he needed. Maybe she could try to figure out a way to stay here in the city. She could get into handcycling, and whatever else they did at the rec center. She couldn't imagine there was anything like that in Eureka.

She would talk to Beth about it in the morning. Making that decision felt like a triumph of sorts, and she drifted off to sleep.

17

First thing Monday morning, Beth was on the phone to Linda. She called her cell.

"You're not going to believe this," she said. "I've gone and fractured my ankle. I tripped and fell down the stairs at home. So dumb."

"Oh my god. I'm so sorry. How bad is it?"

"Oblique medial malleolar fracture of the tibia. I'm in a cast, of course. Non-weight-bearing, forearm crutches, the whole nine yards. Hopefully it won't need surgery. I go back for recheck next week."

"Damn. How's your pain level?"

"About six, I guess. Better than it was last night. I've got some Vicodin, but I hate the stuff, so I'm trying to hold off."

"You know better than anyone the importance of keeping the pain and inflammation under control," Linda said. "Take good care of yourself. And don't push yourself too hard. I'll put you down as off for two weeks for now. I'm sure it will be more than that, so keep me posted. Shoot. I'll have to get registry in. With Stan on vacation and Jasmine not yet back from maternity leave. Ah, well. There goes the budget!"

"I'm so sorry, Linda. I feel so bad."

"No worries. I shouldn't be burdening you with this. You focus on getting healed up quickly."

"I'll go stir-crazy here. What about—who will you assign to Tave?"

"I'm not sure yet. Probably the registry therapist."

"No!"

"Beth, please. We'll take care of it, don't you worry."

"You can't give her to someone from the registry, someone who knows nothing about spinal cord injury."

"We'll have to see. Maybe we'll find someone who does have the experience."

"Yes, but—"

"Beth," Linda said, her tone forceful now. "Stop this. I'll take care of it. You're on sick leave. You must let me handle this."

~

Beth tried. She made herself comfortable on the couch, leg elevated on a pillow, and turned on the TV. For a while she watched the local morning news shows, switched to CNN, but got sick of that, and surfed the channels, settling on some cooking thing: a woman with a posh British accent demonstrating how to bake a meat-and-vegetable pie with a puff pastry crust. It looked impressive, but Beth couldn't imagine eating let alone cooking such a thing. She turned off the TV and threw the remote on the floor. She was bored stiff already.

Her thoughts returned to work. There was no remote control for turning that off. She couldn't stop worrying about Tave. Her team conference would be coming up this afternoon, and they would have to make key decisions about her discharge date. Beth knew Dr. Kramer would be under pressure to set a date soon. Yet Tave had no idea where she would live. She had to have an advocate in that team conference. Beth couldn't let Tave be coerced into going to her mother's house.

Katy had gone out to Whole Foods to stock up on healthy items that would be easy for Beth to fix for herself while alone. They had carefully avoided any return to the previous day's argument and had told so many people the story of Beth tripping on the stairs—without any mention of their fight—that it now seemed like the truth, the whole truth, and nothing but the truth. Beth had no desire to force the issue.

Katy returned half an hour later with two bottles of kombucha, grapes, cheese and crackers, and a tub of coleslaw. She settled these within Beth's reach on the couch and cut up some of the banana bread from yesterday, which Beth had forgotten about, and for which she had no appetite at all.

"Look what arrived," Katy said, holding up a slim white envelope. "Our tickets."

"What tickets?"

"Indigo Girls. Remember?" She took out the tickets and waved them in the air. "Jen and Angie are coming too. Yay! I can't wait."

"Cool." Had Katy told her about this? She had a feeling she was supposed to remember a conversation but couldn't. "They must have cost a bunch."

"Hey, I'm a working gal now," Katy said with a swagger of her hips. "I put it on my credit card, but Angie has already given me cash for theirs, so it's all good."

"Okay."

"Do you need anything else?" Katy said. "I've got to go to work."

"I guess the Vicodin tablets from the bedside table." The pain in Beth's ankle was returning with full force. "And the phone." She pointed to the cordless set on its cradle in the corner. She couldn't trust the battery on her cell to last.

"Blanket?"

"Sure."

Katy fluttered like a mother hen. Beth had never seen her so solicitous. Beth was the one who took care of things in their relationship, both the practical and the emotional. When they moved to California, Katy took the lead in searching for an apartment, being more familiar with the different neighborhoods. But Beth had done everything else: set up the cable TV and the utilities, rented the U-Haul. And last year, when first Katy and then Beth came down with an awful stomach flu, Beth acted as nurse for both of them. Beth didn't mind; she preferred it that way. She hated being dependent on anyone else.

"Do you want me to call someone to check in on you?" Katy was saying. "See if Suzanna could pop in?"

"God, no." Suzanna was the downstairs neighbor. She was full of good intentions, Beth recognized, and she knew she should be more tolerant—but she couldn't stand her. Suzanna never stopped talking. She had an endless supply of mindless gossip: about her most recent dispute with the cable company, or what her sister had told her about a burglary across town, or what had happened when she went to the corner store for milk, or her speculation about the old guy who lived next door, and why he wasn't speaking to his son. Once she got going, she hardly stopped to breathe. It drove Beth crazy on the best of days.

"I won't be back until six."

"I'll be fine."

Katy kissed her on the lips, a quick peck, and gave an awkward goodbye wave, before closing the door behind her. Their fight from the day before hung like a vapor between them with neither wanting to be the first to broach the subject. They weren't good at confronting the hard stuff. Beth always preferred to move on and forget about it. Like that fight at the start of their backpacking trip. But this—this was different. A shove down the stairs and a broken ankle were way more serious than a wrong turn on Willow Creek Road. They would have to face it sooner or later. But for now, Beth's foot was hurting too much.

She popped a Vicodin and dozed off.

When she woke several hours later, she was disoriented. She went to jump up but bashed her cast into the knee on her good leg and felt light-headed. The sun was streaming in directly on the couch, and she was hot and sweaty. "Shit," she said, running her sleeve across her face. Her circumstances came rushing back to her. She flipped open her cell. It was twelve thirty. Lunchtime at work. That meant Rebecca would be manning the phones, young enough and dumb enough to give Beth what she wanted.

She had the number on speed dial.

"Hi, Rebecca. It's Beth." She tried for a jocular tone, but her voice came out dry and husky. She took a sip of water.

"Beth! Oh my god. I heard about your accident. I'm so sorry."

"Yeah, it's such a drag. Listen: I'm wondering . . . When is the team conference for Tave Greenwich? It's today, isn't it? I need to know what time."

"Let me check."

The pause was longer than it should be. *Please, just look up the damn schedule. Don't mention this to anyone.*

"Hi! You still there?"

"I'm here." Beth swung her foot back onto the couch, adjusting the pillow under the cast.

"Sorry. Had to deal with a lost visitor. Let's see . . . Tave . . . It's at three thirty."

"Okay, great. Thanks, Rebecca."

"Sure. You get well quick, now."

Three thirty. Beth considered her options. She could call a taxi. But she would have to get herself down the stairs and out to the curb. And for all her years of teaching others how to manipulate steps using forearm crutches, she wasn't confident of her ability to do it alone. Not yet. Not when she still felt woozy and the pain in her ankle was coming back, and damn, she knew she should eat something but had no appetite.

She took a swig of the kombucha and twisted her mouth in disgust. She examined the label: ginger, cranberry, and cucumber. Sounded promising but wasn't. She reached for a few crackers and took more water. She would have to get help. She briefly considered Suzanna, who would likely be available, as she'd recently been laid off from her job at the video store. But Beth couldn't face her. Who else? Most people would be at work. Angie would tell Katy in a flash. There had to be someone. *Think, think.* Her brain felt muddled from the drugs. Then it came to her. Lionel! They'd met him last year at a neighborhood potluck, and he'd become a friend—more Beth's than Katy's. She'd helped him when he was dogsitting his ex-boyfriend's golden retriever, walking the pup for hours to burn off his excess exuberance. Last month he'd invited Beth to the Roxie to see a black-and-white Renoir movie, which Katy said was not her thing. Beth hadn't understood half of it, but she enjoyed hanging out with Lionel. He always made her laugh.

Lionel worked evenings. He should be getting up about now.

He answered on the second ring.

"Lionel, darling. Listen, I had the dumbest thing happen yesterday," Beth said. "I tripped down the stairs and broke my ankle. I know, crazy, right? Look, can you possibly do me a huge favor? I need to go back to the hospital this afternoon. Right, for a checkup. And Katy's at work. Are you free to help me out? I need help getting there. Katy can pick me up when I'm done. Oh, you're such a sweetie. I'll be eternally in your debt. Three o'clock. Well, maybe a bit before. Got to give myself enough time to get down the stairs using these crutches. Thanks, sweetie. Love you."

Beth hung up and nodded, quite pleased with herself. Now she had to get herself to the bathroom. She was yearning for a shower, but knew she could not do that alone, and she would need to get one of those waterproof wraps and figure out some sort of seat. God, she supposed she would need a shower bench, like her little old ladies. For now, she would have to make do with a quick wash up, perching on the toilet seat. Her mind leaped into problem-solving mode. She would have to find some loose pants that she could get on over the cast. She grabbed her crutches and eased herself up to a standing position.

Suddenly, she was desperate to pee. It had been hours. She swung herself down the hall. *Squeeze,* she told herself, good old Kegel exercises, squeeze and breathe. *You got this . . .* But one of the crutches got caught in the strap of Katy's day pack, lying abandoned on the floor outside the bathroom door. *Goddamn it.* She felt the warmth trickle down her legs, and passed some gas that turned out to be—*oh, no.* She lurched for the toilet and sat down to fully relieve herself. *Ooof . . . that's better.* But her underpants were wet—and *fuck*—soiled, a small brown stain in the crotch. For the second time in twenty-four hours, Beth had to clean up crap.

~

Lionel turned up sporting a new beard, neatly trimmed, dark with a hint of gray at the temples. It complemented his fair complexion and might have given him a more distinguished air were it not for his outfit: a flaming red blazer, rainbow boa, and tight leather pants that looked impractical for anything. Yet somehow, he managed to assist Beth in the transition from apartment to car, following her directions to stand one step in front of her on the way down, to help her into the back, to lift her cast onto the seat next to her. She grimaced in pain as he banged her foot into the doorjamb, which caused him so much distress, she had to recover quickly and repeatedly reassure him she was fine.

She reached over from her seat behind him to give his shoulder a squeeze. "You're a doll, Lionel."

They arrived at the hospital at three twenty. Lionel wanted to drop her at the outpatient clinic entrance next to the emergency room—*Don't you have to go in here?*—but accepted Beth's explanation that first she needed to go to the rehab unit in the annex, to drop off paperwork for her sick leave. It occurred to her there might be a form she should complete, but Linda hadn't mentioned it, and Beth didn't want to get sidetracked into that now. She waved Lionel off, took the elevator up to the third floor, and made her way down the hall, hoping she wouldn't run into anyone until she was well on her way to her destination.

The Vicodin was wearing off; she felt her head clearing. And in spite of the throbbing in her foot, she was alert enough to pick up a decent pace, mastering a good swing-through gait on her crutches. Her upper body strengthening routine at the gym was paying off. She reached the door to the soiled utility room, only a few yards from the conference room, before anyone spotted her.

"Beth!" It was Wanda, the nurse. She would surely be an ally. "Oh my god, girl, what happened?"

Beth was surprised the whole world hadn't heard by now. She realized she would have to get used to telling the same story over and over.

"Listen," she said after she brought Wanda up to date. "I thought I'd sit in on Tave's team conference. You know, report on her progress—but it's kind of off the record, so don't say anything to Linda. If you know what I mean." She wasn't sure she was making sense.

Wanda gave her a quizzical look. "Okay, sure. Whatever. Go right ahead. There's a gap in the schedule before her, so the room should be empty. I'll be there in a moment." She took a step away before adding, "I heard the trip to the rec center was a great success."

"Yes, it was." It seemed a long time ago, although it was only the previous afternoon.

Beth ducked into the conference room and seated herself at the far end of the table, propping her foot up on a chair. And waited.

18

Tracy was the first to arrive. She did a double take when she saw Beth: first, a quick nod of hello, and then a *Wait a minute, what are you doing here?* lurch of her head.

"Hi! Oh my god, how are you?" she said, leaning over to peep at Beth's cast.

Beth was going to get sick of this in a hurry. "Fine, fine," she mumbled, as the other team members filed in.

Dr. Kramer was more matter-of-fact. "I hope it heals without surgery," he said with a nod.

And down to business. They sat in tight quarters in the small room. In addition to Dr. Kramer, the leader of the team, and Tracy, whose job it was to take notes and report the outcome to the patient, also present were Laurel, the occupational therapist; a medical student; the dietician; and the temporary physical therapist, a mousy-looking woman in her forties, who became flustered when Dr. Kramer introduced her to Beth and rummaged through a stack of computer printouts, muttering something about not feeling prepared.

"Don't worry about that," Dr. Kramer said with a wry smile. "Luckily, Beth has joined us, cast and all. Okay, folks, let's get started. This is the team conference for Tave Greenwich, twenty-three-year-old female with history of C5–6 spinal cord injury, that occurred on May 7. She was the unrestrained driver in an MVA—"

Wanda entered the room as Dr. Kramer was completing his introductory remarks, and gave Beth a peculiar look, a sort of apologetic grimace. Beth tried to catch her eye again, but she was focused on her notes.

"Tracy," Dr. Kramer said. "Perhaps we could start with an update on the discharge plan."

Tracy began her report. "I'm working with mom on what she would need to do to prepare for Tave to go there. Tave is resistant, but I'm not sure what other options she has."

Beth wanted to blurt out her objection. *She can't possibly go to her mother's.* But she held her tongue. Dr. Kramer insisted on a set format for his conferences: each report given without interruption before any discussion, so she wrapped her arms tight across her chest. It was hot and stuffy in the room, and she wished she'd thought of opening the window before the others arrived. Her armpits were sticky and probably smelly, and boy, if only she'd been able to shower.

Wanda reported on Tave's progress: improved endurance, able to tolerate a full day of therapy without resting in bed, complying with regular weight shifts to relieve pressure and no skin breakdown, learning her medications. "She's doing well with all that. But she had an episode of fecal incontinence after her outing yesterday. We need to work more on her bowel training program, to get that under control."

She glanced at Beth, again with an odd grimace. Beth didn't think she would blame her for the bowel accident; that didn't seem like her. But then the door burst open, and Linda bounded into the room, as though propelled by a fiery dragon.

Fuck, thought Beth.

Not me, mouthed Wanda, surreptitiously waving her finger back and forth on the tabletop, mimicking a shake of the head.

Dr. Kramer looked up in surprise, before returning his attention to Wanda. "Anything to add?" He tapped away on his keyboard, documenting on his laptop.

"I'm done," she said.

"Thank you. Laurel? How are things going in OT?"

Beth tried to fix her attention on Laurel, but Linda was right there in her peripheral vision, perched on the coffee table in the corner, as Beth's elevated leg was occupying the only remaining seat in the room. She could feel the cold stabs of anger directed toward her, although they did nothing to assuage the heat in the room; beads of sweat trickled down her front, under her bra. She felt her face flush and became aware of the throbbing pain returning in her ankle. She hoped she wasn't coming down with a fever.

Laurel must have finished, although Beth hadn't heard a word she said. Dr. Kramer was turning to her now. "I appreciate your coming in today.

Can you give us the PT report?" He squinted at the name badge on the temp. "Muriel, is it? I'm sure you won't mind. Beth has been Tave's primary PT since her admission."

"No, please," the woman said.

"Excuse me, Dr. Kramer," Linda said, in a voice much too loud for the tiny space. "Muriel is the assigned PT of the day, and it is her responsibility to give the report. Beth is not authorized to be here."

Dr. Kramer made no attempt to conceal his astonishment. "With all due respect, Linda," he said, "I'm running this team conference. It's clearly in the best interest of the patient for the team to receive the most comprehensive and up-to-date report."

"Muriel has access to all the documentation," Linda said.

Beth kept her eyes lowered. She felt the urge to drum her fingers on the table, but moved them to her lap, where she rubbed her hands together. Even her palms were sweating.

"Thank you," Dr. Kramer said. "I would like to hear from Beth." He gestured to her. "Go ahead."

Beth took a deep breath. "Thanks." She cleared her throat. She wished she'd brought water. "Tave is making good progress," she said. "I'm particularly excited to see, in the past couple of days, that she is regaining more function in her right upper extremity. I don't know if you've had a chance to examine her today," she continued, addressing Dr. Kramer directly, "but it looks like she's getting more C7 function on the right, with 2 out of 5 strength in elbow extension; wrist extension is now 4 out of 5." Beth had no need for notes; she could remember every detail of her most recent exam. "And on the left, of course," she continued, "she's had 5 out of 5 active elbow extension for a while. I would like to have more time . . . I mean, I think she needs more time . . . to work on the new functional potential this opens up."

"What specifically do you have in mind?" Dr. Kramer asked, looking up from his computer.

"Sliding board transfers for sure. And I think she has the potential for household use of the manual wheelchair, if we can build up her strength and endurance."

Dr. Kramer nodded. "Sounds good. I trust we can provide someone with the appropriate experience to work on that. Are you familiar with sliding board transfer training for a patient with a C7 injury, Muriel?"

"Well, I'm sure . . ." The poor woman squirmed in her seat. Beth almost felt sorry for her.

"We could co-treat with OT," Laurel offered.

"Thank you. That would be helpful. And of course, Laurel, you can help with assessing manual wheelchair capability. Anything else, Beth?"

"Tave had a great time at the rec center on Sunday—yesterday. She was willing to try the individual handcycle, and did very well, propelling herself eight hundred yards without assistance."

"That's wonderful. Good job. I hope she'll have the opportunity to explore that further, wherever she ends up after discharge." Dr. Kramer smiled. "Right. Well, I'll examine Tave myself later this afternoon, and if my findings support Beth's, I agree this warrants a continued stay, with updated goals. I assume we can provide staff with the appropriate skill set to address these." He looked at Linda, who sat with pursed lips. "But we need to finalize discharge placement by next week. Presumably, you can't order equipment until that is established, is that so?" He turned to Laurel, whose responsibility this would be.

"Correct," Laurel said.

"All right. Good. Let's move on. Mrs. Gonzales is next." Dr. Kramer glanced at the clock above Beth's head. He always kept strictly on schedule.

Changing of the guard. The physical therapist for the next patient poked her head in the door to see if they were ready. Chairs screeched as Laurel and Wanda rose to leave; Tracy would be staying for the next conference. Beth had no reason to remain in the room; she had not worked with Mrs. Gonzales. She would have to face Linda, who stood at the door, waiting to pounce. Beth lowered her foot and gathered her crutches.

"Take good care of yourself," Tracy said, scooting her chair forward to allow Beth to pass.

"Thanks for coming in," Dr. Kramer said.

Beth squeezed around the table, trying to ignore Linda. But there was no escape.

"Young lady, we need to talk in my office," Linda said.

Beth considered offering some excuse based on her condition. She knew that would not go over well, considering the circumstances, but she definitely was not feeling well. She closed her eyes and began to sway. She dropped one of her crutches and grabbed hold of the handrail in the hall.

"I'm sorry, I have to . . . I need some water."

"You need to go home and stay home." Linda picked up the fallen crutch and handed it to Beth. "Take care of yourself, for god's sake. But I'm warning you: you need to stay away from here while you're on medical leave. I'm serious. If I see you back here again, I will call security."

Beth was not up to fighting. "Okay, okay." The pain was intense now. And she had to get something to eat. "I just want to go tell Tave why I won't be in."

"No need. I spoke to her this morning. Now go!"

She pointed to the elevator, like a cop directing traffic, blocking Beth's access to the patient rooms or the gym.

Defeated, Beth made her way to the lobby and asked the security guard to call a cab. It came in a few minutes, and she sat in the back seat, with her cast propped up, fighting back tears. She couldn't understand why Linda was treating her this way. She was only trying to support Tave, make sure things were done right. Thank goodness Dr. Kramer stood up for her. But he couldn't and wouldn't do much to interfere with Linda's ban on her returning to the unit. Beth desperately wanted to make sure Tave could take advantage of her recent gains. Maybe she could reach Laurel tomorrow and strategize with her—but Laurel was pretty timid and wouldn't do anything to defy Linda.

She shifted in the seat and winced as a bolt of pain tore through her leg.

"Yes, right here," she said to the cab driver. "The house with the red steps."

She paid the driver and stood at the foot of the steps, bracing for the climb up the stairs.

"Beth!" She spun around to see Katy riding up on her bike. "Where the hell have you been?"

"I thought you were at work until six."

"I got off early to come check on you. Where've you been? You look like shit."

Katy helped her up the stairs. Beth stalled for as long as she could. She was hungry and thirsty and in pain, and she couldn't get comfortable. Katy appeared willing to fuss over her for a while, but once she had made her a grilled cheese sandwich and a cup of chamomile tea, brought her a Vicodin, and propped Beth's cast up on three pillows, she stood in front of her, hands on hips and said, "So, where the hell did you go off to?"

Beth had prepared her answer. "I had to go into work to sign paperwork for my sick leave."

"And that couldn't wait until tomorrow? I don't have to go in until noon, so I could have taken you."

"Linda called. She said I had to take care of it today."

Katy looked skeptical but said nothing more.

19

After dinner, the dining room filled with other people's visitors. Tave saw the wife of one of the old guys approaching and wanted to escape before she started up again about what she called the *tragedy* of Tave's accident. She asked to go to bed early, faking exhaustion and an interest in the movie on TV. She wanted to be alone with her thoughts, but the TV drew her attention. An actress she didn't know, a pretty brunette in a skimpy tank top and tiny shorts was flirting with an actor Tave recognized but couldn't name. They were obviously about to make out. Wow, her outfit didn't leave much to the imagination. He raised her top to reveal her taut abs, deeply tanned, and a belly button ring. They didn't allow nudity on TV, surely, but they were getting close, and wow, she was gorgeous.

Tave became aware of an odd stirring in her core. It wasn't like being turned on in the normal way, but she felt flushed around her neck and shoulders, a tingling behind the ears. She'd always found women's bodies more attractive than men's. For years, she thought there must be something wrong with her. Later, she thought that was the way it was: women were cuter, and everything in the world around her told her this was what sexy was, that it was a woman's job to be sexy for men, that women shouldn't be too concerned with what they might want for themselves. She never lived up to the ideal; her boobs were too small, her thighs too large, her nose too long, her hair unruly—but she tried for a while. And looked at other women in envy. It was a revelation to discover she could enjoy a woman's body for her own pleasure.

She wondered what it would feel like to make out with someone again. Tave shifted her left hand, pushing down the covers, reaching toward her belly, while at the same time trying to use her other hand to hide what she was doing. Rowena had not yet applied the night hand splints, so she was *free to roam around the country*, as Les liked to say. But she couldn't expose herself: *OMG*, Rowena might come back into the room and find her at it. Easier said than done; she didn't have any real grasp in her right hand. She managed to yank the sheet with her wrist, pushing it toward her chin, and grab it between her teeth. *Okay, where was I?* Her left hand, now safely hidden, continued its exploration, reaching to the edge of her gown, inching it upward with the base of her palm, her fingers curled into their usual bent-fist shape. She had some sensation now in the thumb and first two fingers, and as they made contact with the soft mound of her pubic hair, she could feel it—not from *the inside*, not *down there*, but she could feel it as if she were touching someone else. And it felt nice: soft and warm and enticing. She tried to reach further, but she couldn't move her legs, they lay like logs, stuck close together. With a big stretch of her left shoulder, she managed to push the knuckle of her thumb down into the crack, and felt moisture. Maybe it was sweat or . . . *Was her pussy getting turned on, like it had a mind of its own?* She laughed out loud at the thought.

She heard footsteps entering the room, and quickly withdrew her hand. False alarm: they passed by, down the hallway. She looked back at the TV, now switched to commercials: big trucks, and the never-ending ads for medications to cure diseases you'd never heard of. Tave was buzzing from her journey; her hand had ventured only a short distance below, but it felt like a mile. She wanted to go back.

She closed her eyes and thought about touching Les, reaching deep into her mysterious, secret folds, pressing against the hard knob of her clit, feeling the strong pulsing spasms as she arched her back in climax. *Damn*, now something was happening, something weird around Tave's neck and ears, she was feeling flushed and warm, and her breathing had turned to soft panting. She let out a gentle moan and felt relaxed all over.

What was that? Did she jerk herself off? Here in the hospital? She laughed out loud.

"What's so funny?" Rowena came in and looked up at the TV.

"Oh, nothing," Tave said. "Some stupid commercial."

Rowena did her routine, getting Tave settled for the night: turning, putting on the splints. Her hair was different: a bunch of ringlets cascading from a red scrunchie high on her crown. "Looks cute," Tave said.

"Thanks, sweetie." Rowena smiled and chatted as she usually did about her little girl, coming up on her fifth birthday. Tave tuned her out. Her thoughts returned to Les. She missed her so much. They had good times together. She hadn't allowed herself to dwell on those memories; it was too painful. Now they came flooding back.

She thought again about that last road trip to Oregon to visit Les's friends. They'd had a great time, and it was beautiful on the ranch. But they'd argued on the drive home. Les had wanted to leave right after lunch on Sunday, but Raven suggested they swim in the river. Tave was feeling more relaxed, and it sure was hot, even though it was only early May. Tave thought Les had agreed to a trip to the river too, but at the last minute she changed her mind and stayed with Meg, who wanted help changing the fan belt on the tractor.

So Tave went to swim with Raven, and it was fun. Raven told her how she'd met Meg at a music festival back in Missouri or Michigan, or somewhere; they were both working in the kitchen, stirring huge batches of lentil soup. "One thing led to another," she said with a light laugh, "and here we are." That was five years ago, she said, and they were still like crazy lovebirds. Tave thought it weird she was telling her this and was trying to figure out when she was involved with Les. Must have been six or seven years ago. Tave didn't know how long they'd been together. She couldn't help wondering about their relationship, and why they broke up. Les had never told her. But Raven wasn't embarrassed to be talking about it, and Tave felt swept along. They weren't flirting or anything, even though they did go skinny-dipping in the icy cold water, screaming with shock when they jumped in, and splashing and dunking each other. They were only having a good laugh.

But Les was upset. Weird, given how she, Tave, had been worried about feeling jealous and left out. Les never came right out and said anything. But she was irritable on the drive back. Tave suspected she didn't like Tave branching out on her own, even a tiny little bit. Les always liked to be in control. She couldn't imagine how Les was surviving at her mom and dad's place. No matter what her condition was, she couldn't be happy there. Maybe she wasn't in as bad shape as Dan had made out, or could be she was getting better, and was going crazy, and Tave hadn't reached out to her at all. Did Les even know what had happened, where Tave was?

Shit. Tave couldn't believe she hadn't thought of this before. She needed to find a way to get to Les, to check on her, to figure out what she wanted to do. She looked up at the clock on the wall. It was not yet nine o'clock. She needed to have Rowena help her with the speakerphone, try to reach

Dan again, find out if he had any leads on a place for her to live—and if he had any more news about Les. Maybe Tracy was right. She should start acting like a grown-up and take charge for once.

"I just remembered, I need to make a phone call," Tave said. "I've got the number written on a piece of paper in my top drawer." Dan had left it when he visited, but that was ten days ago.

Rowena had her positioned on her side, facing away from the night-stand, so Tave couldn't supervise her rummaging, but after a few moments, she said, "Is this it?"

She leaned across Tave's chest and waved the rumpled scrap of paper in front of her face. Someone had spilled Betadine on one corner, but the number was legible.

"Yeah. That's it."

Rowena brought the table with the phone close to the bedside and dialed the number. The ringing tone echoed through the speaker, eight loud peals, while Tave held her breath. It went to voicemail. Dan's raspy voice: *You know what to do.*

"Dan, this is Tave. Give me a call, for fuck's sake."

20

Tave was bummed out. She'd had a miserable three days. Dan hadn't returned her calls, and she was beginning to think Tracy must be right, that he was a total flake, and wouldn't come through for her. She tried to quell a rising panic, distracting herself with memories of good times she and Les had spent together, and fantasies of Les breezing in and figuring it all out. But the staff wouldn't let her forget.

"Have you figured out where you're going to live?" Wanda asked.

Tave brushed her off, saying something would work out.

"Tracy is going to want to settle on something soon."

"I know." She tried to act cool, but at night the fear returned, an overpowering weight squeezing her chest.

She'd been looking forward to talking this over with Beth. But on Monday, she had a new physical therapist, an older woman who seemed out of it. She didn't know shit about what was going on with Tave and spent most of the session reading stuff on the computer. It was a total waste of time. She said she was filling in for a while but didn't answer any of Tave's questions about why Beth wasn't there, or how long she would be out.

At lunchtime the supervisor woman came in and told her. Beth had been in an accident. No, not seriously hurt, but she had fractured her ankle and wouldn't be able to work for several weeks.

The bottom had fallen out of Tave's world yet again. She hadn't realized how much she'd come to rely on Beth as the center of her team. The other therapists, all the staff here, were nice enough—most of them—but she and Beth had been tight. Ridiculous, now that she thought about it, because most likely it was just a job to Beth. But Tave had felt a special connection. Beth had gone out of her way to connect Tave with Maddy and take her to the rec center on her day off. She hoped the outing hadn't in some way caused Beth to have the accident, that this wasn't another thing that was somehow Tave's fault. Seemed unlikely, but she couldn't help wondering.

Her new PT, who had some stupid name like Mildred or Muriel, was a bit more together on Tuesday. Laurel from OT came into the gym with her, and they talked about a different kind of transfer they wanted to work on, which might have been cool, but Tave was too upset to focus. She sat in her chair and scowled, refusing to answer their questions. Which she knew was kinda dumb, but she felt so down.

She perked up a bit on Wednesday, when Laurel had her try pushing a manual wheelchair, lighter and more practical for in-home use or traveling, she said. She offered a chair with a special rim around the wheels that was supposed to make pushing easier—but it was damn hard work. Tave's shoulders ached, and her wrists cramped up. She quickly became disillusioned.

"I can't fucking do it," she screamed.

Laurel recoiled and held up her hands. "Okay, okay. I guess that's enough for today."

"Sorry," Tave said. She knew she shouldn't take it out on Laurel. "I'm kind of wiped out."

At dinner, she couldn't face the dining room, and asked her nurse if she could eat in her room. Normally, this was a no-no, but she agreed: "Just this once."

Tave sat with her back to the door, staring at the shiny wall of windows on the hospital wing across from her, poking at something they called cottage pie, with her spoon tucked into her wrist cuff. She was a pro at this at least and managed to scoop it up without spillage. But she had little appetite. She sipped at the cranberry juice, which was supposed to be good for her bladder and which usually she didn't mind, but today it tasted too tart. She pushed the table away.

"There you are," a familiar voice came from behind. "What are you doing in here all by yourself?"

Tave spun her chair around, and saw Beth swinging toward her on crutches, one leg bent up at the knee, her foot wrapped in a big plaster cast. She used one crutch to maneuver the straight-backed visitors' chair into position next to Tave. Leaning in, she gave Tave a hug, before flopping down and letting her crutches crash to the floor.

"Just as well you're tucked away here," Beth said. "I'm kind of sneaking in after all the big schmucks are gone for the day."

"It's great to see you," Tave said. "Are you okay? I sure miss you." She looked at the cast. "Sorry to hear about your accident. Shit, how did that happen?"

Beth waved her hand in front of her. "Crazy, stupid stuff . . . you don't want to know."

"I'm so glad you came in."

Beth looked over her shoulder. "Shhh. Don't tell anyone, okay? It sounds crazy, I know, but I'm not supposed to be here. My boss is on my case. I'm officially on sick leave, and all that."

"Got it." Tave grinned. It was fun to have a secret. But she saw Beth wince as she repositioned her leg, hoisting the cast onto Tave's bed. "Is it very painful?"

"It's okay. Hurts mostly at night. But I'm so frustrated. I hate not being able to do stuff I can normally do without thinking."

"Tell me about it," Tave said.

"Oh my god, that was insensitive. Shit. Of course, you know all about that." Beth slapped her forehead. "I'm mostly upset about missing work. I wanted to continue working with you. There's so much more we could do."

"Yeah, I'm bummed too. PT doesn't seem the same without you."

"Now listen, you've got to still work hard at it, okay? Let me look at your hand strength." She lowered her leg and removed the universal cuff from Tave's wrist to put her through the usual testing routine. "Yeah, see—you're getting more strength in your elbows and wrists. And some in these fingers, too. I want you to work on sliding board transfers, okay? Did the new PT talk to you about that?"

"Yeah, I guess. But I couldn't get into it."

"Stop. You can't give up because I'm not here. You've got to keep at it. I'll try to leave a message for the new woman . . . No, I'd better not." Beth bit her lip. "Look, um . . . I'll try to pop in again, see how things are going. It'll have to be in the evening again when my boss isn't here."

"That would be great." Tave smiled. She felt lighter already.

"Did you hear back from Dan?"

"No." The sinking feeling returned. Tave looked at the light reflecting off the windows across the courtyard. "I think he's flaking out on me. Tracy says I'll have to go to a nursing home."

"Shit."

"I know. I don't know what to do . . . And I keep thinking about Les."
Tave turned back to Beth. "My girlfriend."

"I remember."

"Dan said she's in real bad shape, like she has a bad brain injury, or something." Tave's lower lip quivered. "Shit." Tears welled up. "Sorry."
Beth squeezed her hand. "No, it's okay. It must be so hard to hear that." After a moment she said, "Tell me more about Les. How did you guys meet?"

Tave wiped her cheek with the base of her thumb. "We met at the bar where I was working. I was in school at the time, working evenings."

"Wait—you were working in a bar? How old were you?" asked Beth.

"I'd just turned twenty-one. I'd dropped out of school my first semester, the first time around, when I was right out of high school. I was never into it. I only wanted to get away from home. Humboldt was about as far from Riverside as I could get while still being in California. But when I arrived, there was some mix-up with my prerequisites or some bullshit . . . I don't remember exactly, but I said *screw it* and quit." Tave laughed. "I never even told my mom until the end of the semester. I just stayed on in Eureka."

"Wow. You and your mom weren't close even back then," Beth said.

"No, not at all." Tave shook her head. "I went back to school, like, a couple of years later. Dropped out the second time after my sophomore year. See: I'm pretty good at flaking out. Anyways, start of my sophomore year, I got this job, and Les and her friends—the guys she hung out with— they would come in most nights, play pool in the back, stuff like that. I knew right away she liked me. She started hanging out with me at the bar, waiting for me to get off when my shift was done, offered to drive me home. She was real cute. Big brown eyes, a huge smile. Made me melt."

Beth smiled. "That's sweet."

Tave felt a lump in her throat. "Yeah. You could say she swept me off my feet. I'd never been, you know, with . . . like, with a woman before." She sniffed. "I mean, I'd messed around a bit with a girl at summer camp, and another time with a girl on a softball tournament, but nothing real, you know . . . I knew that was what I wanted. I'd just never met anyone."

Beth nodded. She looked like she was about to say something, but she didn't. Tave hoped Beth didn't think she was weird to be talking like that. Didn't seem like she was the type to get easily shocked, but she'd gone all quiet.

"I keep thinking about her," Tave said, "wondering what's going on with her now. I mean, I know she was injured. But maybe it's not as bad as Dan made out. What if she's stuck with her awful parents, and she's feeling trapped, and she's heard nothing from me, and doesn't know what the fuck is going on?"

"So . . . what are you thinking?"

"I've got to figure out a way to see her. Go see for myself. Maybe we need to figure out someplace for both of us to go."

Beth nodded. "Could you try to call her?"

"No . . ." Tave shook her head. She wasn't sure how to explain it. "I don't have her parents' number. I think Tracy found it, but . . . her parents are weird. Her mom, especially. She, like . . . she mostly tried to ignore me, but I think she saw me as a bad influence on Les. Which is such a fucking joke." Tave let out a bitter laugh. "If I call, and she answers the phone, there's no way she's gonna let me speak to her. I feel like the only way is for me to turn up and somehow barge in. Ha, ha. Use this chair as a battering ram." She laughed again. "But of course, I have no idea how the fuck I would get there."

"Where is she?"

"Her parents' place. In Chico."

"Shit. That's hours away."

"I know." Tave bit her lip. It was quivering again, and she could not make it stop.

Beth squeezed her shoulder. "Let me think about this, okay? There's got to be a way."

21

This time, Beth was home well before Katy returned from work. She hauled herself up the stairs, made a cup of tea, and settled on the couch with her laptop, mulling over the challenge of how to get Tave up to Chico.

There was a voice in her head telling her to stop: *This is crazy.* But she argued with it. She had nothing else to do with her time. It had been only three days, but already she was going mad with cabin fever watching the daytime soaps and doing crossword puzzles. She needed something to focus on, keep her occupied. Solving tough problems was right up her alley. If she could come up with suggestions for reconfiguring a small bathroom to allow access with a walker or design an exercise program for a patient terribly crippled with rheumatoid arthritis, she could surely figure out how to get Tave to Chico and back.

It made sense for Tave to want to see for herself the extent of Les's injury. What a sweet, poignant story: her first lover. When they were talking about how she and Les had got together, Beth had almost told her that she, too, was a lesbian—but had decided against it. Tave was still a patient, after all, and to come out violated some unwritten rule. Maybe she'd already figured out Beth was gay. But Beth doubted it; coming from a small town, her gaydar was probably limited.

Beth was determined to help her. Transportation was the first hurdle. They would need a wheelchair-accessible van. But *shit*, Beth couldn't drive. She thumped her cast in anger, sending a bolt of pain through her ankle. *Damn.* Of course, she had to go and break her right ankle, not her left. She needed not only a van, but a driver too. There was Maddy, of course. She had hand controls on her van, but Beth knew she wasn't comfortable having other people drive it. She fretted whenever she had to hand over the keys to parking attendants, afraid they would mess up the settings. And she couldn't ask Maddy to drive them to Chico. She was back in full swing, it seemed, after the infection that sent her to the hospital, but she'd looked frail at the rec center, and the trip would be way too much.

Jorge had a van, but it was a ramshackle old thing that barely made it up the 17th Street hill. There was another woman who came sometimes, Beth couldn't recall her name, but the lift on her van kept breaking; she liked to regale everyone with nightmare stories about getting stuck high and dry, in the up position. She was trying to get a replacement lift. Maybe she had a new one by now, but Beth didn't know her well, and couldn't impose on her.

They could rent a van—but no, way too expensive, and anyway, that wouldn't solve the problem of who would drive. Beth drummed her fingers on the edge of her laptop. Then, she had a flash of inspiration: Billie! She and Tave had been good buddies on the rehab unit, and Billie was home now. Her sister and brother-in-law were planning to buy her a van. Billie had been reluctant to accept, but Beth had encouraged her to take them up on their offer. She tried to think how long ago that was. Three or four weeks. Maybe Billie had her van by now.

She opened her laptop to log on to her work account and find Billie's email address. They'd had some communication back and forth a few weeks ago, trying to resolve the screwup over her shower bench. The messages should be in her sent mail, even if no longer in her inbox. And yes, Billie would love the adventure.

The server was slow to respond. Remote access to the system was always clunky. Finally, Beth reached the log-on screen and entered her username and password.

Username not recognized.

She reentered it.

Username not recognized.

Was the system down or something?

And then it dawned on her. Linda must have blocked her account.

"The bitch," she screamed. She sat bolt upright, placed her elbows on her knees, cradling her head in her hands. This was unprecedented. Last year, when she was off for a few days with that stomach bug, she'd been able to log on and take care of business, sort out some equipment orders, and correspond with a student who wanted to do an internship. Now, Linda was deliberately sabotaging her. Unbelievable.

She sent herself an email from her personal EarthLink account. Within seconds, it bounced back. A message above her personalized signature read: "I am away from the Medical Center on medical leave, until further notice. For all urgent matters, please contact Linda Routledge at . . ."

Linda hadn't even consulted or informed her. Their relationship had always been courteous, professional, and based on mutual respect, Beth thought. It had deteriorated fast. Linda was such a stickler for the rules. She didn't appreciate how vulnerable and isolated Tave was. All the time and resources the team was investing in her rehabilitation would come to nothing if she lacked any support system afterward. The unit paid lip service to the notion of looking at the *whole patient*. Sometimes that required flexibility, thinking outside the box.

She gritted her teeth. Okay, so she would have to find another way to contact Billie. Her phone number . . . It would be in the medical record, of course, and in the paper files Beth kept in her desk. But they might as well be in Fort Knox.

Maybe Billie's number was listed. Beth tried to remember where she lived. South of the city—that's right, in an unincorporated area. She didn't know if she would be listed under Billie, or Wilhelmina. Beth went to the online directory. Anderson was such a common name. Nothing looked right. It was very possible Billie would choose to be unlisted.

She closed the laptop and threw it aside. She was exhausted. And the pain in her ankle was back full force. She took another Vicodin—her first of the day, she reassured herself—and dozed off on the couch. Her dreams were a jumble of running, on a beach, through a forest, and she was in a cabin in the woods, chasing a small animal, a rat or maybe a porcupine, it had a long stringy tail, it was gross, disgusting; it kept darting under furniture, into cracks in the walls. Beth tore after it, almost catching it but not quite; she was outside again, under an eerie sky that turned a brilliant shade of crimson, then turquoise. Rising up through the layers of sleep, she became aware of a noise, a voice, someone shaking her shoulder.

"Beth! Are you okay?"

She opened her eyes. Katy knelt before her on the rug, her face full of concern.

"Yeah, I'm okay," Beth croaked, her throat dry and scratchy.

Katy wiped Beth's forehead. "My god, you had me freaked out. You were kind of shaking and muttering. And you're covered in sweat."

Beth rubbed her eyes, and sat up, trying to bring herself out of her Vicodin-induced fog. "Guess I was having a bad dream."

"I bought stuff to make you chicken soup."

A full grocery bag sat on the coffee table. Katy extracted a bag of crackers, popped one in her mouth, and offered the box to Beth, who took one; the salty, crunchy texture revived her. She examined the ingredients; she was curious to see if they were gluten-free.

Katy noticed and said, "I've given up on the gluten-free thing. I tried some crackers yesterday that were disgusting, tasted like cardboard. I threw them out. I don't think it was helping, anyway. It was kind of a dumb idea, I guess. Besides, there's your banana bread, which is delicious. I took some to work with me. Hope that was okay."

"Of course."

"Would you like a slice now? It toasts up real nice."

Beth shook her head no. She feared she'd lost her taste for banana bread.

"Look what arrived," Katy said, holding a potted plant, some sort of lily, tied with a large yellow bow. "From your mom."

"What?" Beth blinked. She pulled out the small, attached card. *Get well soon*, it read. "Did you tell her . . . ? What did you tell her? When?"

"She called last night. After you'd gone to bed. You were zonked out, so I didn't want to wake you. I told her you fell down the stairs, that you'd broken your ankle."

"Oh my god. What did she say?"

"She was concerned and sends her love. Naturally. Like a mother would."

Beth shook her head, trying to clear the cobwebs from her brain. "Why didn't you tell me she'd called?"

"I did, before I left for work. But I guess you were still out of it. We had a chat. She was telling me what a wet summer they're having."

It amazed Beth how relaxed Katy was talking to Beth's mom. And how much her mom had come around to accepting that she and Katy were together. She hadn't come out to her family before Katy, but it was the only way to explain her move to California. Her mom had taken it surprisingly well and had talked about coming out to visit. But she would never travel without Beth's father, and he showed no interest in seeing San Francisco—probably convinced its sins would rub off on him if he set foot within the city limits.

Katy picked up Beth's cup. "Another cup of tea?"

"Yes, please. Thanks." Beth managed a weak smile. "I'll come in and help."

"No, you won't. Stay and rest. Let me do this." She thumbed through her playlists. "Like some music?"

"Sure."

Katy docked her iPod into the stereo. The sounds of Melissa Etheridge singing "I'm the Only One" filled the room. Beth relaxed back onto the couch, bopping her head to the beat. Beth was never up on who was releasing what album, or who had the best cover for what song. Katy put together all their playlists, her own as well as Beth's.

"Hey!" Katy called from the kitchen, as now the opening bars of "Power of Two" came across the speakers. "*Multiply life by the power of two,*" she sang along, loud and clear. They never had a number designated as "their song," but if they had, this would be it. The Indigo Girls sang it on their first date.

It was strange having Katy so cheerful and solicitous. They'd not resolved the argument about Tave that had led to Beth's accident—and Beth knew they wouldn't unless she brought it up herself.

Or unless she did something else to trigger Katy's anger and jealousy. Which was bound to happen sooner rather than later. She wouldn't be able to conceal for much longer the plan she was hatching.

She noticed her cell phone on the floor, next to the couch. She flipped it open; she had a missed call and a voicemail.

"Hi, Beth. This is Kristy from work. Oh my god. I can't believe you broke your ankle. Hugs and hugs. Give me call when you're up for it."

Kristy: nice of her to call. Beth hadn't seen her when she went in for the team conference on Monday. She sounded nonchalant, so maybe she hadn't heard about Beth's intrusion onto the unit and Linda's big freak-out. Beth's head was clearing now, and she remembered the quest she was working on before she fell asleep. Kristy could help. She glanced toward the kitchen, where Katy was banging pots and pans. She would have to return the call later. And she would have to think of an excuse for needing Billie's telephone number.

22

Tave heard Billie before she saw her: her voice booming out at the nurses' station, teasing them for sitting on their lazy butts, raving about Rowena's new hairdo, and kidding with Feliz about the A's game the night before. Tave stayed in her room. Billie had called earlier in the day and said she was coming in, but she wanted to talk in private, before Tave went to the dining room for dinner. Tave was eager to see her and couldn't imagine what this was about.

"There's my buddy." Billie rolled into the room and leaned forward in her chair to give Tave a hug, grinning with her lopsided smile. "You're looking good, girl. How's it going?"

Tave smiled, but she didn't believe she looked good. She felt worn out, having not slept much the night before. She pushed her hair out of her eyes; her bangs were driving her crazy again. "I'm okay, but I'm kind of freaked out about where I'm going to go after they kick me out of this place."

"I know. Beth called me."

"Wait—so you heard about her accident?"

"Yeah. I couldn't believe it."

"PT isn't the same without her."

"I bet. But you gotta keep working hard, girl. Makes no sense for you to give up because you miss her. You're the only one who loses by that, right?"

Tave nodded. "I know."

"I wanted to tell you something. I hope you don't mind, but I asked Andy, my brother-in-law, to see if he could dig up the police report on your accident. I know you got kind of freaked out when we tried to look for it earlier, but I figured sooner or later you'd want to see it." She paused and looked as if she were waiting for Tave to respond.

"Okay."

"Turns out you can't get the full report unless you're the person involved or a family member or lawyer. I said Andy should pretend to be your uncle, but he wasn't up for that."

"That would've been fine with me."

"That's what I said. But he didn't want to. He did find a site where you can get a summary." Billie rummaged through her purse and extracted a sheet of paper.

Tave's stomach lurched. "Oh, wow. What does it say?"

Billie unfolded the paper and placed it on Tave's lap. Tave scanned the page, trying to focus. It was a computer printout titled *Accident Report Look-up* with colored block ads on the right for various lawyers. A bulleted list on the left summarized the details of the accident—"Date and time: May 7, 2006, approximately 1:43 a.m.; vehicles involved: two, 2003 Toyota pickup truck and 1999 Chevrolet Malibu; weather conditions fine; major injuries reported; driver of Toyota had been drinking, degree of impairment unknown. Officers from the Siskiyou County Sheriff's Department were present at the scene." Below that was an additional note: "Driver of Chevrolet may have fallen asleep at the wheel. Investigation ongoing."

"Shit," Tave said. "So maybe it was all my fault."

"It says investigation ongoing. And seems like maybe the other driver was drunk. I guess they don't know for sure. Do you remember if you said anything at the time to the police or ambulance guys?"

"I don't remember a thing." Tave had tried to conjure up more but was stuck with the same recollections running on constant replay: the dark road, the dotted yellow line, the blinding lights of oncoming traffic. Nothing after the moment of impact.

"Might be good for you to talk to a lawyer, I guess."

"How the hell would I do that? Don't they cost like a shitload of money?"

"I'm not sure. I think you can get a free consultation. I'll see if Andy knows."

"Okay, thanks." Another thing to deal with, to be a grown-up about, as Tracy would say. As if Tave didn't have enough to deal with, figuring out how to push a new kind of wheelchair or use that weird transfer board.

"But listen, that's not the main thing I came to talk about." Billie glanced over her shoulder and lowered her voice. "Beth's cooking up a plan to get you up to Chico to see your friend on Sunday."

"Are you serious? How's she going to do that?"

"Once our gal Beth sets her mind to something, there's no stopping her. But you got to keep this under wraps, okay? And don't mention a word to that manager woman, Linda. She's got it in for Beth, and she would hit the roof if she found out."

"Got it."

"This is what you've got to do. First, do you know the address where Les is at?"

"No. Somewhere in Chico. I never knew her parents' address. Tracy found it, I think. She mentioned the street, but I don't remember what she said."

"Good. In the morning, you go ask Tracy for the address. Tell her you want to send Les a card." She dug into her purse again. "Here's a card, to make it look legit." Billie grinned. "Beth thinks of everything."

The card had a bunch of purple flowers on the front, with the words *Missing You*. "I'll have to get someone to help me write it."

"Sure, that's no big deal. See, it even has a stamp on it—to make it look for real. But don't put it in the mail. We don't want to give Les's folks the heads-up."

Tave laughed. "You guys!"

"This is going to be fun, right? Now, this is how it's going down. You tell Dr. Kramer tomorrow that I want to take you out on Sunday, to my family's picnic, so he needs to write the order for a pass. I'll call him in the morning too, to let him know I want to do this."

"How are we going to get up to Chico? We don't have to take that Paratransit van, do we?"

"No darlin', they don't go that far. And, hell, it would take a week to get there on Paratransit."

"I would think."

"No. You, sweet pea," Billie said, spreading her arms wide, "are looking at the owner of a brand-new van. Fully accessible, hand controls, side-loading lift, all the bells and whistles."

"Wow, that's great."

"I know. It's amazing. My sister, Sandy, and her husband bought it for me. Paid for everything. I think I told you, they're super rich—but still, it's damn good of them."

"That's cool. You're going to drive me up to Chico?"

"Yup."

"Is Beth is coming too?"

"You bet. The Three Musketeers." Billie laughed—that loud laugh Tave found so irresistible. "And what else? Oh yeah, I gotta ask you about Wanda—she was off last weekend, right?"

Tave tried to remember. "Yeah, I think so."

"Good, that's what Beth thought. Means she'll be working this weekend. Perfect. Don't say anything yet, but tomorrow—no, better wait until Saturday—you tell her you want to have an indwelling catheter put in before you leave on Sunday. You know, the one that has a bag attached? Don't worry, they can put the bag out of sight, under your pant leg, so it won't show. Tell her you're worried about the picnic going late, and there won't be any way to take care of that stuff in the park. You with me on this?"

"Sure." Tave nodded.

"Like I say, Beth thinks of everything."

"But shit . . ." Tave looked at her outfit: the usual hand-me-down sweatpants and T-shirt. "I need something to wear. I can't go like this. I gotta get me some jeans or something.

"Hmmm. Okay. What size do you wear?"

"Eight. Maybe ten. They say my weight is stable, but I feel like my thighs are spreading with me sitting here all the time."

"Tell me about it." Billie slapped her own thighs and laughed again. She wore denim leggings and a paisley smock-type thing. "I guess I can pick up something for you at Marshalls."

"I can't ask you to do that. I don't have any way to pay you back."

"Don't worry," Billie said with a flip of her wrist. "We'll figure out something on that. I'll see what I can find and come back tomorrow."

"Something loose, I guess—but not too old-lady-like . . . Sorry, I mean—"

"Got it. Not like this." Billie pointed at her smock. "I'll try. I got a good idea about what you kids like to wear. And I'll get some advice."

"Thanks. Wow," Tave said. That Billie would do all this for her—it was hard to take in.

"Okay. I gotta go. Here's my number. I'll see you tomorrow. Give me a call if you think of anything else. Or if something's not going according to plan. You got that speakerphone, I see. Good. I think we're all set."

"Except for . . . I mean, what the hell are we going to do when we show up at Les's place?"

"You'll figure that out when the time comes," Billie said.

～

Beth was so bored sitting at home. After Katy left for work, she was on her own. She watched CNN for as long as she could stand it but got depressed listening to the talking heads debate the aftermath of the terrorist bombing in Mumbai. The daytime dramas were terrible. The cooking shows drove her nuts. She tried to get caught up with her clinical journals but couldn't concentrate. She picked up a novel she found on the shelf, one she'd started reading last year but hadn't been able to get into: a group of high school girls on a camping trip. But she didn't like any of the characters, and still couldn't read beyond the first chapter.

Lionel came over once, and he was entertaining as always, full of gossip about folks at the gay bar where he worked three nights a week. Beth didn't know most of these people, but it didn't matter. David was breaking up with Michelangelo, Brian was going to be a sperm donor for his brother's ex-girlfriend who was now with a woman—*how crazy is that?*—and Ricardo had a brand-new German shepherd puppy who was the cutest thing you ever saw. Beth was happy to lie back and listen. It beat the trash on TV.

But on Thursday, he had to leave town to visit his uncle in Pasadena.

"I'd love to get out of it, sweetheart. But I can't. I promised I'd help him get the place cleared out. He's putting his house on the market and moving to Phoenix, which I think he's going to loathe. All suburbs and unbearable heat; can you imagine anything worse? I've tried to talk him out of it, but he's determined. There you have it. Sometimes you can't stop someone making a huge mistake; they have to learn their own lessons the hard way. Enough with the sad face, darling. I'll be back in town Sunday evening."

Beth was abandoned. Everyone else worked during the day. After months of wishing Katy would get a regular work schedule and contribute more to the household budget, now she was resentful Katy was picking up extra shifts at the gym.

"Why now, of all times?" she complained.

"Because they're short-staffed. One guy took off all of a sudden for Thailand, and Dee has complications with her pregnancy and has been ordered on bed rest. If I step up now, when they need me, I figure I'm more likely to get a full-time position with benefits. Dave, the manager, pretty much told me as much. I thought you'd approve."

"Yeah, that's great. I'm glad."

"You don't sound glad."

"Honey, I'm just bored and lonely, and I want to go back to work, but they won't let me."

"I know." Katy kissed her. "Oh—and guess what? Dave was telling me about the certification to be a personal fitness trainer. There's this course you can take." She rummaged through her bag and retrieved a brochure. "He thinks I'd be good. The National Academy of Sports Medicine. That's the best one, he says. I'm jazzed. I'm going to check it out."

"Oh. Okay."

"I've got to run. I'm going to get a quick haircut before work. Look at it." She picked at stray strands draping down over the buzzed area around her ears.

"It looks fine."

"It's too long." She ran her fingers across the top of her head, trying to tease her black hair into spikes.

Beth thought it looked cute, but Katy always preferred her hair very short. A few months ago, she'd persuaded Beth to go for a shorter cut, with the longer-on-top look, but it never looked as good on her as it did on Katy. Beth's became scraggly too fast and flopped to the side, and was a real mess now, she thought, sweeping her bangs off her face. She watched as Katy walked across the room. Her arms looked buff in her black sleeveless T-shirt. She must be working out, being there at the gym every day. While Beth was sitting here, becoming a slob. She should at least get out the dumbbells this afternoon, do some upper body work.

"What's your schedule this weekend?" she asked, as Katy stood at the door. "Can we plan something fun on Saturday? I can't bike ride, obviously. But we could go for a drive. Go out to eat some place nice. Or go see your folks. We're way overdue for a visit."

"I may have to work on Saturday. I don't know yet. But I have Sunday off for sure."

Sunday? *Shit.* Sunday was the day Billie was going to take Tave up to Chico. *Oh my god.* She'd walked right into this one, and now didn't know how to handle it. Maybe she should step away and let Billie do the Chico trip on her own. Billie could manage. Sounded like her van was all set up; she'd given it a test run to Costco and all had gone smoothly. The lift worked perfectly; she was getting the hang of the hand controls. And Billie would take good care of Tave. If Tave got the catheter put in before she left, she wouldn't need too much that Billie couldn't handle. Maybe Linda was right; Beth needed to let go some. She should stay home. Check in with Billie again, make sure everything was set. And spend the day with Katy.

But no. Beth couldn't. The whole Chico thing was her idea; she had to be there. It wasn't only the logistics. She wanted to support Tave. She understood why Tave wanted to see Les, and it was great she'd suggested it, but Beth was apprehensive about the outcome. She was pretty sure Les would be in bad shape. Seeing her would be traumatic.

Billie was a great cheerleader. But she didn't have any clinical experience. She couldn't be expected to shoulder the heavy emotional fallout from the visit. That wasn't fair to her, or to Tave. This would be a long outing, Tave's first big foray out into the real world. A big deal. It would be irresponsible for Beth to leave her to her own devices.

And, hell, yes: she wanted to go along. When she thought of them driving up the highway, heading for Chico, she buzzed with excitement. It would be a glorious adventure.

But Katy would freak out. There was no way around that. No way for Beth to creep away for the whole day. And with Katy being off and expecting to do something together: there could be no escape. The proverbial shit was going to hit the fan. She had to think of a credible story.

She shook her head and exhaled deeply. There was no good way to do this. She felt as if she was standing on a precipice, close to the edge. She could step back, forget the whole idea. But she knew she wouldn't.

23

Tave asked Leticia to dress her in the outfit Billie had dropped off the previous evening: pale-blue cotton pants, white T-shirt, gray-and-white striped long-sleeved shirt. Not exactly what she would have chosen herself, but for sure an improvement over her usual rehab garb. Wanda had approved: the pants were soft, not too tight, and with no hard seams that might dig in and cause skin problems. And the shirt sleeves felt soft too, against Tave's forearms.

"Could you roll up the sleeves? Please," she added. She was trying for a less dorky look. "Yeah, that's better." A couple of turns of the cuffs helped.

Wanda was checking the placement of the leg bag when Billie rolled in.

"Okay," Wanda said. "I think you're all set. Have a good time." She winked.

They paraded out to the parking lot, Billie in the lead, Tave following, and Leticia bringing up the rear. Tave noticed Billie seemed upset that Leticia was seeing them out to the van, but Wanda insisted. As they rounded the corner to the blue handicapped spots, she saw Beth standing off to the side, leaning on her crutches.

"Shit, Leticia," she said. "Don't say a word about me being here, okay?"

Leticia grinned. "Don't worry." She slid a finger across her lips. "I don't see nothing."

"I think Wanda's already figured it out," Tave said. "She said as much to me yesterday. But she's cool."

"Hope so," Beth said. She looked kind of stressed out.

"Looking good, kid," Billie said, nodding at Tave's new clothes. "They fit you okay?"

"Yeah." Tave smiled. "Thanks so much."

"Okay. Let's get this show on the road."

Billie's van was bright blue and sparkling clean. From the outside, it looked like a regular family-size van that might be ferrying kids to soccer practice. But when Beth slid open the side door behind the front passenger seat, Tave saw the second row of seats had been removed, leaving a large space for a wheelchair—or two. Billie pressed a button on the side panel, and a lift platform rose up, swung out, and lowered to ground level.

"Cool," Tave said.

"Now," Billie said, looking from Tave to Beth. "How are we going to do this?"

"You get in first," Beth said. "And transfer into the driver's seat. Then I'll lower the lift, and Tave can get into the back."

Billie said, "First time I've taken any passengers. Gee, I'm sure glad you're here, Beth. This would be kind of tricky if it was only the two of us."

Beth nodded. "Go ahead."

Tave watched from the sidewalk as the lift rose. When it came to a halt, Billie rolled into the van and stood up out of her wheelchair. Holding on to the car seat armrests, she took a few slow, unsteady steps into the driver's seat. Her legs, weak as they were, could at least manage that much. *That's way more than I can do,* Tave thought. A few months ago, she would have looked at Billie and seen someone weak and pathetic. Now she seemed like a superwoman compared to Tave. Billie turned and yanked her chair into a folded position, tucking it out of the way behind her seat.

Once Billie was settled, Beth lowered the lift again, and it was Tave's turn to ease onto it. Beth pressed the button to raise her up. It was way smoother than the lift on the Paratransit bus, no jolts, no grinding noises.

"Sit behind the driver's seat," Beth said. "And I'll fasten the seatbelt."

There was a specially adapted seatbelt that Beth fixed around Tave and her chair. "Where did you get this van?" Tave asked. It had that new-car smell.

"Place called Mobility Works. They're the pros. They fixed everything up real nice."

Beth took the front passenger seat and placed her crutches on the floor next to Tave. She smiled. She seemed to be cheering up.

Leticia waved them off. "Have a great time, you guys. Don't get into too much mischief."

"You have no idea," Beth said as they pulled out into the street. "Did they believe the Billie family picnic story?"

"Yeah, I think so," Tave said.

"Good. We'll have to call the unit in a few hours and make up some excuse. Some explanation for you being gone so long."

"I'll invent a cousin who's flying in from Albuquerque, and who insists on meeting Tave, and whose flight is delayed. By fog."

"There's no fog!" Beth protested.

"Sure there is. In Albuquerque."

"No one will believe that. It's always sunny in New Mexico."

"Calgary, then," Billie said, with a loud chuckle. "My cousin Cookie from Calgary."

Tave and Beth laughed with her. Billie eased the van through the city streets toward the bridge. Tave couldn't see well from her position behind the driver's seat, but she was fascinated by the hand controls Billie was using.

"You, like, control the gas pedal and the brake right there on the steering wheel?"

Billie leaned to the left to give Tave a better view. "Yeah," she demonstrated. "Like this." She pointed to a lever. "I twist it toward me for the gas; push it down for the brake."

"Cool. But I guess you need pretty good use of your hands to do that, huh?"

"They have adaptations for quads," Beth said. Tave was trying to get used to thinking of herself as a quad: not the leg muscles her high school coach used to yell about all the time: *pump those quads.* No, now Tave was a quad, as in quadriplegic. Beth held up her own hands in a fist-shape. "You can get hand grips that you slot your fists into. And push buttons for the blinkers and wipers, and such. There are quads who drive. You can get a removable driver's seat and drive right from the wheelchair."

"All that must be hella expensive."

"Well, sure."

Tave sighed. There was no way she'd ever be able to buy wheels like this.

Soon, they were crossing the bridge and heading for the open highway.

"Whoopee!" Billie raised her hands in the air. "This is her first road trip. She needs a name, don't you think?"

"Hey! Keep your hands on the steering wheel," Beth said.

"Okay, okay. What do you think about Lucille? Or Matilda?"

"I like Matilda," Beth said. "Waltzing Matilda."

"Matilda it is. Okay, Matilda, take it away." Billie accelerated into the fast lane.

~

Tave watched the miles of flat fields whizzing by, with the mountains off in the distance. The hills were brown now, the lush green of spring all gone. It felt great to be on the open road, the first time she'd been out of the big city in—what? Must be over two months. Even sitting in her wheelchair in the back of a van, she felt a little uplift, as her lungs expanded to embrace the view. Tufts of golden grass at the roadside swayed in the breeze, and the sun streamed across her lap and onto her forearms. Billie had turned on the air conditioning, but Tave could feel the warmth. It was obviously hot out there; a blue haze shimmered over the valley. She tried to harness that warmth to quell her anxiety about what would happen once they reached Chico.

Beth said the drive was about three hours total, but they should stop for a break. "I don't know about you guys, but I need a cup of coffee. And you, my dear, need a weight shift," she said, looking at Tave.

"Oh, for god's sake."

"I can't have you going back with skin breakdown. That would definitely get my ass fried."

"I thought you weren't officially with me on this pass."

"True, I'm not. But I'm going to feel responsible." She pointed to an exit. "Try here."

"This should work," Billie said. She steered the van into a small shopping mall with a pizza parlor, a pet food store, a tax office, and nail salon. There was a coffee shop in the corner.

"There," Beth said, pointing to a blue parking spot. "Good thing no jerk has gone and parked in the striped zone on the side."

"Yay," Billie said, pulling into the space. "Made it. And it's in the shade: perfect. Now . . . I guess we get out in the reverse order to how we got in. Beth, you go first."

Once they were gathered on the sidewalk, and the van locked, Billie stopped and laughed. "Look at us. A power wheelchair, a manual wheelchair, and a pair of crutches. Sounds like the setup for a joke: *Three crips roll into a bar . . .*"

And in they rolled. Half a dozen customers were seated in the café, and two women worked behind the counter. Tave felt the buzz of conversation come to a sudden halt. They all turned and stared.

"Morning, y'all!" Billie said, her voice filling the room.

There was a mumble of *good mornings* and furtive glances as Beth used one of her crutches to push chairs away from a table by the window, to make room for the two wheelchairs. The young girl from behind the counter came over to help. Once they were settled, she presented Beth with a menu.

"Can we have three menus, please?" Beth said.

The girl blushed, and looked from Tave to Billie, and back to Beth. "Oh, but I thought . . ."

"There are three of us," Beth said. She shook her head as the girl returned to the counter.

"I only want coffee," Billie said.

"I know. Me too. But it's the principle. She assumed you guys were incapable of ordering for yourselves. Makes me mad every time." She turned to Tave. "Do you want anything to eat?"

"Nah, I'm good."

"You'd better do your weight shift." Beth pointed at Tave's wheelchair control.

"In here? It's going to look very weird."

"Sweetheart," Billie said. "We look pretty weird already."

Tave laughed. "I guess you're right."

She pulled on the recline switch, until she was leaning all the way back, with the weight off her butt. There was a large yellow stain on the ceiling above her head, next to the vent blowing cool air onto her face and shoulders. She remembered the white ceiling panels she'd stared at when she was first in the hospital, right after the accident—or maybe not—she had no idea when it was, and at the time she had no idea what was going on—but she recalled the blur of the ceiling, and wondering when Les was going to come and rescue her.

Now Tave was a few miles away from trying to rescue her. She had no idea what she would find, if it was as bad as Dan had made out. She bit her lip as she felt tears pressing on her eyeballs.

Billie said, "You better tell us more about your pal Les before we show up."

"I don't know what to expect," Tave said. Her stomach heaved. Maybe this whole expedition was a crazy idea.

"What was she . . . I mean, what *is* she like?" Beth said, moving her chair back, closer to Tave's head. "What's she into?"

Tave didn't know if she should think about Les as the person she was or how she might be now. "She's tough, I know that much. Strong. She worked as a carpenter, a landscaper, a truck driver. She loved the outdoors, hiking, camping. She loved karaoke, even though she couldn't hold a tune. She could be very funny. Shit . . ." Tave's eyes filled with tears.

"Hey." Beth took hold of Tave's hand.

"It's like I'm talking about someone who died. But she's not dead. I just have no idea what she's like now."

"That's what we're fixing to find out," Billie said.

~

They got lost coming into town, and circled around a park twice, ending up back at the intersection next to Walmart, which was where they'd started. But eventually they found Lifton Avenue and came to a halt outside Number 72.

"This look right?" Beth asked Tave.

"I dunno. I've never been here before."

"Oh, that's right."

Tave had always been curious about the house where Les grew up. Les had described it often enough, but never allowed Tave to visit. "You know you'd hate being with my folks," she always said. Tave knew that wasn't the real reason. Les tried to kid herself that her parents believed she was straight—which was nuts. They must have known. Everyone knew. Les wasn't a large woman, but she walked with a bold swagger and wore flannel shirts and big boots, always wore her hair short. She'd never dated guys. But Les didn't want her parents to know she and Tave were together. Or, Tave suspected, she was ashamed of Tave, she wasn't good enough in some way.

The house was ranch-style, like all the others on the block, with a well-manicured lawn, shaded by two large oak trees, and a porch with two chairs and a table, bordered by a bed of red and yellow flowers. A kid about ten years old rode by on his bike and disappeared around the corner. Otherwise, the street was deserted. A couple of cars were parked farther down, and one or two stood in driveways, but all signs of life were safely hidden behind closed doors. It was eerily quiet.

"What do we do now?" Tave said. They sat in the van, like criminals casing the joint. She wondered if people were peering at them from behind their shutters, about to call the cops.

"Go knock on the door, I guess," Beth said.

"Maybe you should go knock," Billie said. "Before we do the whole rigmarole with the lift and all."

"That okay with you?" Beth asked Tave.

Tave shrugged. "Sure."

Beth opened the door—but stopped. "No. Tave, you should go first. Come on, I'll lower the lift."

"I'm scared," Tave said.

"Go on, hon," Billie said. "We're right here."

Once her wheelchair was lowered to the sidewalk, Tave took three deep breaths. Then she noticed the steps. Her path to the front door was blocked by three small steps up to the porch. She turned back to Beth. "I can't get there," she said.

Beth was leaning against the side of the van. She lifted one of her crutches and pointed to the side of the house. A driveway led up a slight incline to another door, next to the garage. "Try that door," Beth said.

Tave rolled up to the side door. She noticed a small ramp over the threshold step. She gasped; it looked like a wheelchair ramp, newly installed. She took another big breath and positioned herself sideways next to the door. There was no bell, so she swung her arm out, and used the side of her fist to knock on the door as loudly as she could. The heat bounced off the concrete, and she could feel beads of sweat gathering on her cheeks and upper lip. She was tempted to squeeze her eyes tight, terrified of what would happen when the door opened. *It's okay, it's okay*, she told herself. *You need to face this. You need to find out.* She could feel her heart thumping.

But there was no answer. Maybe she hadn't knocked hard enough. She tried again, attempting to be more forceful, banging her wrist against the door. She heard a kitty meowing from behind the fence, but not a sound from inside the house.

She looked back at Beth, who was busy on her phone. Tave stared at the door. Now what? She hadn't considered the possibility of no one being home.

"Can I help you?" a voice called out from behind, at the end of the driveway.

Tave spun around to see a woman with gray hair, dressed in matching lilac capris and top, staring at her, arms crossed tight across her chest. It wasn't a helpful sort of *Can I help you?* More a *What on earth are you doing here?* Tave gaped at her, speechless.

"Can I help you?" she repeated, even less helpfully.

"Er . . . I'm . . . we're looking for Leslie Saunders," Tave stammered.

The woman appeared to suddenly notice Beth, who swung toward her on her crutches. "Who are you? What are you doing here?" she said, taking a step back.

"We're friends of Leslie's, and we're hoping to see her," Beth said.

"Oh." She looked from Beth to Tave and back again. "Are you from the hospital?"

"We're friends of Leslie's," Beth repeated.

"I see." The woman inspected Tave again. "They're out. They've gone to church."

Church? Of course. Tave should have realized.

"Thank you so much." Beth smiled at her. "Do you know when they'll return?"

The woman looked at her watch. "Most likely within the hour," she said.

"Thank you," Beth said again. "We'll wait here, if that's all right with you, ma'am."

Now it was the woman's turn to be at a loss for words. She retreated across the street without looking back and entered a house two doors down. Billie lowered herself from the van and joined Tave and Beth on the sidewalk.

"What was all that with the yes ma'am, no ma'am?" she said.

"No point rattling the neighbors," Beth said.

"She looked pretty rattled."

"Just nosy, I think."

"Well, it ain't a crime to be parked on the street, for heaven's sake," Billie said, checking her watch. "I guess we wait it out, huh?"

"Might as well," Tave said. "We've come this far."

"We've got a good shady spot here," Billie said, glancing up at the large oak trees. "Let's have a snack." She rolled around to the rear hatchback, lifting it open with the press of a button. "I've got cheese, crackers, granola bars, juice. Help yourselves."

"Hey, thanks, Billie. A tailgate party!" Beth dug in.

Tave took a cracker between her thumbs and nibbled at it. But she was too nervous to eat much. "Is that woman staring at us from her house?"

"Who cares?" Billie said.

No, Tave didn't care about her. That wasn't what was making her stomach twist in knots.

～

It was way more than an hour. "I'm going to have to pee soon," Beth said.

"Me too," Billie said. "You're lucky," she said to Tave. "You have that bag."

"It's gonna need to be emptied." Tave hated the thought of asking either Beth or Billie to help with that. But she would have no choice.

"What do you think? Do you want to pile back in the van and go find someplace?"

"Let's wait a while longer," Beth said.

Tave heard a vehicle approaching. A van, bigger than Billie's, and older, was slowing down, its turn signal blinking. Tave gulped. "That must be them," she said.

The van turned into the driveway. Tave looked up to the sight of Les's mom staring down at her from the passenger seat. She opened her mouth in shock and turned away to say something to Les's father. Tave sat, floating in a moment of time, a boundary between *before* and *after*. She felt light-headed; her ears buzzed. She was unsure if it was only seconds or minutes that passed in silence.

Finally, the door opened. "Tave?" Les's mother said, her voice timid. "Is that you, Tave?" She climbed down and stared. She was dressed in her Sunday best: yellow flowery dress, white high heels.

Tave moved toward her. "Hello, Mrs. Saunders." Her voice shook.

Mrs. Saunders took in the wheelchair and clasped her hand to her mouth. "Oh my god. I thought you were . . . I mean I knew you were . . . But what are you doing here?"

"I've come to see Les."

"Oh. I don't know . . . Leslie is tired. We've been out for a while. She needs to rest."

"I've come a very long way," Tave said. She held her head higher.

Mrs. Saunders glanced up again at her husband, who had made no move. "Ted," she said, appealing for help.

Mr. Saunders opened his door and came around the van to face Tave. She couldn't recall ever having seen him standing; he'd always been seated in his truck, waiting for his wife outside Tave and Les's apartment, like he might become contaminated if he entered. He stood tall in front of Tave now, glaring at her, hands on his hips. A huge belly hung over his belt, straining against the buttons of his starched white shirt. It took all of Tave's willpower to hold his gaze.

"I've come to see Les," she repeated. She heard Billie wheel up behind her, and the snap of Beth's crutches on the pavement; they had her back. "I need to see her."

Mr. Saunders looked at the others over Tave's head and gave a quick nod. Wordlessly, he moved to the rear of the van, and pulled open the door. Tave turned her wheelchair to follow him, but she stopped parallel to the back door, afraid to turn and peek inside. The van was more like a commercial van, way different from Billie's, a dark maroon color, with rust around the bumpers. She heard a scraping sound as Mr. Saunders extended a heavy metal ramp and placed the far end on the driveway. The ramp was at least eight feet long, and looked way too steep, kind of unstable. Tave thought she heard Beth give a sharp intake of breath in disapproval, but she couldn't look at her. She was transfixed, her heart pounding, her mouth dry.

He disappeared behind the other side of the van, and Tave heard him climb back in. She closed her eyes and tried to control her breathing. She looked up again at the sound of wheels on the metal ramp, and saw first the footrests, then the chair, tipped back onto its large rear wheels, being inched down by Mr. Saunders, puffing and straining with the effort. Beth had positioned herself at the end, one crutch placed on the ramp to steady it. Once on the level driveway, he turned Les around to face Tave.

Tave raised both hands to her cheeks. "Les?" she whispered. And then louder: "Les!"

She would never forget the sight in front of her. Les sat in a manual wheelchair that at first seemed far too big—but it was Les who had shrunk, shriveled. She was pale and skinny, with sunken cheeks and, *oh my god*, her head: the right side of her skull was deformed, indented above her ear. The eyebrow on that side had disappeared, with the eye itself twisted off at an angle. Tave shifted her head slightly to the left, and to the right, trying to make eye contact, but Les's right eye didn't move at all and the other darted in seemingly random movements, not settling in any one place. Her mouth was twisted too, drooping to the side and drooling. Both her arms were bent at the elbows, each hand clenched tight around a white washcloth placed in the palm. She was dressed in a pink—*pink*, of all colors—outfit that looked like a pair of pajamas, made from a thin polyester material. Les must be outraged.

But this wasn't Les. This was some empty shadow, a remnant of the Les that was.

"Les," Tave said, her voice choking. "It's me, Tave."

The Les who wasn't Les jerked in her chair, her back arching into a spasm, her arms flailing.

Her mom approached and grabbed the wheelchair handles. "She's very tired. She needs to go inside for her tube feeding and then back to bed." Her tone was abrupt. She turned Les's chair around. It was clear that Tave and her companions would not be invited in.

"Wait," Tave cried. "What is she . . . ? Is Les in therapy? What does she need?"

Les and her mom disappeared into the house. Tave felt Beth's hand on her shoulder and heard her sniffle. Tears poured down Tave's cheeks.

Mr. Saunders pushed the ramp back into the van and closed the door with a loud thud. He turned to face Tave and spoke for the first time. "Get out of here," he said, pointing toward the street. "Leave. And don't come back. Don't you think you've done enough damage already?"

He entered the house, slamming the door behind him.

24

Tave had only a vague memory of getting back into Billie's van, and the bathroom-break stop at McDonald's; she had no idea who emptied her leg bag, or how she ended up with a soda in the slot on her armrest. She remembered sobbing so hard her whole body shook, and somebody—Beth, it must have been—wrapping her in a hug, stroking her head. Now she was wrung dry, and her chest ached, a dead weight pressing on her shoulders. She sat in a daze, vaguely aware of Billie and Beth discussing the best route back, and if the traffic would be bad as they got closer to the city. Beth turned to look at her from the front seat, like she was expecting the answer to a question she had asked. Tave shook her head, choking back tears.

She closed her eyes but all she could see was the haunting image of Les writhing in her wheelchair, the side of her head crushed, her eyes roaming all over the place, and the *emptiness*. There was no other word for it. She had no idea if Les had seen or heard her. Les had jerked her arms when Tave called her name, but it seemed like a random thing, not like she knew Tave was there. She couldn't make eye contact. It was like she was locked in. Destroyed.

Fuck. Tave wished she could help Les. But there was nothing she could do. Not right now. Maybe someday down the road when she'd gotten her own life together. But the fantasy she'd been holding on to, that Les would be the one to swoop in and rescue *her*: that sure was dead. It was stupid to believe that somehow Les was okay, that Dan had been exaggerating or had misunderstood, or that Les had gotten a lot better than when Dan had seen her in the hospital. Les was not better. *Shit.* Tave wiped her cheeks with her shirt cuff. Les was totally messed up.

Tave wanted to go back and rewind the movie of that terrible night, stop for the night before it got so late, or leave earlier: anything to change the script, make like it had never happened, wake up from this nightmare. Go back to her and Les laughing and running and rolling in the sand at Samoa Dunes, hanging out downtown, having a beer at Ernie's: all those normal things she and Les would never do again.

And it was all Tave's fault. At least, Les's dad seemed to think so. His parting words spun around in her head.

"Why the hell did he have to say that?" she blurted out, sometime, maybe hours, later. *"I'd done enough damage already.* Why did he have to be so mean?"

It was only when she saw Beth and Billie exchange glances that she realized she had spoken her thoughts out loud. After a short silence, Billie said, "I think he blames you for the accident, hon. With you being the driver and all."

"That's so fucked up," Tave said. "As if I've come out of this okay? Look at me. Shit. And what about the other driver? He was drunk, wasn't he?"

"I guess so, sweetheart," Billie said. "The report said they were looking into that, right?"

"And of course, they didn't think to let me know what their lawyer has found out. Maybe see if their lawyer could help me too. No, just put all the blame on me."

Another silence, then: "For Les's parents," Beth said, "you know . . . after something like this, looking for someone, anyone, to blame is only natural. It's their way of coping right now."

"They didn't have to be so damn nasty about it. Can't they see I'm dealing with enough of my own shit right now?"

"Didn't seem like they saw you at all, hon," Billie said. "Her mom didn't ask you a thing about how you're doing, did she?"

"No. Of course not."

Beth scooted her seat back, way back into the space next to Tave. "Ouch," she said. She shifted in her seat, and raised her foot, the one in the cast, up onto the dashboard. "Goddamn, this thing is hurting now."

"You have any pain pills with you?" Billie said.

"I do. But I hate how they make me so spacey."

"Yeah, I know," Billie said. "But you've been sitting a long time. You can space out and doze off. We won't mind."

"Oh my god, you guys." Tave was suddenly shaken awake. "I'm such an idiot. I'm sorry. I really do . . ." Now she was choking up again. "I appreciate you doing this, driving me up all this way. And Beth, you with your broken ankle and all. I'm sorry it turned out to be such a bust."

"It wasn't a bust," Beth said. "You needed to see Les. You said you wanted to see for yourself how she was doing. And now you know."

"She looks pretty bad, huh? Do you . . . I mean, do you think she could get better?"

Beth made a soft puffing-out-air sound. "Well, I hate to say *never* about anyone. I've certainly seen times when all the doctors, all the experts, said a patient would never regain much function, or would be basically a vegetable, and they've gone on to wake up and surprise everyone. But it's rare. And Les . . ." She shook her head. "This far out after the accident—it's almost three months now—with her clearly having such severe deficits . . . I'd say it doesn't look good. I'm sorry. I know it's not what you want to hear."

No, it wasn't what Tave wanted to hear. And seeing Les that way was not what she wanted to see. But—at least, now she knew. Whatever she might sort out about where to live after rehab, it wasn't going to include Les. And she didn't think she could go back to Eureka, to live among Les's friends. Hell—maybe they blamed her for the accident too. She was no stranger to getting blamed for stuff; she was always messing up. But that was for little things that didn't matter when you thought about it, like picking up the wrong kind of bread, or overcooking the eggs, or suggesting a bar that turned out to be a bust. But to be blamed for what happened to Les, to hang out with people and wonder all the time if they were thinking that about her: no. She had enough crap to deal with, without that bullshit.

No, better to start over someplace new. Tracy was right, she needed to act like an adult and take control over her situation, as much as she could, figure something out. She could do that. She could have a say in where she would go, unlike poor Les.

Poor Les. Tave shook her head, trying to stop the tears welling up again, remembering Les sitting there, unable to respond, at the mercy of her awful parents. Tave looked at her own crippled legs, her weak arms, her useless hands. But at least she had her brain; her mind was intact. She might not be able to walk, and she couldn't control many of her body functions, but inside, she was the same person. Her core was not shattered. Her soul had not vanished.

She looked at Billie driving up front, and remembered how earlier in the day, she'd felt jealous of Billie being able to do things that she, Tave, could not: stand to move into the driver's seat, have full control of her hands. And afford a fancy new vehicle. But Tave herself had a lot to be grateful for. Starting with these two good buddies. She had to stop feeling sorry for herself and get on with her life. She could get help from friends like these guys, but most of it was up to her.

She would have to look for somewhere to live in the city. Stay and build a new life there. She would ask Beth if any of the guys at the rec center might have a lead on a place she could stay.

"Beth," she said.

But Beth had dozed off. She jolted awake. "What?" She looked at her watch. "Oh my god, look at the time. We forgot about calling the unit. They'll be freaking out. They've probably put out an all-points bulletin or sent out a search party. Here—" She pulled out her phone. "Damn. I don't have service. Where's your phone?"

"In my purse," Billie said.

Beth retrieved it. "Okay, this is better. Three bars. Uh oh. Looks like they tried to call you. You'd better check in. Here. I'll dial, and you talk." She held the phone up to Billie's ear.

Billie got the charge nurse and told her story. "We're running late. Yeah, sorry, I meant to call earlier. No, everything is going great. But we're waiting for my cousin who is flying in, and she wants to meet Tave. Her flight is delayed. Fog in Albuquerque."

"Calgary," Beth hissed.

"I mean Calgary," Billie said. "Cousin Cookie from Calgary." She turned away from the phone, choking up with laughter, while Beth pressed the phone to her sleeve.

"What?" Billie said when she had regained control, the phone back at her ear. "Sorry, you were breaking up. We'll be back by . . ." She looked at Beth, who mouthed *five*. "We'll be back by five o'clock. Yes, Tave is doing just fine, aren't you hon?" Billie held the phone up in Tave's direction.

"Yes, I'm okay," Tave shouted, managing to find her voice.

~

Beth's phone buzzed back to life when they had less than fifty miles to go: a frantic series of pings in her pocket. It would be Katy, of course. She had welcomed the break in cell phone service, but she would have to face the music now.

She flipped open the phone and saw the alert: three text messages, two missed calls, one voicemail. *Oh, shit.* She didn't know which to look at first. The texts commanded attention. The most recent was merely a series of question marks, preceded by *WTF?* and *Why aren't you answering me?* Beth groaned.

"What's up?" Billie said. She ejected the Coldplay CD and handed it to Beth. "Bad news?"

"Katy's freaking out."

"Who's Katy?" Tave asked.

"My girlfriend. Maybe my ex-girlfriend by now."

"Oh."

Beth figured there was no harm coming out to Tave now. She couldn't think of Tave as simply "a patient" anymore, after spending the whole day with her, away from the hospital. And she'd overstepped all sorts of other boundaries, as Linda had pointed out, so what the heck? She looked behind her to gauge Tave's reaction, but she was looking ahead, out the front window, probably absorbed in her own emotions. She wouldn't care about Beth's personal life.

But then Tave spoke up. "What are you guys fighting about?" she said.

"The usual garbage," Beth said. *That sounds ridiculous. Meaningless.* "Actually, she was pissed I spent all day away from her doing this trip."

"For real?" Tave said. "Shit. You never said."

No, thought Beth. *I never said. And I shouldn't be laying this on you now.* "It's not just that. We've been struggling for a while now." Which wasn't what she would have said—to herself or anyone else—until a few days ago. But which now seemed to be the rewritten narrative of their relationship. The months of tension over Katy's lack of money, her sitting on her butt, lying about jobs she said she'd applied for but hadn't, her building resentment of the time Beth spent at her job had now burgeoned into a mountain that could no longer be ignored. Even the squabbles they'd had on vacation, about where to camp or which trail to choose— so unusual, as they typically traveled together well—had felt minor at the time, and Beth had pushed them out of her mind, but they now seemed harbingers of what was to come.

Yet Katy seemed to be settling into her new job and was paying half the rent. She too was working long hours now, and—what had she said about pursuing a personal fitness certification? Beth hadn't acknowledged her when she'd mentioned it. *Damn.* She should have. Personal training would be a good fit for Katy. She would make a point of encouraging her when she got home.

She knew she'd have to make amends. When it became clear Katy was going to be off on Sunday, Beth had struggled to come up with a strategy for getting out of spending the day together. She had no trouble devising a web of lies and tricks to cover for the semi-illicit springing of Tave out of the rehab unit, but she was stumped at a plausible excuse to offer Katy. She was mortified now when she thought of how she'd messed up. First, she told Katy she had to get together with Lionel, that he needed help sorting through papers his father had left after his death, and she squirmed her way through Katy's interrogation about why that had to be done on Sunday, and why at his place and not hers, and why Beth was the only person who could possibly help him, with Beth giving ludicrous answers that she knew wouldn't hold up. But it all crumbled when Katy came home on Friday evening having run into Matthew at Whole Foods, who told her Lionel was in Pasadena. Beth had resorted to bursting into tears, blaming the Vicodin for her confusion, and finally having to admit she was actually going into work for a baby shower for one of the nurses, but had been afraid Katy would get upset about her going in to work, so yes, she felt terrible, but she had lied.

When Billie swung by in her van to pick up Beth, she'd said Billie was a former patient—well, that part was true at least—who was very fond of this nurse, and who had helped organize the shower, and was giving her a ride, and they might go hang out for a while afterward.

She knew this would boomerang. A baby shower starting at nine o'clock in the morning and lasting all day was completely implausible. She would have to scramble to cover her tracks when she got home. She'd shoved those thoughts aside to focus on the outing to Chico, embracing the camaraderie with Billie and Tave, and doing what she did best, acting as chief planner, the voice of comfort and reason. And champion avoider of conflict in her own life, compartmentalizing everything into watertight containers.

Now, the sluices would open and create a giant fiasco. Katy would be furious. Beth would have to apologize, come clean, and think of how to make it up to her.

Another ping, another text from Katy: *You asshole. I called the unit. There was no baby shower. And your favorite patient is AWOL.*

25

Beth knew it would be bad but had not anticipated this: Katy standing in the hallway, lying in wait. She must have seen Beth arriving from the living room window.

"Hi," Beth said in a pathetic squeak.

"I can't believe you lied to me." Katy held her arms crossed tight. "You bitch." She spat out the words. "How the fuck am I ever supposed to trust you again? Are you having an affair with this chick?"

"Who?"

"Don't give me that *who* crap. You know who I'm talking about. The chick from the hospital."

"Of course not. Look, I'm sorry, I know I lied to you, and I shouldn't have. I understand you're upset about that. I fucked up. But it's not a romantic thing. She's a patient and she's . . . she's a baby, only twenty-three, for heaven's sake. A very young twenty-three."

"Oh yeah? Why all the fucking deceit then? The creeping behind my back, not telling me she's a dyke." Katy stood in front of Beth, towering above her. Her eyes blazed with fury.

Beth recoiled, swinging two steps back on her crutches. That's when she saw the duffel bag at Katy's feet. But she didn't absorb its meaning.

Katy continued to rant. "I made a complete fool of myself, calling your unit and asking about the so-called baby shower. I've never felt such a fucking idiot in all my life."

Beth's ankle was throbbing, and she was exhausted. "I know. I messed up. I'm sorry, okay? I need to lie down." She elbowed her way past Katy and reached the couch, lifting her cast onto a pillow and closing her eyes.

"And after everything I've done, taking care of you," Katy said. "You ungrateful bitch."

"I'm sorry," Beth said again. "I guess I'm strung out on all those pain meds and not thinking right." She flung her arm across her face, trying to hide, and buy time.

"Bullshit. You've hardly touched the stuff. I checked your prescription bottle before you left this morning. It's more than half full."

"Please stop harassing me. I said I'm sorry." Now Beth was getting irritated. She wanted to make things right, but she was overwhelmed and exhausted, and couldn't gather her thoughts.

"I'm harassing you?" Katy was shouting now. Beth opened her eyes and flinched as Katy approached. "That's rich," Katy screamed. "You're the one—"

Beth's anger rose to meet Katy's. She wasn't going to be bullied. She sat up. "You're the one who pushed me down the fucking stairs and got me into this mess in the first place. Or have you conveniently forgotten that?"

"Oh, of course, nothing is ever your fault. Little miss perfect. You always do everything right, you always have your shit together, unlike us mere mortals." Katy twisted her mouth around the words. "Well, guess what? You've fucked up big-time now, sister. I'm not putting up with this crap."

Beth took a deep breath. She needed to start over. "Please calm down. I said I'm sorry. I shouldn't have lied. I understand you being upset about me spending so much time on work stuff, and with this patient. But there's nothing else going on. I didn't mean to deceive you."

"Too late for that." Katy grabbed the duffel bag from the hall. "Get out," she said, pointing toward the door, her eyes on fire.

"What the fuck?" Beth blinked. She'd never seen Katy so angry.

"You heard me. I've packed your bag. Now get out before I push you down the stairs and break your other leg."

"You can't be serious," Beth said.

"I said, get out."

"Where am I supposed to go?"

"That's for you to figure out. Go back to your girlfriend in the hospital. Or stay with that broad who picked you up in her van this morning. She must have been in on your little scheme. Making a big fool out of me. Go shack up with her for all I care."

"But . . ." Beth tried to protest. "This doesn't make sense. You can't kick me out. This is my home."

In the days to come, Beth would revisit this moment many times. Katy had no right to evict her. Beth should have stood her ground. But she was too racked by guilt, maybe, or too shocked, or too exhausted to fight anymore. Katy opened the door and tossed the duffel bag to the landing below, where it fell with a loud thud. Stunned, Beth gathered her crutches and scooped up the newly arrived issue of *Outside* from the hall table, trying to assert a modicum of control over the situation. She tucked the magazine under her arm and hobbled down to join her bag. She was met by Suzanne, the downstairs neighbor, looking up from the door to her apartment.

"Everything all right?" she said, her eyes alight, eager for gossip.

"Fine, thank you," Beth said, slinging the bag over her shoulder and making for the front door. Once on the street, she flipped open her phone and called a cab.

26

Monday morning, Tave was drained. She'd asked for a sleeping pill, which normally she refused, but she was haunted by the image of Les in her wheelchair, and afraid it would keep her awake; she wanted to be knocked out. Now she regretted it. She felt hungover and yearned to stay in bed all morning.

"Sorry, mate," her nurse said. Wanda was off, as she'd worked the weekend. Tave had a male nurse, a guy with an accent, from Australia or something. He'd never taken care of her before, and at first Tave thought he might take pity on her. No such luck. "Staying in bed ain't an option here on rehab. It's business as usual, mate. PT at nine." He winked. "No matter what jinx you got yourself into over the weekend."

So, the whole staff knew. Or thought they knew. They didn't know she had gone to Chico. That she'd seen Les. That would be her little secret.

In PT, Muriel, that stupid new woman, did nothing except set her up for exercises at the pulley weights. Tave went through the motions, unenthusiastically at first. But her blood got pumping, waking her up some. She remembered what Billie had said, that she had to keep working. She remembered her resolve to move on with her life. No one else was going to do it for her. She pulled harder, straining, letting the weights bang down to their resting position.

"Duane," she called out to the PT aide. Muriel was nowhere in sight. "Add another five pounds to this, will you?"

⁓

The phone rang as Tave was returning to her room. She was excited; she rarely received a phone call. She had to use her footrests to shove the wastebasket out of the way to reach the bed table where the speakerphone sat. A stack of clean washcloths rested over the keypad, which was irritating.

Why the fuck did everyone assume she wouldn't want to use her phone? The rings persisted as she knocked the washcloths to the floor and managed to tap the speaker button with the knuckles of her left hand.

"Hello? This is Tave."

"Hey, babe. How you doing?"

"Dan? Shit, I'd given up on you."

"I know, babe. I'm sorry. I've been out of town. I had a construction job down in Shasta. Made a shitload of dough, so I couldn't say no. But now I'm back, and that feels good. Hanging with the guys. Sammy says to say hi. How are things going?"

"I left you, like, tons of messages."

"I'm sorry. Like I say, I was gone. And my answering machine is all messed up. What's happening?"

Tave felt a surge of anger. "What's happening is I'm stuck here in this wheelchair, and I have to find some place to live, and you said you were going to help me, and you fucking disappeared like you've fallen off the face of the earth." She knew she sounded mad but fuck it. "And they keep getting on my case here about where I'm going."

"I'll get on it, I promise."

"No, Dan, forget it. You won't. You don't understand. It's not like I get to hang out here until you maybe kind of think about getting your act together. They have their rules and stuff with insurance and all. I'm supposed to be gone, moving on."

"Whoa. But, like, you still in that wheelchair?"

"Yes, Dan." Boy, he really didn't get it. "Looks like I'm stuck with this wheelchair. But, whatever. It helps me get around."

Dan did not respond.

"But you know what? I've decided I'm not coming back to Eureka. I don't think it's going to work out. I'm going to stay here in the city. There's some cool stuff for me here that I wouldn't find up there. Like sports and stuff."

"Wait . . . I thought you said you're still in a wheelchair."

"I am. I'm talking about cycling and shit I can do even if I can't walk. I mean, it's different, but there are guys here who do all kinds of stuff."

"For real? What, you mean like, the Special Olympics?"

Tave screwed up her nose. *What?* She didn't know much about it, but she was pretty sure the Special Olympics were something else. "I'm not talking about going to the Olympics, or shit like that," she said. "Just doing normal, day-to-day stuff, trying to live my life, figuring out how to move on. And have fun."

"Oh, right."

He didn't get it; that was obvious. But that was okay. It confirmed she was making the right decision, staying in the city.

"And you know what else? I went to see Les."

"You mean, like, at her parents' place? How the hell did you do that?"

Tave smiled to herself. "It's a long story. But you were right. She's totally messed up. It's so sad. I don't know if she has any idea where she is or what's happened to her. And I don't know if she's ever going to get any better. But I don't know, I guess, like . . . Well, shit, seeing her made me realize . . . at least I can talk, and think for myself. I have to make the most of that."

"Wow, babe. You're so brave."

Brave? "No. It's not brave or un-brave. It's me doing what I need to do. Because no one else is going to do it for me."

⁓

Tracy came into her room when Tave was taking her obligatory weight shift. She pulled up a chair next to where Tave's head lay in her fully reclined position. Tracy's face hovered over her, purple earrings dangling inches from Tave's nose. Not the best bargaining position.

"Decision time," Tracy said.

"I know."

"I had another call from your mother. She wants to come up and attend your family discharge conference. She's very keen."

"I told you, no."

"I can't stop her coming. She's your only family. You should at least listen to what she's proposing."

"I am *not* going to even *think* about going to live with her." Tave tried to reach the controls to get upright, but the power button was off, and she couldn't reach it. She had not been reclining for long, but she needed to sit up for this conversation. "Turn this on. Please," she added.

Tracy poked at the button with a finger decorated with purple nail polish. "As we discussed last week, I'm not sure what other options are available to you. And we need to set a discharge date."

Tave closed her eyes, steeling herself to stand firm. Or sit firm, she thought with a silent, wry smirk. *I am not going to my mom's . . . I am not going to my mom's,* she repeated to herself. She'd never visited her mom's new place, but she imagined it must be similar to the street where Les's parents lived: barren, dead, crazy-making. She thought of Mrs. Saunders pushing Les in the wheelchair, taking her back inside, returning her to the prison behind those walls. An image flashed before her now: her own mother, propelling *her*, Tave, in her wheelchair, taking her off to some crackpot Bible-thumper to get "cured." No, no, no. Not going to happen. Les was powerless, stuck with her parents, and who knows if she even knew where she was. It was so goddamn awful, and she had no way to resist her fate. *But I do.*

Tave swallowed hard. "There's no way I'm going to live with my mom. You told me I needed to start acting like an adult. So, here I am. Ta-da! It's me—all grown up." She tried to spread her arms wide, going for the Y effect in the YMCA dance, but she couldn't lift her arms above her shoulders, her wrists dangled limp, and her fists remained curled, so it looked more like a flattened, wimpy W. But hey, she told herself, it's the thought that counts. "I get to decide who comes to any conference where you guys talk about where I'm going."

"Okay. Fair enough." Tracy strummed her purple nails on the manila folder on her lap. "I'll have to look for a nursing home placement, then." She pursed her lips. "Unless you have any other ideas."

"How much time do I have? I mean, when will you kick me out of here?"

"We need to set a discharge date, a goal of getting you out by . . . say, in one to two weeks, max. But, like I told you, we won't—we can't—literally kick you out onto the street."

"I'm going to look for a place to live here, in the city."

Tracy widened her eyes in surprise and scribbled some notes in her folder. "That's going to take a while. It's hard to find apartments around here. And it would have to be fully accessible."

"I know."

"Most likely, I'll have to look for a nursing home placement for you in the meantime. I don't know how long that will take."

Tave shrugged. "I'll be here."

"You want me to look for places down here—not in Eureka?"

"Yeah. Here, in the city." A thought was taking shape in her mind. "There is someone I'd like to invite to that meeting you're all going to have," she said.

"Yes?"

"Billie."

"Who?"

"Billie Anderson."

"You mean . . . Billie, the patient who . . . ?" Tracy's eyes widened again. "Oh, of course, she took you out on pass yesterday."

"Yeah."

"How did that go?" She evidently was not up to speed with what Billie would call yesterday's *shenanigans*.

"Good."

"And you want her to come to your family conference?"

"Yeah. She's my buddy."

"Really? Well . . . I suppose that would be all right."

Tave hadn't asked Billie but hoped she would agree. Billie would know what questions Tave should ask about where they might want to send her, all that shit. Beth would know too, but Tave couldn't ask her. Not with everything that was going on with her, with her girlfriend and all. And it seemed like she wasn't even supposed to come into the hospital anymore, which Tave didn't understand. Tave didn't want to get her into any more trouble. Billie was her only other option.

"Okay," Tave said to Tracy, "let me know when you're having that meeting."

~

For the next few days, the whole rehab team was focused on what was usually called *family training*. Wanda crossed out the *FT* on the schedule and substituted *DT*: *discharge teaching* being more like it in Tave's case. Her schedule was full of *DT* sessions every day.

"No matter where you end up, you're going to have to be commander in chief," Wanda told her. "Anything you can't do for yourself you'll have to tell your caregivers how to do it. And how to do it right."

It was like cramming for a final, and Wanda made sure there was a pop quiz each morning. How should the resting hand splints be applied at night? How often should she be catheterized? What was the right way to hold the catheter? When should she do her weight shifts? When should she do her bowel program? What areas on her body should be checked for skin breakdown? What were the early signs of skin breakdown?

"Damn," Tave complained, "it's like being in school."

"It is. And this is a school where you can't drop out," Wanda said. She was making a poster of all Tave's meds. "Well, you can. Some people do, for sure—with disastrous results: infections, skin breakdown, being confined to bed for months. It's not pretty. But I don't think that's you. You're better than that. You can live a good life if you take care of yourself. I can see you getting into handcycling, or adaptive skiing, sailing, all sorts of great stuff. I'm not saying it's easy. It's hard. Especially if you don't have family behind you."

"Right. I have no one."

"I know. It's tough. You have to create your own family of support." She looked up from her writing and fixed her eyes on Tave, holding a purple magic marker like a conductor's baton. "You have to learn not only *what* needs to be done, but *how* to communicate that to those who're helping you. Too bossy, and no one will want to work for you: they'll quit; not assertive enough, and your health will suffer." She held up the completed list. "Now, what's the Ditropan for?"

"My bladder."

It was overwhelming, and sure, there were moments when Tave felt like throwing up her hands and saying *fuck it*. But then what would become of her? She wasn't going to curl up and die. She felt like she had been given a second chance. Unlike Les. There was no way to understand why Les had come off so much worse—Les, who'd been sitting two feet from her, in the same car. She sometimes wished she could change places with her—no that wasn't it—of course she wouldn't want to be in Les's condition, but if the accident was her fault, there was no way she would have wished this on Les. But it was useless to beat herself up. She could do nothing to help Les. At least, not now. Maybe one day in the distant future, when she had her own setup, maybe she could find a way to rescue Les, find a better place for her to stay. For now, she had to focus on getting her own shit together, or she would be no use to anyone.

It was weird, but Tave felt more energized than she had in a long time. She couldn't remember when she'd been so determined to do something right. Well, making the softball team at Humboldt, for sure. She hadn't won a scholarship; she had to walk on and try out and she worked hard to get on that team. She knew she deserved a spot, and she got a lucky break. Or rather, the catcher, a senior, had an unlucky break: fractured her collarbone. Tave took her place. She was given her chance.

Now, here in rehab, she had a new chance. And she was determined to do it right.

She was working in PT on a new way of transferring from bed to wheelchair and back again. Muriel was gone, thank goodness. In her place was another temp, Sorrel. She was tiny, no more than a hundred pounds, super cute. She seemed very young but must be older than she looked; it turned out she had a husband and a two-year-old and had recently moved up from Los Angeles. She hoped to get a permanent job on the unit. She was super smart. She told Tave her brother had a spinal cord injury, from a bike accident when he was sixteen; that was how Sorrel first got interested in becoming a physical therapist. He was doing well, she said. He was an accountant in a big fancy investment firm.

Sorrel worked with Tave on using a sliding board, a long wooden board that looked kind of like a skateboard, but with no wheels, obviously. This was what Muriel had been going on about, but Tave hadn't wanted to listen to her. Sorrel demonstrated how it slid under Tave's hips and acted as a bridge between the bed and the chair. Tave wouldn't have been able to do this even two weeks ago, but now she had way more strength in her arms, at least on the left, enough to pull herself across this bridge. She still needed help; her trunk muscles were missing in action, so she flopped to the side or did a nosedive if there was no one to stabilize her torso. "But this is a whole lot easier than doing a full pivot, or using a mechanical lift," Sorrel said. "There'll be less excuse for not getting you up. You can't let them leave you in bed all day."

Them being the staff at whatever place Tave would end up. "You'll have to instruct them how to help you with this," was the mantra. She felt like she was preparing for a military expedition, with a plan for any barrier she might face. And the equipment to match. Laurel sat with her to review her wheelchair specs. She had a massive catalog set out on the table in the OT room.

"The wheelchair you've been using belongs to the unit," she explained, flipping through the book. Some of the pages had the corners turned down in little triangles, reminding Tave of the way her mother would mark her

Sears catalog years ago. "We'll have to order your permanent one, and that may take several weeks. In the meantime, we'll set you up with a rental. You'll also need a backup manual wheelchair for use inside."

Laurel would put in for everything Tave needed on her wheelchair—recline function: obviously; elevating footrests: absolutely; adjustable seat height: nice, but it might get denied and they would have to appeal, so Tave had to keep her posted, okay?

"Got it."

27

The week following the trip to Chico passed by in a blur of discharge preparation. In the evenings, Feliz, who usually watched *Jeopardy!* with Tave, insisted on changing the channel. He was obsessed with the A's because they had a hot new outfielder from his village in the Dominican Republic. Tave liked his company but would have preferred the Giants.

Her mind drifted, dwelling on Les's plight, and how mean her parents had been. They could have explained what was going on with Les, what therapy she was receiving, and *fuck*—they might have asked her one damn question about how she was doing or shown a speck of sympathy for her being in the wheelchair. Or asked if she'd gotten herself a lawyer or needed help with that. *Bastards*, she thought. She shuddered thinking about the way Les's mom pushed her into the house, controlling everything she did, only now caring about what Les needed, when she'd never seen her for who she was before the accident.

Apart from the disastrous events in Chico itself, the day had been fun: the first time out of the hospital in weeks and getting to hang out with Beth and Billie. She missed them. On Wednesday, Billie came in briefly for the team meeting. She didn't talk much in the conference, but her presence gave Tave the confidence to speak up and stick to her plan. Billie had to leave immediately afterward—she had a contractor coming to look at her bathroom, she said—and Tave didn't know when she might see her again. She thought often about the fun she'd had handcycling. She needed to figure out how she could get back to the rec center, but had no idea how to make that happen, or how to contact any of those guys. She had moments of panic; maybe it was crazy to think she could find a new set of friends in the city.

But late Thursday afternoon, as Tave was whizzing down the hall, she heard another motorized wheelchair behind her, a smoother sound than her own, lower-pitched. She swiveled around and saw Maddy approaching.

"Hi, Tave," she said. "I came to see how things were going. Is this a good time?"

"Sure. I'm finished with therapy for the day."

Tave recalled how freaky she thought Maddy looked the first time they'd met, with her crooked body and writhing movements. Now she was thrilled to see her. Maddy beamed at her with warm, sparkling eyes. She wore her signature *Life is Good* baseball hat. They went to Tave's room.

"I saw Beth a few days ago," Maddy said. "She came to our board meeting. She asked me to stop by."

"Oh my god. How is she?"

Maddy twisted her jaw in what could have been a *not good* kind of face, or one of those twitchy movements of her body. "She's not doing great, to be honest. But she probably wouldn't want me telling you that."

"Oh, shit. What's going on?"

"Well . . . I guess it's okay to tell you. Looks like she's breaking up with her girlfriend."

"Damn. It's all my fault."

Maddy shook her head. "Don't even go there. It's never anyone else's fault. If there's something outside the relationship creating problems, it was on shaky ground already."

"I guess."

Tave sure hoped that was true. She'd never wanted to get between Beth and her girlfriend. Until a few days ago she never even realized Beth was gay. Although now that she knew, it kind of made sense, like she'd known all along. There had always been a special connection between them, with Beth doing all kinds of extra stuff, taking her to the rec center and up to Chico, of course. But she was sure it hadn't been a flirting kind of thing. She would have picked up on that at least. Tave had never thought of Beth in *that* way—in a way that could possibly make her girlfriend jealous. That was crazy. Tave couldn't imagine ever getting involved with anyone again. Not with her being the way she was. And certainly not with Beth. Beth was more like a sister—kind of like the older sister she'd always wished for—not someone Tave would date.

She didn't understand how Beth's girlfriend could think such a thing. She must not know much about Tave, not know what a loser she was. And that she could hardly move a damn thing. But wait—Tave looked at Maddy, married to that handsome dude. Tave wasn't sure how that worked, and she could never ask, but somehow it did. Maybe one day, some way, it might be possible to have another girlfriend. But not now. She had way too much on her mind to think about getting hooked up with anyone. She had to figure out where she was going to live, how she was going to get attendant help, and all that crap, not be thinking about sex, for god's sake. And certainly not breaking up someone's relationship. She didn't want to be blamed for that, on top of everything else.

"Beth's pretty upset about being unable to work," Maddy was saying. "Any idea when she'll come back?"

"I don't know. She might have to have surgery on her ankle."

"Shit," Tave said.

Maddy took a sip from the long straw attached to the cup on her armrest. "Beth wanted me to check in with you and see what's up with your discharge planning," she said.

"We had a meeting, with the whole team and all. My friend Billie came too. Do you know Billie? She used to be a patient here. She's been in here several times, I guess."

"I haven't met her, but Beth told me about her."

"She helped me stand up for myself. They wanted me to go to my mom's. But I told them I wasn't having any of it. I'm going to stay here, in the city. I want to look for a place to live down here," Tave said. "Eventually, I mean. For now, they're going to send me to a nursing home. Whenever they find a place that will take me, I guess."

"A nursing home, huh? Or SNF, as they call it: skilled nursing facility. Or *Snif*, as in better not, it will stink of urine."

"I know. I'm dreading it. But I don't have a choice. I'm going to work on getting a real place to stay."

"For sure. You can make it happen." Maddy took another sip of water, and looked back at Tave, holding her in a steady gaze. "I was in a SNF once."

"For real?"

"Yeah. This was years ago, before I met Ryan. I'd been gradually getting weaker, more unable to take care of myself, and then I got a bad bout of pneumonia. I was in the hospital, and it was clear I couldn't manage at home, so they sent me to a SNF. I was there, I guess, two months. Or three, I'm not sure. Eventually I found an apartment, and got in-home supportive service set up and hired attendants, and I got out of there."

"Yeah. That's my plan, too. But it feels kind of overwhelming. I don't know where to start. I mean, I don't even know anyone in the city. Or how to go about looking for somewhere to live."

"I have a friend," Maddy said. "Jess. She works for an organization called Independence Now. Their whole gig is working with people who don't belong in nursing homes, getting them out into the community and living independently. Helping them find apartments, hire attendants, the whole shtick. They're great. I don't know of anything like that up in Eureka, but if you're planning to stay around here, I could set you up with them. Would it be okay for me to ask Jess to come in and meet you, and tell you about their program?"

"Sure. That would be . . . sorry." Her eyes brimmed with tears.

"Hey. It's okay."

Tave nodded. "I get kind of scared sometimes." She swallowed a lump in her throat.

"Of course. It's scary. But you don't have to face it alone. Jess is a good soul. A big woman, she towers above me. She has a loud booming voice that can be disconcerting at first, but don't let that put you off. We've become real good friends."

Tave smiled at the image of Maddy hanging out with a big, tall woman. Then she remembered the trip up to Chico, and what an odd crew they'd been, and Billie's *three crips roll into a bar* joke. I guess these are my peeps now, she thought.

"Jess knows how to get stuff done," Maddy said. "She's super busy, so she might not be able to see you before you leave here. But I'll be sure to have her come to wherever you end up. Has the social worker told you which SNFs she's looking at?"

"She mentioned some names, but they didn't mean anything to me. I guess there might not be much available. She said I might have to go with whatever I can get."

"Some are a lot better than others. Let's hope for the best. We'll have to work on springing you out of there as soon as possible." Maddy grinned.

"Seems like it's going to cost a lot to find someplace," Tave said. "And I have nothing. But I keep thinking about, you know, if I could get a settlement or something. I see these ads on TV all the time. Some chick who looks fine to me, but says she was injured and got a ton of money. I don't understand how that works."

"Hmmm. I don't know much about that either."

Tave told Maddy about the accident report Billie had found online. "It said something about the other driver, like he was maybe drunk, I guess, but they're still checking into it. I'm stuck in here and I don't know what to do. I have no one . . ." Tave felt herself tearing up again, throwing herself a damn pity party. She didn't want to cry.

"It's a lot to deal with. Let me ask Jess about that too. I bet she knows someone who could help."

"That would be great." Tave sniffed.

"What about the Department of Rehab? Have the folks here set you up with an appointment?"

"I don't think so."

"Okay. Well, that might be too much to focus on right now. But once you're settled, you'll want to get moving on that too. The Department of Rehab takes forever, but they can offer amazing things. Like, help going back to school, or getting retrained for a new career. A friend of mine got them to buy him a van, because he was going to need it for school."

"Cool." That was something Tave could definitely get into. She had an image of herself behind the wheel of a fully equipped van like Billie's. Red, she decided.

"Don't worry. I know it's a lot to take in. But I'm here to help. We're not going to let you go through this on your own."

The lump in Tave's throat returned. "I'm so lucky to have you guys," she managed to say.

"Hey, that's what friends are for, right?"

It was a wonderful evening. Maddy stayed through dinner, which Tave was permitted to take in her room, as she had a visitor. Maddy had already eaten, she said. She asked Tave about the trip to Chico, and what it was like seeing Les, and what she'd heard from her friends in Eureka—nothing more—and they talked about the volunteer work Maddy did at the rec center, and where she grew up on the East Coast. Maddy told her she could sign up for Paratransit and order a ride to the rec center from the SNF, come any Sunday for handcycling.

Tave realized she'd stopped paying attention to Maddy's jerky movements. It *was* like hanging out with a friend.

28

Lionel's couch was a huge white leather sectional that was great for lounging during the day, but at night, the sheets kept slipping off. Every time Beth turned over, the weight of her cast sent the bedding tumbling into a heap on the floor. She had to get up twice to tuck everything in, pulling the cushions out a bit and shoving the bottom sheet back into position. The neon lights from the bar three doors down, flashing full of life at 2 a.m., cast a blinking orange glow through the room, which was driving her nuts. There were no shades. Being high up on the third floor, Lionel apparently felt he didn't need them for privacy, but Beth yearned for blackout curtains.

She was glad to have a place to crash, but she would need to find something more workable. She'd called Katy repeatedly since Sunday, but Katy was not picking up. Beth resorted to sending multiple texts and pleading voice messages, even though she knew she sounded pathetic. She apologized for lying. She should have been up front about her plan to go to Chico with Tave. It was dumb of her, she recognized that. She did. The lying part was stupid.

But Beth couldn't believe Katy thought she was having an *affair* with Tave, for god's sake. Tave was much too young; cute, yes—but hooking up with a patient was a line Beth would never cross. She'd been overinvolved and obsessed maybe, because Tave had an extreme set of needs Beth couldn't ignore, and she'd felt compelled to rescue her. She recognized now that she had let Katy down. She'd screwed up big-time, which wasn't easy for her to admit. She'd tried to be perfect but had utterly failed.

Clearly, Katy had resented her work for a long time. Beth had known on some level but hadn't tried to reassure Katy. She'd taken her for granted. Katy had been so sweet recently, taking care of her since she broke her ankle. And acting more responsibly, getting into her new job. *Damn*, Beth thought, she'd been so careless. She checked her phone again, to see if there was any word from Katy since she last looked at midnight: nothing. Only the voicemail Beth's mom had left the day before, which she'd been ignoring. *OMG . . .* she hoped her mom hadn't called the landline, that Katy hadn't told her she'd kicked Beth out. Surely, Katy wouldn't do that. Telling other people would give their separation a life of its own, legs it shouldn't have. This was temporary, a little blip, they would get over it soon, they had to. Beth had told no one—apart from Lionel, of course, but even then, she'd made it sound more like a mutually agreed-upon arrangement.

She let out a loud groan. What would become of them? They could go to couples counseling. Jan and Rachel had gone to someone good; she should get the details. She wasn't sure Katy would agree, but she could try to persuade her. Beth had been to counseling with Pam, back in Chicago. It hadn't helped in the end, as Beth had come to understand they had completely different perspectives. Pam fundamentally didn't believe in monogamy; she wanted the freedom to explore any fleeting attraction that came her way and wasn't going to change. But with Katy: Beth didn't believe they were so very different. They both wanted a stable relationship. They had moved out here together, invested four years of their lives. You don't throw all that away.

The light from the bar illuminated a large calendar hung above the couch. The July page featured a black-and-white Mapplethorpe self-portrait. The month was almost over. Next month—*oh god!* Jenny's birthday was coming up. Beth clasped her hand to her mouth. If she and Katy broke up, she'd lose Katy's family too. *No.* That couldn't happen. "Damn," she said, out loud this time. She shook her head in disbelief. Only six weeks ago they'd been backpacking among the Santa Lucia wildflowers, blissfully unaware of the turmoil to come.

The covers slid again. Beth tugged at the blanket and turned over, scraping her good leg with her cast. A spasm of pain shot through her ankle. *Goddamn it.* It was going to be a while before she could take on any exciting adventures again. She'd seen the ankle specialist on Tuesday, and he wasn't happy with the alignment in her foot. He was going to give it another week, before deciding about surgery. Beth knew she would have a better outcome with internal fixation, but she dreaded it. Recommending it for patients was one thing, but to contemplate it for herself was scary.

And meanwhile, here she was on crutches, dragging her ass up three flights at Lionel's. Because, she reminded herself, Katy had shoved her down the stairs. It wasn't fair. If anyone had to get out of their apartment, it should be Katy. If Beth stayed at home, she would have only the five steps up from the street, and the half flight inside. Let Katy go and crash somewhere else until they resolve things.

The blinking green light on the stereo showed 3:21. She could not get back to sleep. She sat up and reached for her laptop, logged on to her email. She saw a new message from Kristy: *How you doing?* Kind of her. Beth composed a quick reply, keeping it superficial; she wasn't going to let her know about her fight with Katy. She decided to wait until morning to send it. She didn't want Kristy to see she was awake at this hour.

There was nothing else of much interest—the usual junk and spam. Then she reread the message Maddy had sent the previous evening, that Tave was asking about legal compensation. Beth needed to do more research on this. She'd asked Lionel if he knew any lawyers, and he'd called his friend Brian. But Brian worked in corporate law and said he wasn't up to speed with current law in the personal injury field.

"I don't need the latest and greatest, for god's sake," Beth had protested. "I'm sure he knows a hundred percent more than I do. I only need to understand the basics."

"Maybe he's concerned about liability if he gave you any inaccurate information," Lionel said. "Being a lawyer and all. But he said he was going to find someone. He will."

Beth was impatient. In the meantime, she would do her own research. For all her years working in rehab, she had surprisingly little knowledge about personal injury lawsuits. Almost none of her patients won settlements. There was no money in crashing your mountain bike or getting shot in a drive-by shooting or diving into a shallow section of the river. If Beth had her way, everyone who sustained a spinal cord injury would get everything they needed, because they needed it, not because they managed to sue someone. A few of her patients had workers' comp. They were the lucky ones. She always thought if you were going to get yourself a catastrophic injury in this crazy health care system, do it at work, for god's sake; it was the best way to get everything fully covered, for sure. Fernando, a patient on their unit two years ago, fell off a roof, working for a construction company: he'd gotten all his attendant care paid for, for life, and all the best equipment you could imagine. She did recall one young girl—she couldn't remember her name; it was back in Chicago. The patient was a pedestrian run over by a number 38 bus making a right turn onto Dearborn Avenue. Beth shuddered recalling that girl's gruesome injuries. But she'd won a huge settlement: thirty-six million dollars, if Beth remembered correctly. The bus company was held liable; they had the deep pocket. But most run-of-the-mill car accidents? You weren't going to get much, if anything.

But what about the other driver in Tave's accident? *How did this all work?* Maybe he was super rich, with tons of assets—or did it depend on what kind of car insurance you carried? She couldn't believe she knew so little about this.

Beth yawned. Her neck and shoulders were tight with tension. She rotated her head, rubbed the back of her neck. She ought to try to get back to sleep. And, she told herself, she should be fully focused on mending her relationship with Katy. And yet . . . she felt compelled to pursue her search for answers. A few more minutes. She googled personal injury law. California, it would have to be, each state being different, no doubt. She blinked at the glow from her laptop, fighting off fatigue. *Shit.* Seven million results. And top of the page, even on to the second page, tons of paid listings, ads from lawyers. Ambulance chasers. Just the idea of it Beth found repulsive. Probably a bunch of sharks, the lot of them. It would be impossible to know whom to trust.

Tave must know even less about the legal aspects than she did. Beth could see Tave getting manipulated, taken advantage of by some jerk. She couldn't let that happen. Beth wasn't her physical therapist anymore, but she could do this, make herself useful. She was so bored sitting on the couch all day. She'd done nothing productive apart from drag herself out to the DSR board meeting on Monday night—taking a cab there and back. It had been good to see people, and she'd been able to chat about Tave with Maddy, who'd promised to go see her again on the unit. But Beth needed an ongoing assignment. Educating herself on the legal issues would be perfect.

With this new sense of purpose, Beth felt better, ready to try to get some sleep. She stood and, balancing on her good foot, used a new method of fixing the bedding, using two small cushions from the rocking chair as wedges stuffed down tight into the gap between the larger cushions of the couch. She placed her T-shirt over her head to create a blindfold. This was ridiculous, she thought. In the morning, she would text Katy and tell her she was returning to the apartment. Either they would work out how to be in the same place, or Katy could be the one to find somewhere else.

Beth was awakened by an intermittent buzzing. The blinking clock on the stereo showed nine fifteen, so she must have slept after all. The buzzing was her phone, she realized. She fumbled through the pile of cushions on the floor to locate it, her head in a fog. She had a raging headache, and her mouth was parched. She finally found the phone and flipped it open: a missed call and a text from Maddy. *Jess knows a good personal injury lawyer. She's going to send her in to see Tave.*

Beth flopped back on the couch. *Wait,* she thought, I was working on that. Lionel talked to Brian who was going to . . . "Stop it," she said out loud, and quickly looked around to make sure Lionel hadn't entered the living room. She shook her head. "Shut up with this nonsense." She couldn't believe she was being so selfish. It was great Jess could respond so quickly and get Tave the help she needed. But—Beth had been looking forward to plunging into more online research later in the day. Maybe she would look into it anyway. Wouldn't hurt. This person Jess knows might flake out or be no good. Yes, she would continue her research, and tomorrow, Saturday, when Linda would be unlikely to be there, Beth would go visit Tave and give her the scoop.

29

Wanda came into Tave's room as she was about to take off for her morning OT therapy. She placed a piece of paper on Tave's bedside table.

"I just took a call at the front desk," she said. She checked the paper again. "An attorney—Miranda Davenport—wants to come see you later today. Someone your friend Maddy knows referred her, I guess. I told her your schedule, and she said she'd come at noon. You can take your lunch in here if you like, so you can have privacy."

When Tave returned to her room at lunch, the woman was already waiting for her, sitting with her back to the door, working on her laptop. She jumped up when Tave approached.

"Good morning," she said, extending her hand. "Or is it afternoon?" She smiled and clasped Tave's fist. She placed her business card on Tave's bedside table and sat down again. She must be old, Tave thought, because her hair was gray, but she wore it in a cute, stylish cut, and her face looked much younger, with no makeup. She was petite and smartly dressed, in a bright-red suit: a short pencil skirt and well-fitted jacket. She put her laptop in her briefcase and pulled out a black leather file folder. "I'm Miranda Davenport. Please call me Miranda. I hope you received the message I left with the nurse earlier this morning. I'm a personal injury attorney. I'd like to help you with your case."

"Thanks. That's great. But er . . . not meaning to be rude, or anything, but I don't have any money for a lawyer."

"There's no charge for this."

"What, I'm a charity case?" Tave didn't know why she said that. It was like her mother's voice tumbling out. She and Les were always up for free stuff: free clothes from the Rescue Mission box, the chest of drawers someone left out on the street, and sure, even the food bank sometimes—like when Tave was out of work for four weeks. "Sorry," she said now.

The woman did a little wave of her hand. "No, no. This is normal. Jess is a friend of mine, so I'm happy to help. You may have a claim to compensate you for your injuries. I don't know yet if you have a case, we'll have to see. But if you do, you wouldn't pay me anything up front. If I were to win you a settlement, I would take my fees out of those funds. Does that make sense?"

"Okay." Tave nodded.

"I took the liberty of pulling up the police report of your accident," Miranda said, opening the file folder. "Have you seen it?" She held up a bunch of papers. The front page was a tightly packed form, filled with tiny boxes and x's and notes in scrawly handwriting.

Tave shook her head. "No. I haven't. My friend found something online, but it was only a short summary."

"This is the full report filed by the officer at the scene." She flicked through three additional pages of boxes, and a last page containing a diagram. "I've made a copy for you." She placed it on Tave's bedside table.

Tave stared at the columns, the report she'd been afraid to see. Now it just looked like an obscure stack of paper, oddly old-fashioned, like the bookkeeping records her mom brought home from the nail salon when Tave was very young. Yet it signified the most consequential event of her life.

"Does it say the accident was my fault?"

Miranda looked up from studying her copy and gave a gentle smile. "We'll get to that in a moment. I need to clarify a few things first. You were the driver, right? Whose car were you in?" she asked.

"Yeah, I was driving. My car."

"Were you insured?"

"Yeah. I wasn't for a while, but I'd gotten insurance a few months before the crash. That was Les—I mean, Les thought I should get it."

"Good for her. Les is your friend—Leslie Saunders, right?" She glanced at her papers again. "Do you happen to know what the per-incident liability limit was on your policy?"

"I don't have a clue. I know it was the cheapest policy I could find."

Miranda nodded. "It's probably very little in that case. The minimum is fifteen thousand dollars per person. Perhaps you have twenty-five thousand, maybe fifty thousand if you're lucky. But that's nothing for a catastrophic injury like yours. And I understand Leslie was severely injured too?"

Tave nodded.

"Do you have any information about the other driver? Was he insured?"

"I dunno."

"Have the people here at the hospital asked you for any details about your car insurance policy? They must want to access that for billing."

"I don't know. I think there was some woman who asked me a bunch of questions, but I don't remember much about that."

Miranda made more notes and continued the grilling. "Did you have health insurance at the time of the accident?"

"No."

"Do you have any assets? Do you own a house or any other property?"

Tave shook her head.

"Any stocks, shares, trust fund?"

Tave laughed. "No, hardly."

Miranda smiled. "I didn't think so, but I have to ask." She looked at the papers again. "You must be on MediCal now?"

"I guess." Tave shrugged again. She felt dumb. She didn't know this stuff. "I think that's what the social worker told me. MediCal pending, I think."

"Okay. Good." Miranda looked up and smiled again at Tave. "I know this must seem overwhelming. And I'm sure you're expected to under-stand a lot of other detailed information that seems foreign to you right now. But it's kind of important."

Tave took a deep breath and straightened her shoulders. "Okay."

Miranda shuffled through the papers some more. "Was your car totaled in the accident?"

"I don't know." All these questions Tave had never thought to ask. It didn't seem to matter until now. And she had no one on the outside taking care of any of it.

"And this was the '99 Chevy Malibu, right?"

"Yes. Over a hundred thousand miles on it. Kind of a beat-up old thing. But it ran well. I'd had it, let's see . . . three years."

"Brakes okay?"

"Sure. As far as I know."

"What about the tires?"

"We replaced those, like, I don't know, maybe a year ago."

"All right. Good. Had you had any recent work done on it at a shop, or anything?"

"No." Tave added, "I never took it into a shop. Les did all the maintenance on it. Like changing the oil, that kind of thing. She didn't believe in paying anyone else to do that."

Miranda's eyebrows shot up. "That's interesting." She made a note.

Leticia stood at the door with Tave's lunch tray, hesitating. Tave didn't want to be rude, but she was hungry, and her next therapy session would start in half an hour. "Is it okay with you if I eat while we talk?"

"Of course, go ahead. We're almost done. I need to check one more thing here."

Miranda went through the papers again and took another sheet from her black folder. She waited while Leticia opened containers, cut up the cantaloupe, and set Tave up with her utensils. She sat with a polite little smile on her face, like she didn't want to say more with Leticia in the room, though Tave didn't care. As soon as Leticia left, she said, "I would like to do some research on the other driver, and what his insurance and his resources are, if that's all right with you."

Tave nodded, her mouth full of pasta salad.

"Good. I need you to sign this contract for me to represent you." She placed the form on the table next to Tave's tray. "An x will do. Here." The lawyer steadied a pen in Tave's right hand. Her stronger left hand was occupied with her adapted fork, so her squiggly mark looked really goofy, but Miranda seemed satisfied.

"Great," she said, packing up her folder. "I don't want you to worry about this too much, okay?" She stood in front of Tave. "I'll take care of it. Your insurance company should have assigned someone, a lawyer, to the case. I need to check on that, but it's good to have your own personal attorney too, someone who's looking out for your interests. At some point the insurance company lawyer or one acting for Leslie may want to take a deposition from you."

Tave felt lost, like she was following about half of what Miranda was saying. She must have been looking cross-eyed because Miranda paused and said, "I'm sorry; I don't mean to confuse you. Do you know what a deposition is?"

Tave shook her head. "No."

"It's a statement under oath. They ask you lots of questions about the accident."

"But I don't remember the accident itself." She glanced at the papers Miranda had given her. "Does it say . . . ? When I first woke up in the hospital, I thought I must have fallen asleep at the wheel, but I don't know if that's true. Like I say I don't remember." She still had only the vague memories of the urge, the irresistible urge to close her eyes.

Miranda sat down again. "It appears that was a question raised by the officer at the scene, but this is considered hearsay evidence. Nothing is proven at this point. If you're questioned, you simply answer truthfully, as best you can, and you're entitled to have an attorney present. I'll inform all the parties I'm representing you, but if anyone contacts you, let me know, okay? Don't meet with anyone without me. Okay?"

"Got it." Tave stabbed a piece of cantaloupe with her fork.

"Good. I have to wait until I know more about the other driver, but I suspect that will not change the overall picture. Most likely, there's going to be very little money available for either you or Leslie. Something maybe, but I suspect not much. Based on what I see so far, I think it's unlikely there will be a huge settlement here."

"Oh." Figures: she'd been stupid to get her hopes up. Then Tave remembered. "But the other driver . . . if he was drunk . . ."

"I will be checking into what they've concluded from the investigation. If that's the case, he'll be facing DUI charges at least, and possibly vehicular assault."

"So that would make a difference, right?"

"Unless he has a lot of assets or was acting in a nonpersonal capacity, it probably won't change much in terms of any monetary settlement." Miranda leaned forward and squeezed Tave's forearm. "I'm not giving up. I'll look into it, see if there's some deep pocket that could be held liable, if there was, for example, a documented problem with road safety on that stretch of highway neglected by the county. But I don't want to leave you with unrealistic expectations."

"Okay. But . . ." Tave hesitated. "What if the accident was all my fault?"

"Try not to worry about that. We don't know yet if you were legally negligent. That would have to be proved. Perhaps the fault lies partly or wholly with the other driver. But none of this means you're in trouble, or that anything bad is going to happen to you, okay? You don't have any assets anyone can go after, so nothing much will come of it."

"But I can't bear the thought that I did this to Les."

"That must be so hard. I'm so sorry this happened." Miranda's mouth twisted in an odd movement that made Tave wonder if she was on the verge of tears. But she quickly regained her composure. "But you know you didn't intentionally do this to yourself or anyone else. You should be focused on your rehabilitation, as I'm sure you are. You don't need to put any energy into self-blame." She stood to take her leave and smiled. "It's been nice meeting you, and I'll be in touch, okay?"

"Sure." The woman was already at the door before Tave remembered to add: "Thanks for coming . . . and everything."

Tave was mulling over what she'd said, trying to keep it straight in her mind, when Laurel popped in.

"Hey," she said. "Your new wheelchair has arrived. The rental you're going to use until your permanent one comes in?"

This seemed to be a question, so Tave said, "Okay."

"We'll get you set up in it this afternoon," Laurel said. "I think you'll like it. It's much spiffier than that thing." She nodded at the hospital-issued one Tave had been using.

"Great." Tave smiled. A few weeks ago, she would have made some sarcastic remark. But now—it was true: she was excited about checking out her new chair.

～

And it was kind of cool. Much quieter than the one she'd been driving, a smooth recline function, the armrests all clean, a shiny new joystick, and no cracks in the backrest. At the end of her therapy day, Tave hung out at the nurses' station showing off, zipping up and down the hall, turning tight 360s. It wasn't exactly zero-to-sixty in six seconds, but Feliz, the evening shift aide, was super impressed.

"Look at you, girl," he said, extending his arm for a fist bump. "You'll be ready for the Indy 500 soon!"

"Your phone's ringing," one of the nurses shouted from the other end of the hall. She was standing at the door to Tave's room. "Want me to get it?"

"Sure, thanks." Tave hurried back. Getting a call was always exciting. "Who is it?"

"Dunno. She wouldn't say."

She, huh? It wasn't Dan, then. Tave had not heard back from him since their conversation over a week ago. She would be in a real mess if she was waiting on him to find her a place to live.

The nurse had set the phone on speaker.

"Hello," Tave said.

"Hi. It's Beth. How are things going?"

"Oh, wow. Great. I mean, great to hear from you."

"Just wanted to check in. How are things going with your discharge planning?" Beth's voice was kind of gravelly.

"Okay, I guess. Did you hear I decided I'm not going back to Eureka? It will be better for me to be here in the city, I think. Tracy is looking for a nursing home. For right now. You know, until I can work out something else, get my shit together. Maddy knows someone who, like, can help me get my own place."

"That's good."

"And I got me my new wheelchair. You should see it. It's cool."

"Great."

Beth sounded spacey, Tave thought. "How's your ankle doing?"

"It still hurts. And I'm worried I'm going to need surgery, which would be a real drag."

"Shit. You're going to be off work for a while I guess."

"Yeah, I think so."

Beth didn't sound like her usual self. It must be true, Tave thought— what Maddy had said: that she was breaking up with her girlfriend. She wanted to ask but felt awkward. "Listen," she tried.

But at the same time, Beth said, "Hey."

"What?"

"I heard you want to look into getting compensation for your injury."

"Yeah, but . . ."

"I've been checking out some good lawyers for you."

"Oh. Well, Maddy got me someone. She came to see me today. The lawyer, I mean."

"She did? Already?"

"Yeah, and she's cool. She told me not to worry too much. She's going to take care of it. And I don't have to pay her or anything."

"Oh. But what did she say about the other driver? Going after him, I mean?"

"She's going to check it out and all. But she didn't . . . um . . ." Tave tried to recall what Miranda had said about the other driver.

"I've been trying to find out if the police have charged him with vehicular assault. And what his insurance is, what assets he has."

Something about this made Tave uncomfortable. "Well, I don't know . . ."

"I'm going to contact this guy, a lawyer my friend Lionel knows," Beth said.

"No," Tave heard herself say, surprised at how firm it came out. "I don't think that's a good idea. This woman . . ." Miranda's card was on the bed table where she'd left it earlier in the day. "I have a lawyer. Miranda Davenport. Seems like she knows what she's doing. I think . . . I'm going to stick with her."

"Oh. Right. Sure."

A pause hung in the air. With her newfound confidence, Tave asked, "What's happening with you . . . and your girlfriend? You guys doing okay?"

Another pause before Beth answered, "We . . . we went through a bad patch but we're working it out."

"That's good." Tave was relieved to hear it.

"Listen, I've got to go. But I thought I might come in and see you on the weekend. To hang out for a while. Saturday, most likely. Wait—that's tomorrow, right?"

"Sure. I'll be here," Tave said.

30

Saturday morning, Lionel was all smiles and cups of coffee brought to Beth in the living room, and *At your service ma'am, what do you need?* Beth didn't have the heart to tell him about her sleepless nights or how uncomfortable she was on the couch. But when he said he was free all morning and would be happy to drive her anywhere she needed, she said she had to make a trip to the hospital, and after that, she wanted to go home.

She was about to fabricate a story about needing to pick up something from work, and pretend Katy had invited her back, but she stopped herself. *Enough with all the lies.* Instead, she said, "I'm going to try to work things out with Katy. But first, I want to visit with a patient for a while, so if you could drop me and return, say, an hour later, that would be great."

"This is the kid you took on that wild jaunt up to Chico, right?" he said.

"You heard about that?"

"It's all over town, sweetheart." Lionel laughed with an exaggerated flick of his wrist. "It sounded hilarious, although maybe it got embellished in the retelling. I'm surprised you're not wanted on charges of kidnapping and endangering a minor."

"That's definitely embellished. She's not a minor and she was not kidnapped! Nor in any danger. Seriously, where did you hear this stuff?"

"My lips are sealed." He covered his mouth with both hands. The beard was gone, but now he was experimenting with a pencil-thin mustache.

Beth threw a cushion at him. Katy must have told her friend Angie, who told Lionel. "It was an important thing for her—the patient—to do. And there was no other way to get her up to Chico. Tave. That's her name. And yes, I want to go see her."

"So, do you have a crazy crush on her?"

"No! Of course not. She's a patient, for god's sake. It wouldn't be appropriate."

"Inappropriate things happen, darling. Especially in matters of the heart."

"Well, it's not like that at all. I do feel—well, very connected to her, I guess. She's a young dyke, and she's had a terrible injury, and she has no one in her family who's any use to her. I want to help her, that's all." She lay down to elevate her foot again. "And because of this fucking ankle, I can't be treating her at work. I want to go see how she's doing. They're getting ready to discharge her to some shitty nursing home. It will be full of old ladies screaming their heads off and peeing all over the place."

"Sounds grim."

"I know. She wants to look for a place to live independently here in the city, but she's going to need a lot of support for that to happen. And she has no money."

"Right. This is the same patient you said needs a lawyer. Got it. Okay, I'm happy to drop you off at the hospital. I'll go get groceries and swing by to pick you up later." He looked at her, all serious. "Sweetie, I know you're super committed to your job, I get it. But be careful, darling. You can't solve every problem. Sometimes things are fucked up."

He was beginning to sound like Linda. But Beth smiled and said, "Thanks so much. You're an angel."

"With wings on." He laughed, fluttering his arms behind his back. "I'm going to take a shower, and then I'll be ready when you are."

~

This should be safe, Beth thought. Linda, like all the managers, would be off, and the weekend crew would be a chill bunch; they wouldn't snitch on her. She stepped off the elevator at the third floor and was immediately welcomed by shrieks and a huge hug from Leticia, and a high five from Duane.

"It's so great to see you!"

"We miss you, girl!"

"Hey! How's that ankle doing?"

The commotion brought out Wanda and Julie, one of the weekend PTs, emerging from a patient room. Soon, there was a small throng around her. It was like a homecoming. Which it was.

"Still non-weight-bearing?" Julie asked, nodding at Beth's ankle.

"Oh, yes, for a while, I think."

She made her way to the nurse's station, where there were more hugs and more questions. Beth was happy to hang out. Saturdays were always calmer than weekdays; the patients had a therapy schedule, but a lighter one, and the whole atmosphere was more laidback. The doctors made quick morning rounds and were gone. Unless there was an emergency, there were no staff from ancillary departments such as x-ray or the lab milling around the unit, there were no insurance case managers poking through the charts, interrogating staff about the patients' progress and discharge plans, there were no team conferences. And no bosses around either.

Beth got caught up on Leticia's daughter's college applications and Julie's engagement party to be held at the Mark Hopkins, of all places—*Wow!* and *Congratulations!*—and Wanda had brought in her famous chocolate chip cookies that Beth had to sample. The chocolate oozed into her mouth. She helped herself to another one.

"Mmmm, these are delicious. I shouldn't," she said, her hand going to her belly. "With so little exercise, I'm sure I've gained ten pounds."

"You look fine," Wanda said. "Using those crutches burns a ton of calories, I'm sure. Any idea when you'll be back at work?"

"I have no idea. Have to wait until I see ortho again next week." Beth pulled another rolling chair toward her to elevate her foot. "Several more weeks is my guess. I'm going crazy sitting at home." She didn't mention she wasn't sitting at her own home. "I'm so damn bored."

"We got word that Joint Commission is coming within the month," Sarah, one of the other nurses, told Beth, raising her hands to rearrange her long red hair in its ponytail. "You're lucky to be out of that mess. You know how it goes. Everyone's already getting themselves in a tizzy, making sure everything's spic and span."

"Obsessing about the temperature of the refrigerators, and the crash cart checklists, I bet." The inspections never focused on anything of substance, in Beth's opinion.

"Help!" A shout came from a patient room close to the nurses' station. "Help me!"

Leticia jumped up and ran to the room. "There she goes again," she said.

"A new stroke patient," Sarah said. "Very confused, easily agitated."

Patient care must go on, no matter what day of the week. Beth grabbed her crutches and stood up. "I should let you guys get back to work. I wanted to say hi to Tave. Is she in her room?"

Sarah scrutinized the therapy schedule on her computer. "Looks like she's in the PT gym. She's with the new registry PT, Sorrel. She's great. She's a real expert on spinal cord injury. Tave loves her."

"Oh," Beth said. "That's great." She made her way down the hall to the gym. Sorrel: a real expert on spinal cord injury, huh? Beth was glad for Tave, of course she was. Good she had someone who knew what she was doing. Especially important now, with all the teaching Tave would need to carry with her to the nursing home. But Beth was disappointed she wasn't the one getting her ready for discharge.

"Beth?" A stern voice behind her. A voice she knew only too well. "What are you doing here?" She turned to see Linda coming toward her.

"What are *you* doing here?" Beth said before she could stop herself.

"Excuse me?" Linda let her mouth hang open in a pose of exaggerated surprise. "I'm here catching up on work before the Joint Commission survey. But you, Miss Farringdon, have no business being here at all. I've told you before, and I mean it. You need to stay away. Especially after what happened with Tave last weekend. Don't think I don't know you were behind that escapade. I am very disappointed in you. You placed the patient in danger; she was at risk of significant harm, being gone for so long, and without proper authorization. And no one knew where she was. I have discussed this with HR. I'm going to issue a written warning that will go in your file. And I'm now going to add an addendum, to the effect that you violated my instructions to stay away from the unit until you're off medical leave." She stood in front of Beth, her arms crossed. "Now leave at once. Or I will call security."

∿

Beth sat in Lionel's car and wept, burying her head in her hands. He stayed silent, a warm, embracing stillness that seemed to allow the space to be present with her pain and sadness. He had turned on the car with a push of a button on the dashboard; he had a new hybrid that idled in complete silence. After a few moments, the engine sprang to life, offering a prompt for action.

Lionel tapped her knee. "Tell you what: I have groceries. I need to run home, pop the chicken in the fridge. But after that, let's go for a drive."

Beth managed to nod. She didn't have any better idea. It felt good to have someone else take charge. They drove in silence back to his house, and she sat motionless while he ran inside, staring ahead of her but seeing nothing.

She jumped when he opened her door and presented her with a travel mug. "You're definitely in need of coffee," he said.

"You're so sweet. Thanks." She took a sip. It must have been left over from earlier in the morning, well stewed and lukewarm, but she wasn't going to complain. "Thank you, Lionel. You're a doll."

"It's a beautiful day. I'm taking you across the bridge to the Marin Headlands." He turned on his CD player and skipped through two discs, before nodding in approval. "This," he said, bobbing his head and swaying his shoulders, as the first bars of "Don't Cry for Me Argentina" filled the car. *It won't be easy; you'll think it strange . . .*

It was irresistible. Lionel knew all the lyrics and soon Beth was singing along too. *The truth is I never left you . . .* As they crossed the Presidio, she caught sight of the Golden Gate Bridge and opened her window to stick out her head. The wind took her breath away more than she expected, so she withdrew until only the top of her head was exposed to the elements, the breeze ruffling through her hair.

"I've been such a goddamn idiot," she said, turning back to Lionel. "I've screwed up big-time."

"Welcome to the human race, darling."

"I blew it. I let my work become the most important thing. And it's not."

"It's understandable, sweetheart, with the kind of work you do. I'm sure it becomes all-consuming. Most people couldn't do it."

"Yeah, but . . . I thought I was so special, and that I was the only one who could help Tave. And that's bullshit. I'm good, but I'm not the only one; there are a lot of other good people who can help her. For all my paying lip service to the idea that rehab is all about *team*, I acted like I was alone. That I alone could save her. And that's so fucking stupid. And I screwed up my relationship in the process. The best relationship I've ever had."

"I'm not the one who needs to hear this, sweetheart," Lionel said.

"I know."

～

They returned to Lionel's apartment to pick up Beth's stuff, and he then drove her back to hers. He said he would wait outside in the car, telling her to leave her duffel bag in his trunk until she was sure everything was cool.

"This may take a while," Beth said.

"Take your time." He retrieved his copy of the *New York Times* weekend edition from the back seat. "I'm all set here. Text me, okay?"

"I will. And thanks, Lionel. I mean . . ." Beth tried to give him a hug, awkward with the center console between them. She was going to cry again.

"Go." Lionel gave her a gentle shove.

She made her way up the front steps on her crutches. It was harder going than usual because she felt exhausted and drained. She paused for breath in the hallway before attempting the short flight up to her apartment and caught her reflection in the mirror. *What a sight for sore eyes*, she thought. Her eyes were red, her cheeks pale, her hair a mess. She tried to tweak her hair back into shape, but it remained stubbornly lopsided. *Oh well . . .*

She didn't even know if Katy would be home, but some instinct told her she was. As she fumbled with the key while balancing on her crutches, the door opened. Katy stood in front of her, staring open-mouthed.

"Beth," she said, her voice not unkind. "Oh my god, what happened to you?"

"Katy . . . I've made a total, complete mess of everything. I am so, so sorry. Can you ever . . . I mean . . . Can we try to start over?"

Katy hesitated for a moment while Beth waited in suspense. Then Katy opened her arms. "Come here," she said, pulling Beth into a hug.

Beth rested her head against Katy's chest, inhaling her warmth and the musty scent of her T-shirt. She flung her arms around Katy's waist, causing her crutches to tumble to the floor, and she started to cry. Huge sobs wracked her body, layers of hurt bubbling up from somewhere deep inside her, unleashed from years of being pushed down, in the need to keep it all together, to be the perfect one, the successful one. She wept so hard she felt her chest might crack open. She could not stop. "I'm sorry, I . . ."

"Shhhh," Katy said. "Come, lean on me."

Katy threw Beth's left arm over her shoulder and gripped her right hip, supporting her as Beth hopped into the living room. They collapsed together onto the couch. Beth closed her eyes, resting on Katy's shoulder, overcome with fatigue. She lost track of time, dozed off for a moment, until Katy shifted underneath her, releasing her arm.

"Hey," Katy said.

Beth opened her eyes and wiped her face with the back of her hand. Bright sunlight streamed across the room, revealing a swarm of dust motes hovering above the coffee table. She shielded her face from the glare and looked around. The room was disheveled, matching her own appearance and state of mind. Two magazines, a pair of socks, and the TV remote lay tossed on the floor; a sweatshirt dangled from the arm of the chair in the corner. The table was littered with junk mail, dirty cups and plates, and an empty takeout food container. She resisted the urge to tidy up. She needed to talk, to apologize.

"I know I totally messed up." *No.* She would have to do better than that. She tried again. "You were right to be upset with me. I was way over-the-top in my involvement with Tave—that patient. Not romantically, it wasn't that, but I *was* having strong feelings and I spent too much time with her, above and beyond what was called for. And I should never have lied to you."

Beth shifted to look up at Katy, who stared straight ahead, her jaw set, face blank. But she gave Beth's shoulder a gentle squeeze. Encouraged, Beth continued, "It wasn't necessarily a bad idea to take her to Chico. That's where her girlfriend is—I don't know if I told you—but her girlfriend was also in the car crash and very badly injured, and is now living with her parents, who are, like, totally homophobic. Tave needed to go see for herself, not hear it from people she doesn't know if she can trust. But . . ." *Shit. Stop talking about Tave.* Beth's jaw quivered. The tears welled up again. "It was so dumb of me. I didn't mean to hurt you. I should never have . . . You mean the world to me. Please . . ."

She sobbed again, burying her head in her hands. Katy rubbed her back in gentle movements between her shoulder blades, but the stroking felt robotic, as if on automatic pilot. Katy had not yet said a word. When Beth looked up, she saw Katy was crying now too.

"I love you," she said, kissing Katy's cheek, salty with tears. "Oh, sweetie, are we going to get through this?"

Katy sniffed. "I hope so," she said. "But . . ."

"But what?"

"Um . . . well, see . . ."

"What?" Beth sat up straighter, pulling back.

"You're not the only one who messed up."

"What do you mean?"

Katy bit her lip, staring straight ahead. Following her gaze, Beth noticed there sure were a lot of cups and plates on that table. And *two* takeout food containers, wedged on top of each other. Several empty beer bottles lay scattered on the floor under the table. And the sweatshirt on the armchair, now that Beth focused on it—bright orange with an unfamiliar logo—belonged to neither her nor Katy.

"Shit," she said. She blinked, trying to absorb this new shift in the scenery. "Who?"

"You don't know her. Some friend of Angie's. Visiting from LA."

"What the—?"

"I'm sorry," Katy said shaking her head. "It was . . . it wasn't good. In fact, she was kind of a wacko, to tell you the truth. I was upset and missing you and it was totally stupid."

Beth gasped, gut-punched. *Wow*, she had *not* seen that coming. "Wait . . . Is she here now?" She turned sharply to look behind her, her eyes darting around the room in panic. The door to the bedroom was closed. She hauled herself upright, and remembered her crutches were in the hall. She was trapped.

Katy pulled her back down. "No, no," she said. "It's okay. She left."

Beth sank into the couch. She tried to respond but gagged, the taste of bile hitting the back of her throat, her words wedged in a morass of jealousy and rage and fear and sadness. Her stomach rumbled in an odd combination of nausea and hunger; she'd had nothing to eat all morning, only Lionel's strong coffee. Clasping her belly, she took deep inhalations in and out, lips pursed, trying to refocus, feeling as if she had to regain her land legs after a week at sea.

Katy reached for Beth's hand and held it between hers, massaging the knuckles, twirling the braided silver ring Beth wore on her pinky finger, the ring she'd bought on their trip to Oaxaca three years ago. Beth stared at their intertwined fingers as they sat side by side in silence. A fire truck passed up the street, sirens screeching. The refrigerator hummed in the kitchen. A door slammed downstairs.

Finally, Beth found her voice. "We're better than this," she said.

31

Three days later, Tracy appeared after lunch. She sat on the bed, next to Tave's wheelchair, and patted the file folder on her lap. "I've found a place for you," she said.

Tave's stomach lurched. "Where?"

"Oakridge Gardens. Here in the city. It's one of the better ones. And I'm told they have a few younger patients right now. You're lucky. They have an unexpected vacancy." She twisted her mouth in an odd movement.

"Oh." *Unexpected vacancy* means someone has died, Tave supposed, but she pushed that ugly thought away.

"And they accept your insurance." Tracy waved the folder in triumph.

"Wow . . ." Tave took a deep breath. She'd known this moment would come, but it felt like a blast of cold air. "I guess my rehab is over," she said.

"No, not over, dear. You'll get therapy at Oakridge Gardens. It won't be an intense daily schedule like here, but they have decent PT and OT there. They'll treat you three times a week, something like that. And the therapists here will provide detailed discharge instructions and reach out in person to make sure there's a smooth transition."

Tave nodded but couldn't find any words.

Tracy leaned across and squeezed Tave's forearm. "It will be another big adjustment for you, for sure," she said. "But you can do it. I've seen all the therapists' and nurses' reports. You're ready. You're strong. You can do this."

"When would I go?"

"Tomorrow."

"Tomorrow?" Tave gulped.

"Oh yes. That bed won't stay cold for long. Got to seize the day, as they say."

~

Tave had been awake for hours. "It's D-Day," Wanda said, bouncing into the room, arms spread wide in salute, a broad grin on her face.

Leticia was right behind her. "Gotta get you packed up, girl," she said.

This was it: discharge day. The nurses had organized a farewell party the night before, with cake and ice cream, a "graduation" certificate, and a song that was totally dopey, but which managed to get Tave choked up, in spite of her attempts to act cool. Laurel had stayed late to join the celebration and presented her with a teddy bear, a gift from all the therapists, she said, for Tave to take home—well, not home exactly, but to her next port of call. All that was left was for Dr. Kramer to come by for one last check and Paratransit would be on the way.

Leticia was loading a cart with more than a dozen clear plastic Patient Belongings bags. For a girl who arrived with nothing, she sure had a lot of gear: braces and splints and special utensils, creams and lotions, exercise bands and elastic stockings, pads and catheter supplies. And all her written discharge instructions and the educational posters Wanda had created for Tave's future caretakers.

"Where do you want this?" Leticia said, picking up the teddy bear. It was real soft, with a cute red bow and the perfect size for Tave to easily hold herself.

"I'll take it," Tave said. She placed it on her shoulder and snuggled against it as she watched Leticia moving calmly and smoothly, managing and organizing, on this unit that had been Tave's home for the last seven weeks—the only home she'd known in this, her new body. Now she was being launched out into the big wide world without these guys.

"Your speakerphone has arrived," Wanda said, returning to the room with a box.

"For real? I thought Tracy said I had to apply to some program, and it would take, like, weeks."

"Yeah, the CTAP program. It does usually take a while." Wanda examined the box, turning it over in her hands. "I have a sneaky feeling Tracy bought this for you out of her own pocket. She's off today, but she left it at the nurses' station yesterday evening, with a note to give it to you."

Tave gaped. She couldn't believe it. After all Tave's snarky thoughts about how ditzy Tracy was. "I can't . . . I mean, she shouldn't have done that."

"Well, she did, and I don't see her taking it back. So, you get to take this with you," Wanda said. "Have them set it up in your new room." She added it to the pile of possessions on the cart. "Give us a call and let us know how it's going, okay?" She leaned in and gave Tave a hug, stroking the top of her head. "It's going to seem awful quiet around here without you."

Tave nodded, overwhelmed. Her stomach twitched with nerves. "Thanks. I . . ." Before she could get any sensible words out her mouth, her phone rang—the hospital speakerphone still at her bedside. She glanced at the clock on the wall: a few minutes after nine.

"That will be my lawyer," she said. How fancy that sounded. Tave had left a message the previous afternoon with Miranda's assistant or whatever she was, letting her know she was moving, and wanting to talk with her before she left. The assistant said Miranda would call first thing in the morning. "This is Tave," she said, hitting the speaker button with her knuckle.

"Hello. This is Miranda Davenport."

Wanda gestured that she would leave her to take her call. After Tave told Miranda she was getting ready to be discharged, she asked, "Did you find out any more about the other driver?"

"I have some additional information. He was indeed over the legal blood alcohol limit, and with a previous DUI, so his license has been suspended, and he's looking at some hefty fines, possible prison time for that alone. But it appears no other charges have been filed against him. They've not yet determined comparative negligence. In other words, they don't know for sure if his being drunk was the sole cause of the accident."

"So, it was my fault?" Tave couldn't shake the feeling she must be to blame.

"Well, maybe partially. There will be a process for determining what we call comparative negligence. But no charges are being filed against you. As I said, I don't want you worrying about it, okay? Nothing good can come from that."

"Okay."

"And as for a monetary settlement, the other driver doesn't appear to have any significant assets. In terms of insurance, he had decent coverage, a hundred thousand dollars per person, and he sustained fairly minor injuries. But proportional negligence has yet to be determined and . . ."

Tave was losing her again, buried under a wave of jargon. "So, do I get that money?" It wasn't millions but hey, she wouldn't say no to a hundred thousand dollars.

"Well, probably not, I'm afraid. Depending on how proportional responsibility is finally determined, you and Leslie would both be entitled to the maximum available under each policy, split between you. But there's something else I may not have explained."

This sounded like more bad news. Tave didn't know if she was supposed to say something. She didn't.

"The thing is," Miranda continued, "you will have already incurred enormous costs from your hospital stay. MediCal—the state—will have first dibs on any funds, to recoup what they have been billed. I doubt there'll be much left after they take their cut."

"That's not fair."

"Maybe not. But that's the way the system works, I'm afraid."

"Fuck," Tave said. "Oops, sorry." Probably not a good idea to swear at your lawyer.

"I know that's not what you want to hear, and I understand it's disappointing. If anything changes, I'll let you know. I have the number for Oakridge Gardens. I'll get in touch with you there."

"I'll have my own phone there. I mean, I don't know the number yet or anything, but I got a speakerphone and all." She didn't know why she said that. It sounded kind of dumb.

"Great. I'm glad to hear it." Miranda said. "I hope things go well for you, Tave. I'll be rooting for you, and I'm sure Jess will keep me informed as to how things are going."

This Jess woman Tave kept hearing about: she hadn't even met her yet. But it was Maddy who recommended Jess, and she trusted Maddy. She had to. Her thoughts turned to Beth, who had introduced her to Maddy. She would like to let Beth know where she was going, to keep in touch, but she didn't have her number, and felt awkward about the whole thing. Beth had sounded weird when they spoke on the phone, and kept going on about the lawsuit stuff, like she knew more than Tave's lawyer. And she said she was going to come see her on Saturday, but never showed up. Maybe Beth was trying to get back together with her girlfriend, and it wasn't going so well. Tave didn't need to get mixed up with that.

Dr. Kramer came in and listened to her lungs one last time. He took her hands between his and smiled and nodded. "You've done well, really well. We're all extremely proud of you."

Behind him, Wanda returned carrying a large flower arrangement. "One more thing for your pile," she said. It was a gorgeous display of yellow roses and something purple and those highly scented white lilies. Tave was no expert, but it looked super expensive.

"Where did those come from?"

Wanda took a small card from a plastic stem stuck between the roses and opened it up for Tave. It read:

Wishing you all the best. If you change your mind at any time, my door will always be open for you. Love you, Mom

Tave's eyes filled with tears. She wasn't going to change her mind about living with her mom. But maybe—just maybe—one day her mom might stop criticizing her all the time, and she, Tave, might forgive her for all the mean stuff she'd said in the past, and they could try to start over. Like she was starting over with every other aspect of her life.

"What time are they coming for me?" she asked, swallowing a lump in her throat.

"Eleven," Wanda said.

"Can I go outside for a bit? You know, just to chill."

"Sure. Go ahead. We'll leave everything here, ready for your pickup."

Tave rolled toward the elevator, past the familiar landmarks of the nurses' station and the hallway leading to the therapy gym, and rode down to the first floor, out into the sunshine, heading for the small garden area between the two wings of the hospital. She looked up at the tinted windows of both buildings, the only places she'd known since her life had been turned upside down and gradually rebuilt. She looked at her legs, her still useless legs, dressed in the pants Billie had bought her for the trip to Chico, with the teddy bear tucked in her lap, seated in her brand-new wheelchair, which could swivel and turn like a finely tuned machine. She didn't know what lay ahead—but *hell*, in her old life she'd never known what she was doing, or where she was going. Now, she felt she had to take charge. She was going to get her act together and make something of herself. She would get help, from Maddy and that Jess person, and whoever else she might find along the way. But like when you play on a team, your coach can give you guidance, and your teammates are there cheering, but when you step up to the plate and hold the bat: you're the one who has to make the play.

An ambulance pulled up at the emergency room entrance across the courtyard, beneath the high retaining wall against the hillside. The paramedics jumped out, rushing inside with a gurney. That must have been how she arrived—although she had no memory of it. But she remembered the ICU, the whirl of the machines, the noise and the bustle, the smell of the wound dressings and the disinfectant, and the hollow fear of what was to become of her. And the weeks of rehab with the daily grind of therapy sessions, the set schedule and the dreary food: macaroni and cheese every damn Friday night, burgers on Saturday, meatloaf Sunday. Now, she was leaving; she was getting out. She would be free. She imagined herself soaring over the wall; she heard the solid thwack of the bat, and the announcer bellowing: *"This one is high . . . this one is deep . . . this one is . . . outta here."*

32

"I'm off to get beautified," Billie said, rolling into Tave's room. She ran her hand through her chestnut bangs. Her roots were coming back gray. She returned from the hairdresser with a slightly different color each time. "Hopeless task, but a girl's gotta try. Gotta look my best for the big day tomorrow."

"You always look great," Tave said. And she did. This morning, she was wearing purple leggings and a white top, and an assortment of purple and silver beads around her neck. "But I don't understand why you're making such a big deal about tomorrow. It's only a formality, right?"

"I know, hon. But come on, I'm just having fun with it. I'm excited! And Andy will want to take photos, so I can't look a mess."

Tomorrow they would sign off on the final approval and inspection of the remodeling project. Well, Billie would. She was very generously including Tave in every stage of the process, but Tave still thought of it as Billie's thing. Billie had left her rented house that was way smaller and not truly accessible, bought this property, and stripped it down to the studs. Her brother-in-law, Andy, had paid for every cent. He could easily afford it, according to Billie, but Tave thought it was amazing to be living in such a beautiful place. She was paying rent—a small amount, what she could afford out of her SSI check—but she knew she was getting a bargain, thanks to Billie's kindness. She had her own bedroom, now equipped with a roll-in shower, and Billie was in the other "wing," as she liked to call it, the bedroom at the other end of the house. "I'm returning to the East Wing, my dear," she liked to joke, in a fake posh accent. And at the back, they had a smaller bedroom, almost completed, where a live-in attendant could stay.

They hadn't found that attendant yet, but Tave hoped they would soon. Being able to offer a rent-free room as part payment would hopefully avoid some of the disasters she'd heard about. Her most recent roommate at Oakridge Gardens was a woman with cerebral palsy, as disabled as Tave, who'd been trying to live on her own, but her attendants kept flaking out. She wept whenever she talked about it: she'd ended up with a pressure sore on her butt because, as she put it, "some no-good useless piece of shit" who was supposed to be working for her had decided she had something better to do. The sore became infected, landing her in the hospital and then in the nursing home, and she didn't know if she'd ever get out.

Tave was scared she'd end up the same way. Right now, she was piecing together help from five different people. Trying to juggle everyone's schedules was a pain. Rosa came this morning but announced she wasn't available tomorrow. Tave had to spend an hour on the phone getting coverage. She longed to have a consistent person, someone she could rely on.

"Are you going to be around at one o'clock?" Billie said. "The carpenter is supposed to finish up the windows in the back bedroom. He's coming from another job, said it shouldn't take him long. If you're not going to be here, I can call Andy."

"I'll be here, if he's on time. Paratransit is coming to pick me up at three."

"Okay. I'll tell him it's one o'clock sharp. Is today your final?"

"Yup. One more after this, on Thursday, and I'll be done for the semester. Yay!"

"Good luck, girl. I know you'll ace it."

Tave wasn't so sure. She had no confidence in herself as a student. The math class was way too hard. But she enjoyed her computer class and loved working with the new iPhones the school had recently purchased. She was trying to save up to get her own. Tapping away with her knuckles on the touchscreen opened up a whole new world of independence— surfing the web, doing her own email, playing her own music. Her mother had sent her two hundred dollars for her birthday—surprise, surprise— so she had almost enough money.

She rolled out to the rear patio. This was what she loved best about the house. The backyard wasn't huge and had bare dirt around the edges that needed to be filled, and some construction gear in the far corner, but it was heaven to have somewhere she could easily go catch a few rays. It faced east and south, getting full sun for most of the morning and early afternoon. The neighbors had a large bush with orange-red flowers that cascaded over the fence: trumpet vine, Billie said.

As Tave reclined her chair for a weight shift, a hummingbird hovered above her head, flitting from one flower to the next. She watched as it landed, resting for a moment on one thin branch, its tiny green breast shimmering in the sunlight. At Oakridge Gardens there wasn't much of a garden at all, so Tave couldn't figure out how they came up with that name, but she did have a bush outside her window, one with dangly pink flowers. The hummingbirds loved those flowers, and there was one particular hummingbird—at least, Tave liked to think it was one special hummingbird, which was crazy, because how would she know—but she liked to think there was one special bird that always returned, like it was watching over her. Stupid, really, but Tave always smiled when she saw it and whispered, *Yes, I'm going to get out of here one day.*

"Hello! You out back?" That was Jess, stopping by for her midday check-in.

"I'm here."

Jess bounded onto the patio and leaned down to give Tave a hug. She unwound the long, woven scarf she always wore, and plopped a brown paper bag on the wrought iron table. "I bought peaches at the farmers' market. Oh my god, you should see all the beautiful stone fruit they have. I love this time of year, don't you? Will you have a peach with me?"

"Sure. In a bit. I just began my weight shift."

"Okay. I'll sit here with you." Jess pulled up a chair close to Tave's and tipped back to turn her face to the sun. Tave saw fine wrinkles around her eyes that she'd not noticed before. "Hmmm. It's so nice out here," Jess said.

"I know. I love it."

"How was the morning attendant today? Which one was it?"

"Rosa. She's all right. But turns out she can't come tomorrow, which is not what she said last week. So, I had to scramble. And now I'm nervous about Thursday. I can't have her flaking out again. I have to get to my final." She couldn't risk another incomplete. She had to prove to Howard, her Department of Rehab counselor, that she was serious about school, to have any chance of getting a van.

"Let me talk to her. You focus on your studying. I'll make sure someone is there."

"Grrrr . . . I don't want to have to think about this all the time. And I'm so sick of having to always train someone new."

"I know. We'll get there."

"Do you have any applicants for the live-in position?"

"Nothing very promising. One is a maybe. I'm checking it out."

"Fuck. How long is this going to take?"

"Hang in there, Tave. You've got to be patient. You can do it. You've been through worse."

"I know. I just . . . I don't want to get stranded. And I don't want to have to rely too much on Billie. I mean, she can't do everything I need, obviously, but she can do a shitload more than I can." Billie always reminded her she had MS, and her condition could deteriorate—but she had been stable now for over a year. "I don't want to have to ask her for stuff. She's not my attendant; she's my roommate. I can't mess this up. It's the best chance I'll ever have for a great place to live."

"We'll find the right person. And you're not going to mess up."

Tave smiled at Jess. "My cheerleader."

Jess stood up and tapped Tave on her chest, above her breastbone. "You know all this yourself, deep inside here. I just need to remind you from time to time. Now, I'm going to cut up peaches."

~

Friday was a gorgeous, warm day. A day fit for a celebration. And Tave was in a celebratory mood. She was done for the semester. She wasn't sure how well she'd done on the math final. "Keeping my fingers crossed," she'd told Billie. "Ha, ha, not really, can't cross my fingers." But she was hoping she'd scrape a pass. She didn't want to have to retake the class over the summer. She wanted a break, and to get back into handcycling. What with her school load and moving, she'd not been to the rec center in the past few months, and she missed it. She needed to get in shape, if she was ever going to be ready for the big fundraising ride in Napa in September.

Billie said she would drop her off, as she was going that way, on her route to her sister's house. By now, they had perfected their technique of the two of them getting into Billie's van without help. Tave got on the lift first, and once inside, she scooted back as far as possible, right up against the rear seat, to allow room for Billie to get in and transfer to her driver's seat up front. It took time, with the lift having to go up and down twice, but they managed. They turned heads wherever they unloaded. "Yup. Here we come, Laurel and Hardy," Billie would quip. Tave had learned to ignore the looks of astonishment.

As Billie buckled into her seat, and reversed out of the driveway, Tave remembered her first outing in this van, on that trip up to Chico with Beth. It seemed such a long time ago now. What a newbie she was. And what chutzpah they had. Well, Beth and Billie had led, and she'd followed, kind of in a daze most of the time, as she recalled. Certainly, on the way back, after they'd seen Les. Tave remembered little about that part of the journey.

Tave hadn't heard from Beth in months. She'd hardly seen her after Beth broke her ankle and stopped coming to the rehab unit, and she wasn't sure Beth even knew where she'd been discharged. Later, she'd run into her once at the rec center, in passing; she seemed in a hurry, and they'd hardly spoken. Tave always felt awkward around her, like she had to be on guard. She felt responsible in some way for Beth's problems with her girlfriend, when they almost broke up.

"Here we are, my dear," Billie said as she pulled into the rec center parking lot. "What time do you want me to pick you up?"

"I'm good. I've scheduled Paratransit for four o'clock."

"You didn't have to do that."

"No. It's fine. I prefer to. Thanks." Tave didn't want Billie to feel she was taking advantage of her. "I'll see you later." She waved as she rolled full speed ahead into the rec center yard.

The place was buzzing. Everyone had the same idea: get out and enjoy the lovely weather. Brent was busy working with two young kids, aged about twelve, getting them set up for a ride, but he waved at Tave, with a huge smile, and shouted "Hey! Welcome back." He motioned for her to wait until he was done. Jorge was in the back, tools in hand as always, working on a tandem bike. He waved too and rolled toward her.

"Hey. How've you been?"

"Good. What's up?"

"We're getting psyched for Napa. You gonna be there?"

"Hope so. I've got to get back into it, get strong again."

"You can do it." He turned around, like he was looking for something. "Did you meet our new volunteer? Shelby!" He waved at a young woman, bent over a bike in the far corner. "Come and meet Tave."

Shelby dropped what she was doing and came over. "Hi," she said, with a radiant smile, standing in front of Tave. She was maybe five foot three, solid-looking, with strong muscles and deeply tanned arms and legs. She wore short denim shorts and a black tank top. Her hair was platinum blonde with bangs swept off to the side, and she had deep-brown eyes, a pointy little nose and chin. Around her neck, she wore a silver pendant in a wolf-shape design, hanging on a leather strap. She held out both hands to clasp Tave's in hers. "Great to meet you," she said.

She was about the cutest thing Tave had ever seen.

"Hi," Tave said. She couldn't take her eyes off her. She was sure she was blushing.

"Shelby moved up here from San Diego," Jorge said. "She has, like, a ton of experience with adaptive sports."

"That's great," Tave managed to say.

"I can help get you set up if you like," she said. She gestured toward the collection of handcycles in the yard. "Would you like to ride tandem with me? I'd love the exercise."

"Sure," Tave said. She felt compelled to add, as if needing an excuse, "That would be good, because I'm out of shape. I haven't been in for a while. Been busy with school and stuff."

"I'm in school, too. Or I will be, in the fall. I came up here to go to pharmacy school."

"Cool."

Shelby selected one of the handcycles and waved to Brent for him to come help with the transfer. He took Tave's upper body, while Shelby bent over to hold Tave's legs and feet. Her tank top fell forward, and Tave caught a glimpse of a red sports bra underneath, and an adorable brown mole in the center of her cleavage. Tave's legs went crazy with spasms as they often did with a change in position, but Shelby knew exactly what to do: she applied gentle pressure to Tave's thighs, and the shaking stopped. As she and Brent settled her feet into the straps, Tave felt little palpitations in her chest. Well sure, she told herself, she was excited to be back.

Shelby brought over a foot-pedaled attachment and connected it to a crossbar between the two large rear wheels of Tave's handcycle, creating a tandem more than ten feet long. Soon, they were gliding through the park, past the lawns with the sprinklers going full force, along the path shaded by eucalyptus trees. The wind and sun embraced her face, and the air was rich with the scent of jasmine. *Back in the saddle,* she thought, with a smile. Tave could feel Shelby pedaling strong behind her, but she knew she was pulling her weight too. She felt the power of her shoulders moving left, right, left, right, gliding ahead; her arms tingled with the effort, alive and strong—arms she'd had to coax back to life, inch by inch, one muscle fiber at a time, through the months of therapy, the weights, the endless flexing and stretching, on an unswerving path, onward to a destination she could not envision. Yet somehow she'd arrived. Her still-useless hands tingled with the burning pain no medication could touch, the buzzing that echoed in her feet, like her fingers and toes were trying to communicate with each other, saying, *Yes, we're still here.* But she'd learned to ignore their chatter and carry on without them.

She saw the lake up ahead. "Do you want to go over the bridge?" Shelby shouted from her seat behind Tave; it was hard to converse while riding tandem.

Tave turned her head. "Sure." With her helmet in place and her hands engaged on the handlebars, all she could see of Shelby was her left leg, but she sensed she was having fun too. "Let's go for it," she said.

This was Tave's favorite part of the trail, but it was steep. She would never have made it up the bridge alone. She released her hand from the grip on the handlebar, engaged the gear shifter into a lower gear, and pulled hard, around and around, as Shelby pedaled hard behind her. They both panted with the effort. Tave steered through the curve at the top of the incline, and onto the bridge itself.

"Whoa! We made it," Shelby yelped in delight.

It was an easy glide across and down to the other side, and along the lakeside path, past the ducks and swans, hidden from time to time behind bunches of tall reeds. They passed bicyclists and kids on skateboards and babies in strollers, and if anyone was staring at Tave on her particular version of wheels, she no longer noticed or cared. Coasting along, getting into the rhythm of her stride, she felt a rekindling of the competitive spirit she'd not felt since her softball days. Maybe she could be good at this. Maddy had told her there were competitions, tournaments, and races you could go to. *Hell,* she thought with a smile, *maybe I could become good. Real good.*

They rode for over an hour. When they returned to the rec center, Tave was exhausted but exhilarated. She sat waiting for help to get back into her wheelchair, just chilling, when she heard a commotion behind her.

"Hey," someone shouted. "Here come the champs."

Tave maneuvered her handcycle half a turn. Approaching on the path to the right were two very fancy handcycles, riding next to each other, moving in perfectly synchronized strokes, gliding forward effortlessly. One was propelled by a rider reclined all the way back, real close to the ground, his front wheel looming so high in front, it was a wonder he could see where he was going. The other machine was different, bright orange, and propelled by a woman with massive shoulders and upper arms. She was older, maybe forty-something, and as they slowed down to enter the yard, Tave could see she wasn't a quad; she was leaning all the way forward and had full use of her hands, which she held up now in triumph, peeling off slim leather gloves. The other rider, coming in behind her, was a young guy equally buff.

"How was it?" Jorge rolled out to greet them.

"Awesome," said the man. "Oh my god, I love this machine. But we need to adjust the torque on the derailleur."

"He's crazy fast on that thing," said the woman, throwing back her head with a laugh.

Shelby was high-fiving the woman and talking to her, but Tave couldn't hear what they were saying. Her stomach plummeted. She'd been feeling so happy, so strong, with ridiculous fantasies about racing. What an idiot. She was a wimp compared to these guys; she could never be as good as them. She didn't have their upper body strength or trunk stability. And she would never be able to afford this type of fancy machine.

Tave felt Shelby's hand on her shoulder. "Steve and Joanie are training for the regional championships. Steve got that Quad Elite paid for in full. There are all sorts of grants out there, if you're interested." It was like Shelby had read her mind. "And if you ever wanted to get involved competitively, they separate paras and quads; they have a whole system of categories. According to level of ability. You wouldn't be in the same group as someone like Joanie, for example." She gave Tave's upper arm a squeeze.

"Okay. Cool."

Shelby crouched, bringing her face level with Tave's, and held her in a firm gaze. She had the cutest eyes, with super long eyelashes. Tave's shoulder still tingled from her touch. "But you don't have to do any of that. You can totally do it just for fun. You don't need to prove anything. You're a champion already for getting yourself this far."

"Yeah, right."

"I mean it. Give yourself credit, girl. You're amazing and strong." Shelby cupped her hands around Tave's cheeks.

Tave could feel herself blushing. She didn't want those hands to move. "Okay, thanks," she said.

Shelby straightened up to standing. "And hey," she said. "I was wondering. Do you want to ride tandem together for the Napa ride? We could, like, train together. If you like."

Tave said there was nothing she'd like better.

33

One week later, Tave sat at the kitchen table flicking through Billie's *People* magazine. She was engrossed in a stupid story about Brad Pitt and Angelina Jolie when she heard Billie at the front door.

"Hey! Guess what?" Billie shouted. "I've got a surprise for you."

For a moment, Tave feared Billie had brought home a kitty. She'd been threatening, but Tave wasn't keen. She never understood the whole cat thing and had told Billie they should at least wait until they were settled on a live-in attendant. Billie remained stuck on the idea. But as Tave swiveled around she saw not a cat—but Beth! Beth walking toward her, arms outstretched for a quick hug, before stepping back to look around her.

"I ran into Billie at Walgreens," Beth said. "She told me you guys are living together. That's so cool." She surveyed the living room and the backyard. "What a great place."

Beth looked good: relaxed, a bit thinner. Her hair was longer, below her ears, in a layered cut. She wore jeans and a plaid shirt, the sleeves rolled up. Tave saw her take in the couch and ottoman, the wide patio doors, and the open-plan kitchen with its lowered, accessible counters, and she thought, *Yeah, see, I've come a long way, baby.*

Then she remembered Beth had never seen her grubby little room at Oakridge Gardens, where she'd had to struggle every day to hold on, to believe she was going to make it, that she had made it only because of the support of Maddy and Jess and Billie, who'd rooted for her every single day. Beth hadn't been there for all of that. But she'd understood why Beth had stayed away, and she wasn't mad at her. But now, seeing Beth again after all this time, she realized she'd been waiting for this moment, that she'd always, somewhere in the back of her mind, been hoping that one day she'd be able to prove to Beth she was worthy, and would live up to Beth's expectations. She'd been doing what she needed to survive, for herself, obviously, but always somewhere in her mind, with an eye to impress Beth.

"Great place," Beth said again, nodding.

"How've you been?" Tave said at the same time.

"Good, good. We got back to town a month ago. Katy and I took some time to go traveling. We were in Argentina and Chile. Had a great time."

"I'm so glad you guys stayed together."

"Yeah, me too." Beth sat opposite Tave, on the couch, and smiled. "We went through a rough patch, but we decided to start over. We both needed to make some big changes. So, after I had the surgery on my ankle, and I recovered from that, I quit my job, and we took off for a while. We always do best when we're traveling, so we up and went, doing it on the cheap, backpacking and staying in hostels, being in the mountains. Now we're back. We're looking to buy a house together."

"Here in the city?"

"Across the Bay probably," Beth said. "More affordable. Katy's parents are going to help with the down payment. It's still going to be stretch, but I'm excited. Katy's doing real well as a fitness coach, she got certified and has a good position at the main YMCA, and she's trying to get private clients on the side. I'm very proud of her. And I'm going to work for home health. I'm hoping it will be less bureaucratic, that I can kind of do my own thing more, working with patients in their own homes. We'll see. They say the paperwork is a nightmare, but I'm hoping it works out."

"You're not going to be in rehab anymore?" Tave said. "But you're, like, you're so good at that."

"I will be doing rehab, but in people's homes. In a more realistic setting. The rehab unit is such a sheltered, artificial environment. It doesn't always prepare folks for the practical issues they'll face back home. I like the idea of problem-solving in the real world." Beth smiled. "And I won't have to deal with the hospital bullshit. The stupid rules and stuff."

"You'll do great in home health," Billie said, coming from the kitchen, rolling her chair with one hand, while the other steadied a tray on her lap, carrying glasses of iced tea for them all. "Your patients will be lucky to have you there too."

"Thanks," Beth said taking a glass. "Tell me about you," she said, turning to Tave.

Tave hardly knew where to start. She was digesting the fact that Beth was sitting in front of her.

"Tave's getting back into handcycling at the rec center," Billie said. "She's training for Napa."

"Fantastic," Beth said, with a huge grin. "Can I sponsor you?"

"Sure. I need to get on it. I've been focusing on the training part, as I was out of it for a while."

"Why don't I take on being your fundraising person?" Beth said. "I would love to. I'm sure I can rustle up sponsors. It would be a good excuse for me to reconnect with folks."

"Sounds good to me."

They drank tea and hung out like no time had gone by, like nothing weird had happened in the past. Tave told Beth about their search for an attendant, asked if she knew anyone who might be good, and talked about school, and about getting back into handcycling. She didn't mention her crush on Shelby. Time enough for that, she thought, if anything comes of it.

"Do you ever hear anything about Les?" Beth asked.

"Not really. I think she's about the same. Her parents haven't reached out to me at all. I heard from my lawyer they were really mad there was no money to be had from anyone."

"That's so sad."

"Sure is. The whole damn thing." When Tave closed her eyes at night, she was often haunted by the image of Les when she'd seen her in Chico, Les looking so damaged and unrecognizable. She tried to erase that image and replace it with memories of their good times together, but those images were much harder to hold on to; they were slipping away.

"What did you find out about the other driver?"

"He was drunk, and I guess he lost his license, and had like some big fine or something. The lawyers argued amongst themselves for months, back and forth, I could hardly follow it all, to be honest. In the end, they decided I was partly to blame. From skid marks on the road or some shit, they said I must have partially swerved into the other lane. But they figured he was speeding. So, they said he was seventy-five percent responsible, me twenty-five percent. Whatever that means." Tave held her hands out in front of her. "I guess I'm responsible for one paralyzed arm. Or leg. Take your pick. I had to let go of worrying about that. Doesn't change anything. Like I say, there was no money in it for any of us. Les's parents wanted to go after me, which freaked me out, but like my lawyer said, I got nothing to give. So, she talked them out of it. The money on the insurance all went to MediCal. Guess I racked up well over a million in medical bills."

"Wow, that's crazy. You're not on the hook for any of that, are you?"

"No, thank god. Can you imagine? No, MediCal covered it all, but when the insurance money finally came through, it was around a hundred thousand dollars, I guess. MediCal got to keep it all, because of what they'd paid out." Tave shrugged. "Anyways, that's all behind me. I figured I've just got to get on and live my life."

Beth looked around the room again. "Looks like you're doing that." She paused. "What about your mom? Are you in touch with her at all?"

"Funny you should ask." Tave rolled over to the counter and pulled out a bunch of papers, grabbing them between her wrists. "I gave her my new address, and she just wrote to me. I'm thinking of inviting her up for a visit, if you can believe that. Seems like she's given up on that crazy minister of hers. She's stopped sending me bullshit about laying-on-hands healing. But now, she's bombarding me with stuff about stem cell research." Tave held up four or five pages of magazine cuttings. "Do you know much about this?"

Beth took the pages and flipped through them. "There are a lot of exciting developments with stem cell research, for sure," she said. "But my understanding is this is mostly at the basic science level. Lab studies with mice, that sort of thing. Very few clinical trials in humans. And the human studies they are doing are focused on newly injured patients, seeing if they can make a difference when they give treatment immediately, at the time of injury. That's where the bang for the buck is. No one's very interested in treating folks who've been injured for months or years."

"See, that's what I said," Billie said. "Plus, you know that shit would be crazy expensive. You think MediCal's gonna cover it?"

"Guess not," Tave said. Lord knows, it was hard enough to get coverage for the kind of catheters she needed. "But one of those . . ." She pointed to the articles Beth was holding. "One of those has something about a guy who went to India."

Beth scanned them again. "I wouldn't trust those stories. And see this one here, this guy . . . he got a change in two spinal cord levels, from C6 to C8. It's not like it cured him of his injury."

"I know," Tave said. She remembered a time when Beth had been so excited because Tave's level had come down one notch. But she didn't say that.

Billie wheeled over to Beth and picked up the papers. "The other thing that gets me about this stuff," she said, "is they always just talk about walking again. As if walking is the only thing that matters. Same with MS." She pushed herself up with both arms fully extended, adjusting her position in her chair. "It's all the other crap that's a far bigger deal, in my humble opinion. I mean, I get around pretty good in this chair. I can't stand it when people say I'm *confined* to a wheelchair. I'm not confined to the chair; I use it to get myself places. I'd be confined without it. But if someone comes up with a full cure, with stem cells or any other shit, and it's a cure for all the bladder and bowel issues I deal with—now you're talking. You can sign me up for that, baby. Yes, please!"

Tave smiled. Billie always entertained her with the way she talked. And Tave understood what she was saying; it made sense, in a way. There was far more to her injury than not being able to walk. But if someone offered to wave a magic wand and make her walk again, would she take it? Sure, she would. She would love to be able to feel the ground beneath her feet, feel the blood pumping through her legs again. In her dreams she was always walking—usually running, in fact, running through fields of long grass. She often woke with a faint, ridiculous hope that maybe *that* was real, and everything else for the past year had been the nightmare. But no, she still couldn't kick the covers off the bed in the morning.

But, Tave thought, she wouldn't want to return to the person she'd been before her accident. She might not be able to run a mile or swing a softball bat, but she was far stronger because of her injury. She couldn't say she was glad it had happened, but at the same time, she knew she wouldn't be where she was now without it.

"It's a beautiful day," Beth said. "Let's go outside. I'd love for you to show me around your neighborhood."

"There's a nice park three blocks away," Tave said.

"Let's go." Beth turned to Billie. "Will you join us?"

"No. You guys go ahead. I'm waiting for a call from Andy."

"Come on," Tave said. "You can reach him later." She rolled over to Billie and hooked her arm through hers. "Let's go."

They strolled down the front ramp and set off toward the park, side by side, Tave in the middle. The sun was warm on her shoulders, the scent of honeysuckle wafted over the neighbor's fence, and she basked in the comfortable silence between friends. But the sidewalk narrowed. Billie held back, and Tave looked at Beth, who signaled for her to take the lead. Tave swerved around a large tree root and switched her chair to its fastest speed.

Glancing back at Beth, she shouted, "Race you to the corner."

And she took off, laughing into the breeze.

Author Statement and Acknowledgments

I started early drafts of this novel back in 2014. Since then, a burgeoning #OwnVoices movement has highlighted the importance of underrepresented groups telling their own stories. Tave, the main protagonist in this novel, is disabled, and I am not. For many years, I worked as a rehabilitation nurse practitioner caring for patients with spinal cord injuries, multiple sclerosis, strokes, and brain injuries as they rebuilt their lives, and I wanted to create characters that defy the stereotypes of people with disabilities as tragic victims. But living with the new onset of a disability is not my own personal experience.

I asked two friends, Judith Smith and Bonnie Lewkowicz, both women with quadriplegia, to read an early draft of the manuscript, and they generously provided feedback and validated the authenticity of the point-of-view character. While their feedback led to revisions, I alone take full responsibility for the portrayal.

In recent years, talented writers with disabilities have emerged, producing memoirs such as those by Judy Heumann, Alice Wong, Rebekah Taussig, Keah Brown, and Shane Burcaw, to name a few. Some have gained thousands of followers on social media. They proudly claim their identity as disabled voices, sharing stories from their day-to-day lives and challenging assumptions about their lack of agency. This is wonderful to see. Fiction by writers with disabilities is harder to find, but Anne Finger, Susan Nussbaum, and Nicola Griffith among others, have led the way and I'm sure more will come. I am in no way trying to usurp that space.

Many scenes in the novel take place on a rehabilitation unit, a setting rarely depicted in fiction or medical dramas. When friends and acquaintances learned what I did for a living, they often assumed the work must be overwhelmingly depressing. Even within the large medical center where I spent most of my career, rehabilitation patients were never chosen for the billboards that touted the hospital's "excellence," despite our center being one of the best in the state. The ads featured instead glowing pregnant women or youthful-appearing heart-attack survivors. Patients with disabilities were apparently seen as unglamorous, best hidden from public view.

I hope readers of this novel gain insights into the world of rehabilitation. The work is challenging, yes, requiring great skill and dedication, but immensely important and fulfilling. My secondary protagonist, Beth, is a dedicated physical therapist who oversteps in her efforts to rescue Tave, highlighting both the rewards and the inherent risks of the job. Tave and Beth are lesbians, as am I. Lesbians come in all shapes and sizes and abilities, as an awareness of intersectionality teaches us.

I have been asked if this novel is based on a true story. *Unswerving* is not taken from any one individual's experience, and the rehabilitation unit depicted here is fictitious. For narrative purposes, to reduce the number of characters for the reader to track, the rehabilitation team in this novel has been limited to the physician, the nursing staff, the physical therapist, the occupational therapist, and the social worker. These characters are also not based on any former colleagues. In reality, the team for a patient like Tave would include other valuable professionals, such as a respiratory therapist, a recreational therapist, a neuropsychologist, a dietician, and hopefully an advanced practice nurse—the role I filled for over twenty-five years. I intend no disrespect to those disciplines by their exclusion here.

I am deeply indebted and inspired by the disability community, especially in Berkeley, California, and to the Bay Area Outreach and Recreation Program (BORP) for their work providing recreational activities for children and adults with disabilities. I am particularly grateful to Bonnie Lewkowicz, who spent time telling me about handcycling, and Cynthia Pereyra Noonan, who took me riding tandem with her, which was informative and a lot of fun. Pam Hansen double-checked my description of the physical therapy assessments, and Tanya Starnes and Fred Feller helped me understand California personal injury law. Alaina Brookmyer provided details on personal training as a career path.

Writing is a lonely, isolated endeavor, with many hours spent staring at a blank screen or a notebook waiting for inspiration, or endlessly tweaking sentences to perfect the prose. But bringing a novel out into the world takes a village, and I am tremendously grateful for the support I have received from my writing community. My early readers David Schweidel, Martina Reaves, and Pamela Feinsilber provided invaluable feedback, and the final manuscript is immensely improved because of their input. I am also grateful to my writing critique partners Gail Kurtz, Alice Feller, and Claudia Marseille, and to my writing classmates Anna Brown, Kathy Moore, Paul Davis, Karen Hunt, Raleigh Ellisen, Molly Hartle, Mike Capbarat, Richard Turner, and Carl Kopman,. I cherish the general support from my cheering section, especially Sue Granzella, Sejal Patel, Devi Laskar, JoAnne Tompkins, and Diane Demeter.

I appreciate the editors of the journal *Please See Me*, who published my short story "A Dreadful Case" (November 2021), based on a chapter deleted from the novel but given a new lease on life in their wonderful publication, which seeks to elevate the voices of vulnerable populations in health-related stories.

And I am immensely grateful to Dennis Lloyd, Jackie Krass, and the whole team at the University of Wisconsin Press, for having faith in this novel and bringing it out into the world.

And to Judy. Living with a writer is not easy, but she patiently supports me in every way.